8/23 $1

THE **UNIT**

LOCK AND LOAD

D0911194

THE **UNIT**

LOCK AND LOAD

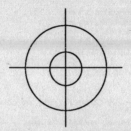

PATRICK ANDREWS

A SIGNET BOOK

SIGNET
Published by New American Library, a division of
Penguin Group (USA) Inc., 375 Hudson Street,
New York, New York 10014, USA
Penguin Group (Canada), 90 Eglinton Avenue East, Suite 700, Toronto,
Ontario M4P 2Y3, Canada (a division of Pearson Penguin Canada Inc.)
Penguin Books Ltd., 80 Strand, London WC2R 0RL, England
Penguin Ireland, 25 St. Stephen's Green, Dublin 2,
Ireland (a division of Penguin Books Ltd.)
Penguin Group (Australia), 250 Camberwell Road, Camberwell, Victoria 3124,
Australia (a division of Pearson Australia Group Pty. Ltd.)
Penguin Books India Pvt. Ltd., 11 Community Centre, Panchsheel Park,
New Delhi - 110 017, India
Penguin Group (NZ), 67 Apollo Drive, Rosedale, North Shore 0632,
New Zealand (a division of Pearson New Zealand Ltd.)
Penguin Books (South Africa) (Pty.) Ltd., 24 Sturdee Avenue,
Rosebank, Johannesburg 2196, South Africa

Penguin Books Ltd., Registered Offices:
80 Strand, London WC2R 0RL, England

First published by Signet, an imprint of New American Library,
a division of Penguin Group (USA) Inc.

First Signet Printing, April 2009
10 9 8 7 6 5 4 3 2 1

Copyright © 2009 Twentieth Century Fox Film Corporation. All Rights Reserved.

 REGISTERED TRADEMARK—MARCA REGISTRADA

Printed in the United States of America

Without limiting the rights under copyright reserved above, no part of this publication
may be reproduced, stored in or introduced into a retrieval system, or transmitted, in
any form, or by any means (electronic, mechanical, photocopying, recording, or
otherwise), without the prior written permission of both the copyright owner and the
above publisher of this book.

PUBLISHER'S NOTE
This is a work of fiction. Names, characters, places, and incidents either are the prod-
uct of the author's imagination or are used fictitiously, and any resemblance to actual
persons, living or dead, business establishments, events, or locales is entirely coinci-
dental.
    The publisher does not have any control over and does not assume any responsibil-
ity for author or third-party Web sites or their content.

If you purchased this book without a cover you should be aware that this book is
stolen property. It was reported as "unsold and destroyed" to the publisher and neither
the author nor the publisher has received any payment for this "stripped book."

The scanning, uploading, and distribution of this book via the Internet or via any other
means without the permission of the publisher is illegal and punishable by law. Please
purchase only authorized electronic editions, and do not participate in or encourage
electronic piracy of copyrighted materials. Your support of the author's rights is
appreciated.

This book is dedicated to my son

Bill Andrews
Veteran of the 2nd Battalion, 75th Airborne Ranger
Regiment

The third of three generations of paratroopers

When planning a campaign, it is necessary to have a complete knowledge of the enemy's capabilities. Then meticulously prepare a proper plan to successfully overcome them.

—Napoleon Bonaparte

PROLOGUE

CIA CONTROL CENTER
SOMEWHERE IN VIRGINIA
15 SEPTEMBER
0945 HOURS LOCAL
1445 HOURS ZULU

Delmar Munger, holding a manila folder under one arm, walked jauntily down the hall, his stride belying his bulk. Normally the heavyset, balding CIA controller-at-large moved deliberately, almost ponderously, but his good mood that morning put a bit of "oomph" in his step.

When he reached the door of his boss's office, he stepped into the outer office with a grin and a wink for Dora Petchley, who, although a perky and attractive young woman, was an extremely efficient, no-nonsense CIA administrative specialist. She immediately sensed Munger's unusually good mood. "Hello, Delmar," she said. "You seem the cheerful guy. Did you run over a kitten on your way to work today?"

Munger's jovial disposition did not diminish an iota. "Not even you can bring me down this morning, my sarcastic little serving wench. Inform Norman that I am here to see him."

Dora picked up the phone and hit the zero button. As soon as Norman DeWitt answered, she quipped, "Delmar has waddled in to see you, sir. Shall I send him in or sic the dogs on him? Very well." She hung up and gave Munger a smirk. "Go right in."

"How about an intimate dinner at the Del Fontaine tonight?" Munger asked. "Followed, of course, by drinks at my place."

Her mind said, *In your dreams, lard-ass*, but her voice said, "I don't think so."

"You're missing a good thing," he remarked, going to the inner door.

Munger stepped into Norman DeWitt's office, going directly to his desk and dropping the manila folder with a grand gesture. Then he took a seat, the grin still on his face.

"What's going on?" DeWitt asked. As a senior controller-at-large, he was Munger's direct superior.

"Just see what I've brought you."

DeWitt opened the folder and pulled out an official communiqué form. He read it carefully, then laid it down in front of him. "It says that one of the main players in the Palestinian Barq-min-Islam terrorist group wishes to defect. His name is Shakeel Bashir."

"Right," Munger said. "He's their liaison officer to all other militant Muslim groups in the West Bank."

"Oh, yeah," DeWitt said. Then he shrugged. "We haven't the slightest bit of interest in him, Delmar. The Mossad are the ones who want to get their hands on this guy."

"That's what's so great about it."

DeWitt leaned back in his swivel chair. "Excuse me, but I can't quite grasp what has you so excited."

"We can work these circumstances to our advantage," Munger said. "I am talking about where the Unit is concerned." The fondest dream of both DeWitt and Munger was to have the Unit deactivated with extreme prejudice, including the imprisonment of its personnel.

DeWitt now leaned forward. "All right. Tell me about it."

"Okay," Munger said. "We don't want this guy Bashir. Fine. The Israelis want him. Fine. So what we do is contact the Unit and make arrangements for them to pick him up. This can be done through our guy Joe Saada in Jordan Station. He also spends time in the West Bank."

"I take it you'll want the Unit to deliver the defector to the Mossad, right?"

"That's what we tell the Mossad," Munger said. "But *not* what we tell the Unit. We instruct those cowboys of Tom Ryan's to get the guy out of the West Bank and back to the States."

A sly smile twisted DeWitt's lips. "Okay. And we don't say anything to them about giving him to the Mossad, or that the Mossad is expecting them to."

"Exactly! And when the Mossad shows up and wants the defector, it will create what is called an awkward situation. The Unit will have to roll over and give the guy up to the Israelis, since they'll be all by their lonesome in the West Bank. With that done, they come home with their tails between their legs. Mission *un*accomplished!"

"I'll admit it might embarrass them," DeWitt said a bit testily. "But that certainly won't bring about what we want, i.e., their utter and complete destruction."

"There is also the chance that the Unit will resist the Jews," Munger said. "The Mossad are a bunch of real badass guys. They might even kill those reprobates if they refuse to surrender the defector. Like I said, the Israelis want him bad. A very serious international situation could come out of this. And we can hedge our advantageous position in this by submitting all our grievances about the Unit to Senator Herbert Kinkaid and his Committee on Intelligence and Special Operations right after the Unit leaves for the Middle East. That will add to their already bad reputation."

"Mmm," DeWitt said thoughtfully. "Particularly if they make some diplomatic blunders where the Israelis are concerned."

"And you know they'll do that," Munger said. "Don't forget all the evidence we've accumulated. The Unit is so far back in the shadows that we can destroy it by strong innuendos they can't disprove without compromising everything they've done since the very minute they were activated."

"We'll need to create some special paperwork involving this defector," DeWitt said. "Everything we produce must indicate that the Unit was supposed to turn the guy over to the Mossad. So we will give only verbal instructions to them that they are to bring the guy back here to the States."

"That also means giving an oral briefing to our CIA colleague Joe Saada that those Unit boys are to bring the guy to us," Munger said. "He may turn in a contradictory after-action report, but there are two of us who will say he misunderstood the mission."

"That'll work," DeWitt said. "If he goes against us there'll be some negative input into his dossier."

"Yeah!" Munger said. "It will be to his advantage to shut up and forget all about it. And all we'll have to do is stick to our story, since neither he nor the Unit will have any written evidence that we gave instructions to haul the defector to the States. We'll insist that we told them to deliver him to the Mossad."

"Right," DeWitt said. "I have one big-ass worry. The Israelis may figure out otherwise. They could blow our little plan apart."

"C'mon, Norman!" Delmar said. "Do you think for one godamn minute that the Mossad or any other Israeli intelligence service is going to appear in public to make comments regarding their operations? That would be like asking nuns in a convent to put on a performance at a strip joint."

Norman DeWitt was quiet for a moment; then he slowly smiled. "Let's do it."

"I like your attitude," Delmar said. "The Unit has shown us up too much in the past. They called that tune too many times, so it's time for them to pay the piper."

CHAPTER ONE

The Cave was actually a one-story cement-block building among the headquarters, warehouses, motor pools, and barracks of the 303rd Logistical Study Unit. The outfit was not quite what it seemed: Instead of being a rear-echelon sanctuary for milquetoast file clerks and overweight senior noncommissioned officers, the edifice was the home of a very distinct and elite Special Forces detachment known only as the Unit.

Below the foundation of the Cave was a double basement. The upper level housed the commanding officer's office, headquarters, team rooms, a briefing room, a commo center, and a small but well-equipped dispensary. Additionally there was a large armory that contained at least half a dozen examples each of all the modern military light weaponry in the known world. Next to that arms chamber was an area especially set apart called isolation. This closely guarded place was where teams chosen to be inserted into special operations were locked away to be briefed and equipped for upcoming missions. Only those particular individuals, along with essential operations and intelligence officers, were allowed in the place. The exception were people called assets, who had critical knowledge that would aid the Unit operators in the conduct and completion of the dangerous assignments given them.

The lower level of the Cave was for shooting. This included not only pistol and small-caliber rifle ranges, but a particularly interesting area referred to as the shooting house. It was here that the teams kept their quick-response shooting skills at a high level by conducting live-firing exercises in various scenarios developed by a particularly masochistic training staff. Although these were closely supervised, even a slight mistake could cause a participant to be wounded or killed. Training standards were rarely more hazardous, but these risks were necessary if expertise with handguns was to be kept honed and primed.

BREIFING ROOM
17 SEPTEMBER
0700 HOURS LOCAL
1300 HOURS ZULU

Colonel Tom Ryan, commanding officer of the detachment known as the Unit, stood by a podium positioned at the front of the room. He looked down at the four men seated in folding chairs facing him, scanning the quartet, thinking they appeared remarkably similar to convicts from an old-fashioned Georgia chain gang; and there were no doubt past episodes in their lives that would put them in such confinement. Sergeant Major Jonas Blane, Master Sergeant Mack Gerhardt, Sergeant First Class Bob Brown, and Staff Sergeant Charles "Carlos" Grey gazed back at him with sleepy-eyed expressions. Jonas was a serious African-American with a demeanor of dignity and proficiency. Mack, on the other hand, had a rugged quality that gave the impression of a hot temper and the courage and strength to back it up. The two other guys, Bob and Carlito, were impetuous, with the arrogance of youth combined with exceptional ability. The "kids" were perfect matches to complement Jonas's logical mind and Mack's violent tendencies.

Ryan cleared his throat before speaking. "Now hear this—as our colleagues in the navy say—you have been called here to receive a briefing for an upcoming mission. There will be no briefback because of the operation's rather unique attributes, which include civilian clothing only." He paused and his gaze turned to a glare. "Now I am going to open yon door and two individuals are going to come through it. One is a stranger to you. The other is someone you hate and despise with a fury that surpasses the passionate abhorrence that the Duke of Wellington and Napoleon Bonaparte had for each other."

A sneer curled Mack's lips. "Delmar Munger!"

"Yes, Sergeant Gerhardt," the colonel replied. "It indeed is Delmar Munger. I wanted you to be mentally prepared for his physical presence with us this morning in order that there are no sudden acts of violence."

Carlito asked, "Who is the other rotten son of a bitch?"

"Now, why do you think this total stranger is a rotten son of a bitch, Sergeant Grey?" Ryan inquired.

"He's with Munger, that's why."

"Yeah," Ryan said. "Now that I think about it, he probably is a rotten son of a bitch. But be that as it may, let's get through this little session this morning with no outward signs of animosity toward either one of 'em." He turned and walked to the door, pulling it open.

Norman DeWitt was the first to enter, followed by Delmar Munger. Both CIA men gave the four Unit operators surprisingly friendly nods. It almost seemed that the duo was happy to be there at Fort Griffith. DeWitt stopped at the podium while Munger went to a chair at the side of the room. Colonel Ryan walked back to his usual station in the rear and leaned against the wall to keep everyone in view.

"Good morning," the speaker said. "My name is Norm DeWitt, and I'm a senior controller-at-large for the Agency. I am here today to give you the poop on a special operation that has popped up out in the West Bank in Palestine."

Jonas Blane looked at the man. "A defector. Am I right?"

"You are indeed correct, sir," DeWitt replied.

"You don't have to 'sir' me," Jonas said. "I am a non-commissioned officer. That means I work for a living and my parents are married."

DeWitt, forewarned by Munger about the team's collective attitude toward the CIA, showed a grin. "All right, I'll keep that in mind. Thank you, Sergeant Major. Now! This defector is a very important one. His name is Shakeel Bashir, and he is a member of the Barq-min-Islam terrorist group. That name, by the way, means 'Lightning of Islam.' This fellow has vital information that will be useful to our national security; thus his value is inestimable."

Bob Brown, slumped comfortably in his chair, raised his index finger to indicate that he had a question. "Will we have to look this guy up?"

"An operative of ours has made arrangements for you to meet him at a safehouse," DeWitt answered. "But let me start from the beginning. You are going by commercial air to Amman, Jordan, using Canadian passports with other ID showing you are civil engineering consultants. You will be met by our operative there, who is using a cover as a businessman with interests in the West Bank. In actuality, these enterprises are legitimate and belong to members of his extended family. He is a native-born American of Jordanian ancestry, and his parents are both legal residents of this country."

"How's this guy gonna get us to the defector?" Mack asked.

"You'll go by automobile across the Jordanian border just north of the Dead Sea," DeWitt explained. "There is a lot of biblical history in the area, so it is a very interesting car ride, they tell me. You will go directly to a safehouse in the town of Musalmar, where you will find this guy happily waiting for you. Once he is in your custody, our agent will radio for a helicopter to pick you up. The chopper will fly from a U.S. Navy vessel, where it is on station in the Mediterranean Sea, to Musalmar and take you and the defector back to the ship. Then, of course, to the USA where you will turn him over to us."

"Hold it," Jonas said. "I don't think the Israelis are going to be too happy to see an unknown aircraft fly through their airspace."

"The flyover has already been approved," DeWitt assured him.

"Weird!" Mack said. "Not the flyover. I'm talking about the defector. You'd think the Israelis would want him. I've heard of that Barq-min-Islam bunch, and they've really been giving grief to that country. If they ain't sending in suicide bombers then they're shelling public areas with mortars and rockets, killing lots of Jewish folks."

Now Delmar Munger stood up and walked to the podium. "That's a good point, Sergeant Gerhardt. But for whatever purposes, both the United States and the Israeli governments have agreed to this arrangement. We are not aware of the reasons behind this, but it's a fact of life. I can well imagine, however, that the people from the Israeli embassy will be in on the guy's debriefing. And that means the Mossad. You will be serving both nations." He paused to check his audience's reaction, then continued. "As a side note, I want to mention that all communication will be handled by the Jordan Station CIA personnel. There will be no transmissions between you and Colonel Ryan."

The colonel interjected, saying to his men, "You won't have any radios anyhow."

"Okay, then," DeWitt said. "That's it in a nutshell. We'll get the passports and other documents to you within a couple of days or so. Meanwhile, you can fit yourselves out as Canadian consultants. I do recommend that you read up a bit on civil engineering in case you're put through any sort of questioning." He looked over at Colonel Ryan. "Munger and I will be here at Fort Griffith until your guys leave, so if you have any questions, comments, or suggestions we'll be available for you."

"Fine," Ryan said, walking to the front of the room. He waited until the two CIA men went out to the hall to be escorted from the area, then turned to his First Team. "You are now going directly into isolation. We'll start outfitting you this afternoon. Dismissed."

The four operators stood up, assuming the position of attention, then followed Sergeant Major Jonas Blane from the room.

THE WEST BANK

Jaleela Qazi was a beautiful, well-educated, independent-minded Arab woman who had been born in Jordan. She enjoyed a privileged childhood, growing up in a wealthy family involved in the business of imports and exports between the USA, Europe, and most of the Middle East nations. These commercial activities gave her the opportunity to travel to Europe and the United States as she was growing up; thus she was exposed to traditions and conditions much different from those of her native land. Her parents raised their only child to be a modern woman with a sense of worth and ambition, along with a full appreciation of all the peoples of the world. They were Muslim, but were very much against fundamentalist terrorist groups and the nation of Iran. They resented the bloody activities of the former, particularly the suicide bombers, and the international threat posed by the latter. These traits were passed on to the daughter, who felt bitter about the suffering of innocent people, while seeing the Iranian government as anachronistic lunatics.

Jaleela attended an American school in the city of Az Zarqa, where she became fluent in the English, French, and German languages. She also received an excellent liberal arts education that stoked her natural intellect to a high level. After she'd completed her local studies, her father sent her to live with his brother and sister-in-law in New York City, where she enrolled at Columbia University.

By then she had matured into a classic Middle Eastern beauty, with dark eyes, deep brunette locks, and a face of beauty that spoke of Scheherazade, Cleopatra, and Salome. American men found her exotic and alluring, and several made romantic overtures toward the stunning Jordanian. But she shunned them all because of a loftier ambition: Jaleela admired Christiane Amanpour, the famous television journalist, and she wanted very much to be like her, and become the first recognized and successful female news reporter in the Arab world. Because of this, she majored in journalism, planning on returning to the Middle East to work in television news.

After graduation she returned to her native country, ready to realize her ambition. That was where she ran straight into a solid wall of resistance.

Women were permitted in the profession, but their roles

were severely limited to public-information announcements, weather reporting, and other mundane assignments.
And worse, they were required to dress modestly, complete
with a head covering and the traditional robelike garment,
as dictated by local custom. Jaleela realized that attaining
her goal was just not going to happen. After a couple of
months, the young woman decided she would have to emigrate permanently to America if she were to advance as she
wished in her chosen profession. Since she spoke English
with barely an accent due to her exposure to the language at
Columbia, Jaleela assumed she would have no trouble
finding a job in the USA even if she had to start with a local
television station. It was while preparing to depart for
America that she met a young man named Omar Hafez.

Hafez worked as a newscaster at the station where
Jaleela had signed on, and it was apparent to the young
man that she was extremely bitter about the situation. After
he heard that Jaleela had given notice, he approached her
one day and told her how much he sympathized with her
frustration, and also resented the state of discrimination
women had to bear in the Middle East.

Omar invited her to join him in the coffee-break room
to be alone, and after they settled down at one of the tables he told her about a clandestine organization known
by the Arabic acronym *Alifhedal,* which stood for *Arab-
min-shan-Dimuqratiya*—Arabs for Democracy. When he
first began talking about it, she immediately dismissed it
as one of those silly youth associations that met weekly in
the members' apartments to have a get-together and com-
plain uselessly about the unfairness of the mullahs who
had such influence over their society. But the more Omar
explained, the more Jaleela began to realize that Alifhedal
was a serious movement. When he invited her to attend a
session of the organization with him the next evening, she
agreed to go.

The meeting was not at an apartment, but in the back of a student coffeehouse near Ummaal University. It was a dark room, smoky from the many lit cigarettes of the attending members, who were seated around tables in front of a small platform. The first thing Jaleela noticed was that the young women present wore makeup and Western-style clothing. These were practices too dangerous to engage on the streets. Omar introduced her around; then they took a seat at a back table as the meeting began. The moderator was a middle-aged man who stepped up on the stage to make a few announcements regarding the collection of dues, purchasing some stamps and stationery, and a few other items such as refreshments for the meetings. With the business taken care of, a round-robin discussion began. It was during this activity that Jaleela found the members were in agreement with her own feelings.

Jaleela Qazi decided she would not go to America, but would join this movement that promised to reform the restrictive laws and customs of Islam, along with dethroning the mullahs to establish a fair and just democratic form of government.

As the months passed and her participation deepened, Jaleela was gradually immersed deeper, through layers of security, until she was close to the inner circle of the membership. Now that she was trusted and fully accepted, she learned that Alifhedal had powerful sponsors among Arab intellectuals and businessmen. There was a secret print shop that cranked out leaflets, pamphlets, and a newspaper called *Hurriya Arabi—Arab Freedom.* Numerous cells in the organization dealt with women's issues, religion, political matters, and other concerns. And there was a very special group known as *al-Askarin*—the Soldiers—that was newly organized. They were to be the fighters, the ones who would put their lives on the line to bring down Arab democracy's enemies in the Middle East. Jaleela wanted nothing to do with armed insurrection even though young women were encouraged to join the combatants.

Jaleela Qazi knew she was really a fully accepted member of Alifhedal when word came down from the higher echelons of the organization requesting her to volunteer to go to the West Bank and take an assignment as a writer for the *Hurriya Arabi* newspaper. This was not broadcast journalism, but it was an important assignment. She said nothing to her parents, other than to leave a note telling them not to worry, that she had left Jordan to work for a wonderful democratic cause.

Jaleela loved the new appointment. She wrote a column especially for young women, urging them to fight back against the oppression forced on them by extremist Islam. Her opposition to armed action evaporated after an incident in Pakistan.

Jaleela's other heroine and inspiration, besides Ms. Amanpour, was a very special Pakistani woman named Benazir Bhutto. Bhutto was Muslim, and had actually been the prime minister of Pakistan before being sent into exile by a military coup. When Bhutto returned to her home country to take on the nation's leader, General Pervez Musharraf, in a struggle for power, Jaleela almost went mad with joy at this very real possibility that Pakistan would once again have a female head of state. But on December 27, 2007, Bhutto was assassinated while leaving a political rally.

That was when Jaleela Qazi volunteered for al-Askarin and became a fighter.

CHAPTER TWO

The outskirts of the city of Sharqmed were a hodge-podge of carelessly built shanties and other structures that looked temporary, though the people either living and/or conducting business in them had no plans to move else-where in the foreseeable future. The area was crowded with people noisily moving through the small lanes and alleys on various errands, and there were the inevitable pushcart merchants selling cheap items as they advertised their wares with chants in singsong voices. Others, sitting at tables outside small cafés, listlessly watched all the activity while snacking or smoking hookah water pipes.

A white, very dusty van bearing the large letters UN on

each front door pulled up to the edge of the impromptu village and came to a halt. It was impossible to drive into the interior, and the driver stepped out and walked down one of the rudimentary streets. He was a blond European with blue eyes and a slim physique, and he replied to the nods and greetings given him by the idle spectators, showing he was a frequent visitor to the neighborhood. He continued on his way down to one of the buildings that was obviously a dwelling, and stopped to knock on the door.

A fat Arab in a sweater and khaki pants answered the summons. "*Sabahil kher*," he said. "Please come in, Lazlo."

"*Kaeyfae haelik?*" Lazlo replied, stepping into the dark interior. The greeter led him through a door to a back room. Another Arab, this one a slim, paunchy middle-aged man wearing a sports jacket and wool pants, was seated at a table with a cup of hot *takhin* coffee. He looked impassively at the visitor. Lazlo pulled out an empty chair and sat down, speaking in English. "I hear you are going on a trip."

The man nodded. "Yes. To a faraway land." With the challenge and password taken care of, he took a sip of coffee. "I am Shakeel Bashir."

"I am Lazlo. Everything is arranged for your journey."

"When do you collect me?" Bashir asked.

"Tomorrow night," Lazlo said. "I will come here to call for you. We will travel in a United Nations van."

"That is good," Bashir said. "No special attention will be called to it." He paused for another drink from the small cup, draining it. "Where do we go?"

"A safehouse," Lazlo replied. "It is a secure and comfortable place to wait."

"What is the location?"

"Sorry."

"I understand," Bashir said. "Do you know how long I will have to wait at this safehouse?"

"No, but I have been assured that within a week you will be on your way."

"If it is a comfortable place, that will not be so bad," Bashir commented.

"I envy you," Lazlo said. "I wish I could go to America." He stood up. "I will return here at twenty-two hundred hours tomorrow. I must go now. Wait at least a half hour before you leave. It is not good that we be seen together."

"I understand," Bashir said.

FORT GRIFfiTH, MISSOURI
THE CAVE—ISOLATION AREA
1400 HOURS LOCAL
2000 HOURS ZULU

The team was taking it easy, locked into one of those traditional military hurry-up-and-wait modes. Their bags and carry-ons were packed with civilian gear in which every item was Canadian, including the magazines, paperback books, and notebooks. The clothing they were to wear on the flight to the Middle East was hung up in wall lockers, ready to be put on when it was time to leave for the trip to Lambert–Saint Louis International Airport. That would begin the first leg of the flight, then on to Amman, Jordan, after a stopover in Orlando, Florida.

Mack Gerhardt was sitting at a table, cheating outrageously at a game of solitaire, unaware that Bob Brown had removed the ten of spades from the deck. Jonas Blane occupied a chair across from Mack, perusing a pro football magazine with rundowns on all the teams for the year's season. Carlito Grey lay on a nearby bunk with his hands behind his head, staring up at the ceiling.

"I don't like it," Jonas said, watching Mack put a black six on a red seven.

Carlito cleared his throat, turning his eyes toward the table. "What don't you like, boss?"

"This whole operation," Jonas said. "The West Bank is the last place I want to go."

Mack chuckled. "Where's the first place?"

"I'd tell you, but you'd have a jealous fit," Jonas said.

"Wouldn't bother me none," Mack stated. "Every time I come back from a mission, I make all kinds of noise at the front door to give her boyfriend enough time to get out the back."

Bob grinned. "You don't want any trouble, right, Mack?"

"Right," Mack said, frowning at the layout of cards. "Y'know, I'm cheating like a mortgage broker and a used-car salesman all rolled into one, but I can't win none of these games."

Bob flipped the missing card onto the table. "Will that help?"

"You bastard," Mack said matter-of-factly, picking up the missing pasteboard.

Carlito sat up on his bunk and looked at Jonas. "Go ahead, boss. Tell us what you don't like about this mission."

Jonas replied, "Let me tell you fine sergeants for sure that Israel, the West Bank, and the Gaza Strip are a big boiling pot of the worst kind of trouble. I've talked to guys who've been there before. They say there're more double-crossers, turncoats, backstabbers, snitchers, two-timers—"

"We get the picture, boss," Bob said, interrupting.

"The chances we have of getting compromised are many and real," Jonas continued. "We could well end up in unmarked graves somewhere out there in the boondocks with bullet holes in the backs of our skulls."

Mack, now with a full deck, quickly finished the game and gathered up the cards. "I wouldn't worry none. This is a pretty simple operation. We go there and get took to a safehouse, where the defector is waiting. The Agency guy then radios for a U.S. Navy chopper and it picks us up. We make a quick flight out to a carrier, then another back to Virginia, where we drop our deserter off. It's as easy as one of Carlito's girlfriends."

"My women are all ladies," Carlito protested.

"Oh, yeah?" Mack said. "What about that one I seen walking around with a mattress on her back offering curb service?"

"Hey!" Jonas said angrily. "You guys knock off playing the dozens and turn a serious eye on this situation we've been put into."

"There is one thing that worries me, though," Mack admitted. "That lying, conniving Munger is behind it."

"My point is made," Jonas said. He stood up and put one foot on the chair seat. "While we're over there I want everybody to stay doubly alert. By that I mean more than just keeping your eyes and ears open. Listen to *what* people say, the *way* they say it, and particularly *who* they're saying it to."

Carlito got off the bunk and walked over to the soda dispenser, retrieving a can of Pepsi, then walking back to join the others. "We ain't gonna be in the boondocks, so at least we don't have to put up any defense perimeters."

"Maybe not," Jonas said. "But we're not all gonna sleep at the same time, understand? At night we'll rotate a one-man-at-a-time guard force. And above all, we stick together. And we're not letting some local yokel split us up. Any questions?" When nobody replied, he sat back down.

"Jesus, boss," Mack said, grinning as he dealt out another hand of solitaire. "You're gonna scare the hell out of us."

"Good," Jonas replied seriously.

AMMAN, JORDAN
QUEEN ALIA INTERNATIONAL AIRPORT
21 SEPTEMBER
2345 HOURS LOCAL
2145 HOURS ZULU

Jonas was in the lead coming off the loading ramp. Mack Gerhardt and Carlito Grey were right behind him, with Bob Brown bringing up the rear. It was Jonas who first sighted the tall, slim Arabic man dressed in a well-cut business suit. The stranger bore a neatly hand-lettered cardboard sign with the words CANADIAN PARTY.

Jonas walked up to him, offering his hand while issuing the challenge: "We are here from the Great White North."

The man shook with him, giving the passwords: "There is no snow here." He showed a friendly smile. "Joe Saada, at your service."

Jonas introduced himself and the other three operators, and Joe gestured for them to follow him. "I've made some special arrangements to get you through customs quickly. That's the advantage of being a local businessman."

They joined the throng of passengers following signs with arrows indicating the direction to customs in a half dozen languages. After going down a hall, Joe led them off through a side door. A small reception area with a couple of inspectors standing behind a long table stood waiting. Joe spoke to them in Arabic, then turned to his guests. "They're ready to process you, gentlemen. Passports ready, please."

Jonas, as usual, took the lead, placing his suitcase on the

table. He started to open it, but Joe interrupted him. "Not necessary, Mr. Blane. Just show him your passport."

The procedure took no more than a couple of minutes as the phony Canadian documents were fully accepted and stamped. The travelers and their escort went out a door opposite the one they'd used as an entrance, and walked past a couple of Jordanian security guards in the general terminal. The pair of men armed with submachine guns regarded them with very little interest.

Jonas grinned over at Joe Saada. "You seem to have everything well arranged."

"Part of the service," Joe joked.

The group went to a van parked at the curb outside the customs building, where the chauffeur took their bags and put them in the back. Bob, Mack, and Carlito sat in the rear seat, while Jonas and Joe took the front one.

"Where are we headed?" Jonas asked.

"We'll be going directly to my office building near downtown Amman," Joe replied. "By the way, the driver is completely trustworthy. He's been with the business since the days my father ran it, but it's always best to be discreet in this part of the world, no matter who you're with."

Jonas turned and looked at his three men. "See? What did I tell you?"

The name of the Saada family business was Nijmi Engineering Limited, and it was a working firm that had been established by Joe's great-grandfather in the 1920s, after the British separated out a region of Transjordan from Palestine. The country was granted full independence from Britain in 1946, becoming a kingdom, and the Saadas' fortunes grew in the new political climate. The West Bank and East Jerusalem were added to the nation during the Arab-Israeli War in 1948, when it was renamed Jordan. However, these were lost to Israel in the 1967 War. A peace treaty with Israel was signed in October 1994. Once again Nijmi Engineering benefited.

Joe Saada's parents eventually emigrated to America in 1970, partly to remove themselves from the precarious goings-on in the Middle East, but mostly because his father had been having run-ins with his own father and an older brother. He eventually got a position with a civil engineering firm in Ohio, where Yusuf "Joe" Saada was born in 1972. The son made several trips back to Jordan during his growing-up years, and enjoyed spending his summers working with engineers on various projects not only in Jordan, but also in Syria, the West Bank, and even a few times in Israel. After his graduation from Ohio State University with a degree in structural engineering, he was recruited into the CIA because of his fluency in Arabic as well as knowledge of the Middle East. Now, after fourteen years with the Agency, he was in charge of the Jordan Station, working in the family firm without his kinsmen's knowledge that he was using the job as a cover for his intelligence work.

During the drive to their destination, Jonas looked with misgivings at the sights through the side window. The view was typically Middle Eastern, with donkeys and carts sharing the streets with late-model sedans and industrial trucks. The pedestrians were typical Arabs, wearing kaffiyehs and long brussa shirts, women draped in the concealing garb of burkas, and a few younger people in Western-style clothing. This was a semimodern area of the world. Jonas considered the environment unnatural, with the enforced separation of men and women that included all the attending taboos. No wonder it was easy to recruit suicide bombers from among a population of sex-starved young men. The story of the seventy beautiful virgins awaiting each martyr in paradise would be exceedingly appealing to some

horny teenager. The Unit team leader shuddered inwardly
and turned his eyes to the front.

The van turned off the highway and into an industrial
park, going around a two-story building to a parking lot.
The passengers disembarked and once again fell in behind
Joe Saada, following him into the interior of the edifice
while the chauffeur tended to the baggage. They were taken
down a hall to an area obviously separated from the rest of
the structure. There were four apartments, well furnished
and well-appointed, available for visitors. Jonas allowed
each man to take one in spite of his instructions that they
weren't to be separated. These were close together and had
interconnecting doors. A common living room was located
at the far end of the hall.

When the luggage was properly distributed, Joe had the
men gather in the parlor. As everyone settled down, the
chauffeur appeared to serve drinks. With that chore accomplished, he withdrew.

Joe took a sip of his scotch and water. "I have some
automatic pistols, shoulder holsters, and magazine belts
with fully loaded magazines, of course, for your use on this
operation. That will give you six extra, though I don't
really expect them to be needed."

"What kind of shooting irons have you got for us, Joe?"
Mack asked.

"SIG Sauer P-two-two-eight nine-millimeter autos with
thirteen-round magazines," Joe replied. "That means you'll
each have a grand total of ninety-one bullets."

"Ninety-two," Mack countered him. "There'll be one in
each chamber."

"I stand corrected," Joe said. "At any rate, they are excellent compact hand weapons that will be perfect for the
job ahead. I know you may have personal preferences for
something else, but you'll have to go along with these."

"Can we keep 'em?" Bob Brown asked.

Joe chuckled. "I'm afraid not. And I want the weapons back, since I signed for them."

Jonas asked, "What about the radio to contact the ship for the chopper?"

"We have several available for that job," Joe said. "No problem."

"How far away is the pickup point for the defector?" Carlito Grey inquired.

"About sixty kilometers from here," Joe answered. "Roughly thirty-seven miles. It's the town of Musalmar."

"And when do we leave to make the snatch?" Mack asked.

"Day after tomorrow at around oh-six-hundred hours," Joe replied. "And it's not a snatch. The guy wants to go with you."

Mack snorted. "Hell, from the way the boss has been bitching, I figured we were gonna have to drag the bastard kicking and screaming clear across the Sahara Desert."

Jonas glared at Mack. "I've never dropped a master sergeant for push-ups, but there's always the first time."

"I get it, boss," Mack said.

CHAPTER THREE

The convoy made up of three battered Toyota pickups roared into the small village, the lack of mufflers on two of them making the entrance noisy and disturbing. The commotion immediately caught the attention of people on the street, and they snapped their heads around to check out the raucous disturbance.

Eight gunmen, facing outward, occupied the back of each vehicle. They hung onto the roll bars of aluminum tubing, leaning against the centrifugal forces of sharp turns. A driver and two more armed men were in the cabs. All wore ski masks to hide their faces, leaving only glaring eyes visible.

The inhabitants in the vicinity of the careening trucks quickly shuffled back next to the buildings lining the dirt street, anticipating serious trouble. The invaders were members of Barq-min-Islam—the Lightning of Islam—a relatively new terrorist group that had sprung up on the scene, and had already made its presence felt in both the West Bank and Israel, causing bloodshed and chaos.

The trucks came to a stop at the ancient well in the town square, and all thirty-three gunsels jumped out onto the street. A half dozen took positions as guards around the Toyotas, holding their AK-47 assault rifles in threatening manners, gesturing and yelling for everyone to stay back. Their twenty-seven buddies fanned out, rushing down three different streets that led off into the residential areas.

A couple of kilometers to the east, on the other side of the border, a pair of Israeli soldiers occupied a watchtower. Their high-power 40x telescope was trained on the scene in the middle of the town. One of the soldiers shook his head ruefully. "Some poor *nebachel* is going to get it," he said, using the Yiddish of his grandfather.

"*B'va'deye!*" his buddy agreed, after taking a look.

Back in the village one of the groups of gunmen appeared, dragging a man with them. Then the other two teams appeared, each also with a single prisoner. The captives were plainly frightened, and they gestured at their tormentors and begged for mercy, asking why they had been pulled from their homes. The terrorists made no reply, dragging the three to the square and throwing them to the stone plaza. Then one of the invaders leaped up on the edge of the well and fired his weapon into the air to make sure he had everyone's attention.

"These three traitors have been identified to us as inform-ers to the Israelis," the man announced. "Each one has a job across the border working for some miserable Jew, and brings information from the West Bank to Mossad agents who visit them at their workplaces. They tell the Zionist dev-ils about us and anything else that is going on around here."

The trio screamed out their innocence of such charges, but the villagers now scowled at the terrified men. One old geezer shouted, pointing at one of the cowering wretches, "I always knew Tabassum was a rotter! He is just like his father!"

The gunmen's spokesman was glad to hear some agreement from the crowd, and he continued. "Normally we would execute these dogs, but our sources tell us they have passed no important information to the Jews. So we will give them a very special Barq-min-Islam punishment."

He jumped down from the truck and motioned a portion of the people to move aside. One of the men was pushed in front of him and stood there terrified, crying out, "*Rahmi*— mercy, please! I have done nothing!"

The terrorist spokesman raised his AK-47 and fired once, hitting the man in his left knee. The victim shrieked loudly as the strike of the bullet spun him around to drop to the pavement. The other two now struggled violently against the hands grasping them, as they stared at their friend rolling on the cobblestones.

The second managed to break loose and run, but the gunman took quick aim and shot him in the back of the head. The 7.62-millimeter slug struck and expanded, blowing off the top of the guy's skull. The militant glared at the third, who stood pale and trembling. "You want it in the knee or the head?"

The man stumbled out by the wounded victim and turned to face his punishment with his eyes shut tight. Another shot sounded, and the man's kneecap was instantly turned into bloody mush. Now the surviving pair lay close together, bleeding heavily from their wounds, sobbing loudly. Members of the victims' families wept in grief and terror for their unfortunate kinsmen, while the women of the dead man fell to their knees and began keening in shrill voices.

"Now they are cripples," the gunman said triumphantly, pointing to the injured men. "I will wager all that I own that the miserable Hebrews for whom they work will dismiss them as useless invalids." He fired another burst from the AK-47 skyward. "Let that be a warning to you all. Whoever cooperates with the Jews or helps them will suffer the wrath of our holy movement. Long live the Barq-min-Islam. *Allah akbar*—God is great!"

The large group of gunmen returned to the trucks and roared out of the village as noisily as they had arrived. Now the people turned their eyes on the two seriously injured men, watching coldly as their families rushed to carry them home.

One kindly villager went into a nearby apothecary to call for a Red Crescent ambulance.

THE JORDAN–WEST BANK BORDER
23 SEPTEMBER
0645 HOURS LOCAL
0445 HOURS ZULU

The Nijmi Engineering van had only to slow down as it approached the Jordanian border guard station. The guards there knew the driver, Joe Saada, very well from his many crossings, and signaled him to continue the short distance over to the Israeli Border Police. When Joe reached the second roadblock he brought the van to a halt as a young policeman approached the vehicle. He glanced in and recognized Joe, but gave Jonas, who shared the front seat, a hard look. Joe hit the button on the dash, causing the right-hand door to slide fully back, exposing the Unit operators in the two rear seats.

"*Darkon gam tuhudat zehhut*," the Israeli said tersely to them.

The Americans couldn't understand one word of what he said, but correctly guessed he wanted to see their papers. They each handed him their personal packets of visas, passports, health certificates, and international driver's licenses.

The guy suddenly grinned and spoke in English. "Canadians, huh? I have an uncle who lives in Ottawa."

Mack smiled back. "Never heard of the place."

"No?" the policeman said surprised. "It is the capital, and—" He suddenly laughed. "You are joking, yes?"

"Yeah," Mack said. "I always try to lighten things up."

"Well!" the Israeli said good-naturedly. "You certainly did fool me."

"Yeah," Mack said, almost leering.

Jonas whipped his head around and gave Mack a look that could have melted a block of cold steel. The Unit operator immediately quieted down.

The policeman checked over the rest of their papers and returned them, then swung his attention back to the driver. "What is your business in the West Bank today, Mr. Saada?"

"The Palestinian government is giving serious consideration to reclaiming several of the abandoned Jewish settlements," Saada said. "They hope to set up more comfortable refugee centers in their places." He pointed his thumb over his shoulder to the backseats. "These are consultants brought over for some advice. They have built several villages for Eskimos up around the Arctic Circle, and we need the benefits of their expertise and experience."

"Those empty communities will be excellent for that purpose," the policeman said. "I know. I helped drag the settlers out of there after our government ordered them expelled. That was a very unpleasant task."

"I'm sure it was," Joe said.

The Israeli waved them on, and Joe gunned the motor to

drive twenty-five meters to the checkpoint manned by the Palestinian police. They were easygoing, like the Jordanian border guards, and simply nodded to let it be known that the van didn't have to stop.

Joe continued down the highway, getting up to speed. "Well, gentlemen," he said cheerfully. "Welcome to the West Bank."

"Any more checkpoints or roadblocks?" Jonas Blane asked glumly.

"Probably," Joe replied.

MUSALMAR
0930 HOURS LOCAL
0730 HOURS ZULU

The safehouse was in a comfortable residential neighborhood where the more affluent citizens of the town had their homes. There were no sidewalks along the street, and each house had a wall around its lot that ran right to the curb. Broken pieces of glass were imbedded in the tops of the barriers, with coils of razor wire added to increase security.

The van with Joe driving went down to the middle of the block, and he hit the electronic door opener clipped to the visor, and an iron gate in the wall on the left opened slowly. He drove into an open courtyard and braked to a stop by the door. A white United Nations sedan was parked on the opposite side of the space.

A blond man stepped out the door of the house, waving as Joe exited the vehicle. "How are you, Lazlo?" the Arab-American called out.

"Fine," the man responded. "I brought the package you wanted." He looked at the Americans, who now stood beside the van with their luggage. "Hello."

"Howdy," Jonas said.

Lazlo turned and went into the interior with the others following. They entered a kitchen, and an Arab man stood by the refrigerator, nervously smoking. He acknowledged the newcomers with only a steady gaze as they set their bags down.

Lazlo looked at the Arab, chuckling. "These are the fellows who are going to take you to America, Shakeel."

Now the man relaxed and nodded a greeting while displaying a smile. "I am happy to be meeting with you," he said in English.

Jonas ignored him, turning his attention to Joe Saada. "We're gonna check the place out."

"Help yourself," Joe invited.

The Americans left the kitchen, stepping into what was probably supposed to be a regular dining room. This area, however, was set up like a minirestaurant for the convenience of a dozen or more people. The living room beyond that had an unusually large number of sofas, easy chairs, and settees. Again, this was obviously a place where numerous guests could be accommodated. Jonas led the team upstairs, where they found four bedrooms. All had a minimum of three beds in them, with the one farthest down the hall having six small cots.

"This is where we'll bunk," Jonas announced.

"Hey, boss," Carlito said, "there ain't gonna be but seven of us here. We could spread out."

"What did I say about staying close together back at Fort Griffith?" Jonas asked testily.

"You said we was gonna stay close together," Carlito said.

"And what are we gonna do?"

Carlito smiled sheepishly. "We're gonna stay close together."

"Right," Jonas said. "And from now on we wear our

shoulder holsters and the ammo belts at all times during waking hours, and especially while pulling guard duty. When you sleep, you have the weaponry under your pillows. Now, Carlito and Bob, go down and bring up the bags. Mack and I are going to check out the basement."

The two youngest members of the team went to tend their bellhop chores, while Jonas and Mack made their way back to the first floor. They found a narrow door and went through it to descend a flight of steps to the basement. This was a wide-open area with a government-issue Shadowfire radio set up on a table in one corner. Across from it was a steel wire-mesh cage that held a weapon rack containing a half dozen M-4A1 carbines. Some metal ammo cans were neatly stacked next to the weaponry. Down on the far end were unlabeled crates stacked three high.

"I wonder what's in them wood boxes," Mack remarked aloud.

"Emergency items, I guess," Jonas said. "C'mon. Let's get back upstairs."

1130 HOURS LOCAL
0930 HOURS ZULU

Lunch was a quiet affair, with everyone in a pensive mood. Since the safehouse had no permanent staff, Joe Saada kept the larder stocked with dehydrated food designed for emergency situations. Each man got into the box and found something suitable to eat. The boiling water needed was prepared on the stove, and in less than fifteen minutes everyone was chomping down on their choice, using plastic spoons kept in one of the kitchen drawers.

Lazlo and the defector, Shakeel Bashir, were not too pleased with the eats, but the Unit operators didn't mind. Most of the time, when they ate such rations, they were out on a mission somewhere in the hinterlands of a foreign country, miserable and isolated. At least they had a roof over their heads and a bed to sleep in under the present circumstances. For Joe Saada this was just another trip to the safehouse, and since it was temporary, he couldn't have cared less what he had to eat.

Jonas looked up from his rice-and-chicken dinner. "When is contact with the ship going to be made?"

"My instructions are to transmit at fourteen hundred hours tomorrow," Joe replied. "We'll get the exact schedule, along with the landing spot for the chopper. You have to keep in mind that this flyover of Israeli territory has to be carefully coordinated."

"Yeah," Jonas said. "That's understandable. One slip and we get an antiaircraft rocket shot up our collective asses."

Mack Gerhardt nodded his agreement. "That's gonna be the trickiest part of the whole operation. Everybody on the ground will be able to hear and see the aircraft, no matter what time of day or night it arrives."

"Another thing," Bob Brown added. "There's not very many of us, so security on the LZ will be another problem to deal with. You were right, boss: This is some real hairy goings-on. God save us from Murphy's Law."

"Say, Joe," Carlito Grey said, "have you got any of that dried ice cream?"

CHAPTER FOUR

MUSALMAR, WEST BANK
24 SEPTEMBER
0945 HOURS LOCAL
0745 HOURS ZULU

The inhabitants of the safehouse lounged around on the many choices of furniture in the building's living room. Breakfast had been another dehydrated feast, washed down with instant coffee. The Unit operators were armed as per the firm instructions of their leader, Jonas Blane, who called for the pistol holsters and magazine belts to be strapped on at all times. However, since he was not subject to the Unit's authority, Joe Saada was weaponless, clad in one of the outfits of tank top, shorts, and sandals he kept in an upstairs bureau for his stays at the house. Lazlo, the mysterious blond man, was stretched out on a sofa taking a nap, while Shakeel Bashir sat stiff and tense in one of the easy chairs. He had yet to feel completely secure in this crowd of foreigners.

It was four hours and fifteen minutes before Joe Saada was scheduled to go down into the basement to the Shadowfire radio to raise the U.S. Navy ship that would dispatch the blessed helicopter to them. There had been a big discussion among the Americans at breakfast about the possible locations of an LZ for the extraction. The consensus reached was that the best place would be somewhere in Israel, west of all Palestinian eyes and authority. The choice also made sense because the Israelis had already cleared the chopper for their airspace.

Suddenly the intercom mounted on the wall by the front door rang. Joe Saada frowned in puzzlement, then went over and pressed the transmit button while leaning close to the mouthpiece. "Do you have a delivery?" he asked in English.

An accented male voice came over the speaker. "Yes. We bring the books you ordered."

"All right," Joe said. "Wait a minute." He turned from the phone, fixing his eyes on Jonas. "This is unexpected. But he has the correct password. It's 'books' for this week."

"You don't seem to be expecting anybody," Jonas said, getting to his feet. "Do you consider this unusual?"

Joe shrugged. "There could be some last-minute instructions sent to the Jordan Station to be passed on to us. Or perhaps something has been changed or gone wrong."

Now Bashir jumped up. "Wrong? Is it wrong something? What is it?"

"Sit down," Jonas said. He snapped his fingers at his team. "I'll take the left side of the room. Mack, to the right. Bob, go to kitchen and stand ready to rush in if something happens. Carlito, get behind the door so that when it's opened by our visitors they won't be able to see you." He pointed to Lazlo and Bashir. "Get upstairs."

As soon as everyone had positioned themselves, Joe turned his attention back to the phone. "I am buzzing you in." He hit a button as Jonas peered through the peephole in the door.

Four casually dressed men came through the gate in the wall, walking down the short sidewalk to the house. Joe opened the door and motioned them to enter. The quartet was made up of dark, husky men with muscular builds that their clothing couldn't hide. They stopped short at seeing Jonas and Mack. The two Americans, with drawn pistols, watched the visitors from both sides of the room. When Joe closed the door, Carlito stepped into view, also showing a hand weapon.

Joe studied the strangers for a quick moment. "What can we do for you?"

One of the men stepped forward. "It should be obvious. We are here to collect the defector."

"What defector?" Joe asked.

The stranger shrugged. "I have already given the password I was told to use on the phone at the gate. My name is Mofaz."

"You are Israeli?" Joe asked.

"The Mossad," Mofaz said. "Our instructions are to take the defector into custody from you."

"How did you know about this place?" Joe demanded angrily.

"The CIA, of course," Mofaz replied impatiently. "What is the problem?"

"We don't know a godamn thing about the Mossad being part of this mission," Jonas interjected.

"That is impossible," Mofaz insisted. "We are well aware that Shakeel Bashir is of no use to you Americans. All of this was arranged between the United States and the Israeli government, and activated through your CIA and those of us in the Mossad. We were told that when we came here he would be turned over to us."

"Well, pal," Jonas said, "our orders are to get him out of the Middle East and back to the States. And that's exactly what we're gonna do."

"We cannot permit that," Mofaz said coldly. "I am sure you are aware of his importance to us."

Mack moved forward, closer to Jonas. "Y'know something, boss, I smell a rat, and it has the name Delmar Munger written all over it."

Joe Saada studied the Israelis for a moment, then looked at Jonas. "We're going to have to give Bashir to them. We have no choice."

"No way!" Jonas snapped. "I have a mission assignment to bring him back to the United States; and there is no question about obeying that order."

"Listen to me, Jonas," Joe said. "You are in my bailiwick, understand? And this is a very sensitive and precarious situation. We have a good working relationship with the Mossad, and something like this could compromise my entire intelligence net in the West Bank."

"I'm not turning Bashir over to them," Jonas said in a determined tone of voice.

"You're going to have to, whether you want to or not," Joe snapped. "And you'll have to surrender yourselves into their custody as well. These guys are going to be nervous with you on the loose in the West Bank."

"That is a fact," Mofaz said. "But we will see that you're sent back to the United States as soon as it is practical to do so."

"Piss up a rope," Jonas said.

One of the Israelis went for his shoulder holster. Jonas and Mack each kicked off simultaneous rounds into the man's head as Carlito jumped back out of the way. The three surviving Israelis returned fire, their bullets smacking into the plaster walls, making dust clouds billow out to float through the room.

Now Bob Brown charged into the room, his SIG Sauer barking three times. Outnumbered, the Israelis made a quick withdrawal through the front door, firing back to cover their exit. The Unit operators ducked down and pumped out more slugs. The dead Mossad agent, with very little of his cranium left, lay crumpled on the doorjamb, his blood running in rivulets into the carpet.

Mack Gerhardt was breathing a bit hard. "Well, all them hours spent in the shooting house have paid off. They weren't quick enough to get any of us."

"Godamn it!" Joe exclaimed. "You killed one of them!"

"He drew his weapon, godamn it!" Jonas growled. "What were we supposed to do, let him shoot us down?"

Joe groaned. "This screws up everything."

"We still have the helicopter," Bob said.

"Yeah," Joe agreed. "But remember it has to cross Israeli sovereign territory to get to us. Then return to the carrier the same way. The Israelis are not going to be in a mood to cooperate after this incident."

"You have that transmission to make at fourteen hundred hours," Jonas said. "That is something that must be done. The diplomats have a tough job ahead of them to calm everybody down. We'll just soldier on like we've been ordered to do."

"We'll probably be stuck here for a couple of weeks while this is straightened out," Joe said.

Now Lazlo and Bashir came gingerly down the stairs. When the Arab defector saw the body of the Israeli, he cried out, "*Shu halmsibi!* This is terrible!"

Lazlo shook his head in dismay. "I have to get out of here as quickly as possible or I am going to be discovered."

"Right," Joe said. "And take a roundabout way back."

Lazlo quickly left the house through the kitchen door.

1415 HOURS LOCAL
1215 HOURS ZULU

Bashir was tucked away in an upstairs bedroom, while Mack, Carlito, and Bob were at security positions in the living room and upstairs. Jonas was in the basement standing next to Joe Saada, who was on the radio trying to contact the U.S. Navy. "Doghouse, this is Checkers. Doghouse, this is Checkers. Over."

"Crap!" Jonas snarled.

"Fifteen minutes of trying and not a peep out of them," Joe said.

"If they were out there, they'd have answered already," Jonas said. "We're royally hosed."

"I can get hold of the CIA station office in Amman," Joe said. "I'll give a full report of what happened. Meanwhile there's another safehouse in Sharqmed. We'll hole up there until new exfiltration plans are organized. If things really go wrong we can use Bashir as a bargaining chip."

"Listen to me," Jonas said in a low, serious voice. "My orders are to get Bashir back to the States. And that's what I'm gonna do, or die trying."

Joe sighed. "Okay, Jonas. And that's probably what you—all of us—are going to do: die trying."

WASHINGTON, D.C.

Senator Herbert Kinkaid was the chairman of the Senate's powerful Committee on Intelligence and Special Operations. This eighty-two-year-old politico from New

England was serving his seventh term in the Senate, and was well-known on the Washington scene as an anachronistic leftist with a near-pathological hatred of all military and police personnel, along with their organizations. He had been born into wealth and privilege and attended the best private prep schools before going on to Harvard University, where he was graduated in the class of 1947. When World War II first started in Europe in 1939, Kinkaid had marched with other Reds and Communists as antiwar protestors. This all changed when the Germans invaded Stalin's Soviet Union, and the young leftists became strident hawks of war. Kinkaid was to never take up arms in the worldwide struggle, because his extremely bad eyesight kept him out of the draft. This afforded him plenty of time to be active in causes to send money and war matériel to the Russians.

Like many young people who had known luxury and unlimited opportunities all their lives, Herbert Kinkaid unaccountably turned against his own social class. He got into politics early, using family funds to finance a run for the state legislature. The young man was a firebrand, espousing causes such as labor strikes, socialized medicine, protection of criminals, abolishing the death penalty, and even introducing a bill that would make it illegal for police officers to carry guns.

But he really found his niche in a particularly zealous antiwar movement during the conflict in Vietnam. This group did the usual protesting, as was their rights as American citizens, but they went a few steps further after escalating legitimate demonstrations into outright riots, in which they pelted the police with rocks. Additionally they conducted rowdy picket lines at the front entrances of military bases. Kinkaid's comrades also made threatening calls to families with relatives serving in the military, and once appeared howling insults at the funeral of a U.S. Air Force

pilot who had been downed over South Vietnam. Kinkaid
was too politically shrewd to participate in such activities,
but he lurked in the background, happily watching the
goings-on through the thick lenses of his glasses.

Kinkaid, taking advantage of widespread frustrations
and discord when the public had turned solidly against the
war in Southeast Asia in 1970, was elected to the United
States Senate, and he had been there ever since. The solid
seniority he had built up brought him the powerful chair-
manship of the Senate Committee on Intelligence and Special Operations, and he used the position to advance his
radical agenda.

THE SENATE BUILDING
1530 HOURS LOCAL
2030 HOURS ZULU

Norman DeWitt and Delmar Munger strode down the
second-floor hall toward the office they sought. It was a
crowded area filled with Senate staff people, security personnel, lobbyists, and others hurrying quickly toward the
areas where they had deals to barter and payouts to make in
the large marble-and-granite edifice.

Senator Herbert Kinkaid, thanks to his many decades of
public service, had one of the best offices in the building. It
was a corner arrangement, in which the ancient politico had
two outside views: through one large window behind him
and another to his left. Both offered excellent vistas of the
nation's capital city.

When DeWitt and Munger reached the office, they went
through the outer door to the reception area, walking up to
the very attractive young lady stationed there. She wore a
low-cut blouse and had a sexually aggressive expression on
her well made-up face. There were no in- or out-boxes on

the desk; nor were there any indications of the tools of stenography, such as pencils or notepads. Only a single piece of paper with names neatly typed on it occupied the expanse of the desktop.

"Good afternoon," DeWitt said. "I'm Mr. DeWitt, and this is Mr. Munger. We have an appointment to see Senator Kinkaid."

The girl checked the list on her desk, then looked up with a smile. "Yes! The senator said to send you in the very moment you arrived."

"Thank you so much," DeWitt said.

After a quick but obvious glance at her cleavage, Munger preceded him to the door, opening it to let his boss pass through. They entered a short, empty hallway leading to a door at the end. Munger chuckled softly. "Do you think the old boy is getting a little of that?"

"Only she, the senator, and the manufacturers of Viagra would know," DeWitt replied with a grin.

When they reached the door and rapped, an old man's voice sounded from behind it: "Come in, gentlemen." They entered to find the senator behind his desk with two chairs conveniently arranged in front of it. "Olivia told me over the intercom you had arrived. Please sit down."

They took their seats, with Munger thinking the receptionist looked more like her name should be Bambi or Candy than just plain Olivia.

DeWitt didn't waste any time getting the ball rolling. "I'm very happy you could see us on such short notice, Senator. We have a very important matter to discuss with you."

"I am not overly fond of the CIA," Kinkaid said. "But you two lads have presented me with some very interesting facts in the past. Am I to assume that you have come here to pass on some additional tidbits about those hired killers referred to as the Unit?"

"That would be the correct assumption," DeWitt said. "Munger here was the man who presented the irregularities of their activities in the Democratic Republic of the Congo back last spring and early summer."

"I recall the shocking details," Kinkaid said. "Especially the massacre of those innocent civilians, and the assassination of two French citizens. Are you here regarding more information on that criminal activity, or is there something more recent?"

"More recent, sir," DeWitt said. "We received word about a defector from a terrorist group that operates in the West Bank as well as the Gaza Strip. Circumstances and protocol, along with an insistent supervisor, forced Mr. Munger and me to turn to the Unit and send them to the Middle East to pick up the fellow. They were to take him to a proper place where he could be turned over to the Israeli Mossad intelligence organization."

"I am very much aware of that gang," Kinkaid said.

"I think we should advise you now that this is a highly classified situation, Senator," Munger said. "You might, at this point in time, prefer that we say no more and take our leave. You may not want to get involved."

"Of course I wish to become involved, gentlemen!" Kinkaid exclaimed. "It is because of dedicated reformers like you that I will be able to bring the baby killers of the Unit to justice."

"Very well, sir," DeWitt said. "The Unit went to the West Bank, and the defector was delivered to them. But when the Mossad arrived at the rendezvous, the Unit leader refused to hand the man over to them."

"I suppose it was that arrogant Sergeant Major Blane," Kinkaid hissed. "People like me worked hard to bring equality to colored . . . er, black . . . that is to say, African-Americans, and some of them have no gratitude. This Blane is a prime example of that ilk."

Munger leaned forward. "This gets worse, Senator. We are certain that Blane demanded money for the man. Of course the Israelis refused. This disagreement led to a gun-fight. One of the Mossad agents was shot down in cold blood before the others could escape."

"What has been Israel's reaction?" the senator asked. "I have heard nothing about this incident."

"It is like Mr. Munger said," DeWitt reiterated. "This is a top-secret operation. It cannot be handled in the open. This is just one more incident of the Unit hiding behind security classifications in order to commit murder and ex-tortion. This case alone justifies the disbanding of that gang and the imprisonment of its personnel."

"I am in total agreement," Senator Kinkaid said. "I shall call my committee together and have a subpoena to drag that miserable Unit commander in front of us for such an intense and thorough questioning that those ridiculous med-als on his chest will tarnish." He paused. "What was his name again?"

"Colonel Tom Ryan," Munger replied.

"Ah, yes!" the senator exclaimed. "Colonel Tom Ryan!"

CHAPTER FIVE

Ishtiaq Naguib was the commander of the Barq-min-Islam mujahideen, and was addressed as *Kumandan* by his subordinates. This tall, bearded man was thirty-six years old, married, with two wives, and seven kids he was raising as he had been raised, i.e., with the powerful belief that the destruction of the nation of Israel was a sacred duty to every Arab man, woman, and child. And when that was done, they would confront all the non-Muslims in the world and slaughter those who would not submit to the tenets of Islam.

Three days before he had personally led a group of his fighters into the village of Bahrsahil, where they rounded up three men who had been spotted at various times carrying on friendly conversations with various persons in the small Israeli town of Yahashfa. This was the community in which the trio had jobs, and they crossed from the West Bank into Israel every day except for the Jewish sabbath to labor as bricklayers. There was no proof they were informers, but the Kumandan disliked his Palestinian countrymen who had any sort of contact—other than the slitting of throats—with Israelis, and he decided to punish them as traitors. But since he really wasn't sure of any particular misconduct on their part, he had decided to be merciful by shooting the men in their kneecaps rather than executing them outright. After all, they were Muslims, and as such had the right to lenient treatment as he interpreted it from the Koran.

The punishment had gone awry when one of the victims suddenly bolted and tried to escape. Kumandan had shot him in the head, killing the unfortunate man instantly. Then he asked the two survivors if they wanted bullets in the skull or the knee. They chose to take the hits in the lower extremities, and the terrorist chief quickly took care of the job. He was pleased to know they would be crippled for life, and his pleasure would have been increased if he had been later informed that the local doctor who treated their massive wounds was forced to amputate one victim's leg.

Now, with that all taken care of, Kumandan was ready to return to a status of business as usual. The Barq-min-Islam's suicide-bombing activities had been thwarted by heightened alertness of the Jewish police, and the last three martyrs-to-be he had sent were now locked away in an army prison outside of the city of Bet Shemesh. Because of those setbacks, the terrorist organization turned to launching a new campaign of hit-and-run raids across the border. These attacks would target small Israeli military installations, shooting them up before making quick withdrawals back to the West Bank.

Barq-min-Islam headquarters was in the slums of Sharqmed, and was a walled area containing four buildings. One was the headquarters, where all administrative and planning was conducted; another served as a combination supply office, armory, and warehouse; the dormitory for the mujahideen was next to that one; and off in a corner by itself was the most sinister structure in the compound: the combination jail and interrogation center, where the group's prisoners were held. In order to fool any Israeli aerial photo reconnaissance, signs were mounted on each building identifying them as innocent businesses, such as a café, greengrocer, clothing store, and—as a sort of joke— the jail/torture center sported a sign identifying it as a butcher shop.

At that particular moment, Kumandan and his planning officer, Taqqee Boudiaff, were studying the large Jordanian military map of Israel, the West Bank, and the Gaza Strip that was located in the planning room of headquarters. The acetate covering over the chart had different-colored marks on it, with red indicating potential targets, blue specifying safe areas, and black showing where suicide bombers had struck. At the moment, the two men were trying to decide which of the red marks would get their immediate attention in the new campaign of hit-and-run guerrilla warfare.

The discussion was interrupted by the arrival of the organization's number one driver. This was a twenty-year-old by the name of Sura Jettou, who was an expert at the wheel of any fast automobile. He had been sent to the house of Shakeel Bashir to pick up the liaison officer and bring him to headquarters for the day's work.

"Shakeel Bashir is not at home," Sura reported. "His servant says he is unaware of where he might be."

Kumandan glanced at Boudiaff with a frown of puzzlement. "Where could he be? He knows we have important business to conduct today."

"I've not seen him now for a week," Boudiaff said. He was a portly, bald man in his mid-forties. "It seems strange that Shakeel has not been around as of late."

"I do not like this," Kumandan said. "Come! Sura will drive us to Shakeel's house to look into this."

They left the building to go out to the light blue Fiat parked between the "clothing store" and the "café." Mabood Gamassy, Kumandan's personal bodyguard, stood by the vehicle cradling an AK-47 in his huge arms. He wore a skullcap over his shaved head, and quickly opened the passenger door to allow his boss to get in. Boudiaff and Sura entered from the other side; then Gamassy followed.

The ride to Bashir's home took a while, since it was necessary to drive through a particularly narrow street that was packed with people going about their business in the densely crowded area. Sura leaned on the horn, driving slowly but steadily through the crowd. Every time he nudged somebody, the person would turn to glare in anger, but as soon as the pedestrian spotted the Kumandan in the front seat he would jump respectfully out of the way. The leader was known to be a short-tempered man who reacted violently if displeased about something.

When they reached the defector's residence, Kumandan leaped out of the car and rushed to the gate. He grabbed the huge knocker and began to bang it hard and fast while his companions joined him.

A couple of minutes passed before Bashir's servant, Jab, appeared. He opened the gate and bowed respectfully. "*Marhaba!* Greetings."

"We wish to speak to your master," Kumandan said, stepping into the yard with the others on his heels.

"I regret he is not here, *sahib*," Jab said. He was a small, elderly man. "I fear I have not seen him for six or seven days, and I have no knowledge of his whereabouts."

"Perhaps he went to visit his wives in Al-Khalil," Kumandan suggested.

"No, *sahib*," Jab replied. "Late last evening one of the ladies called asking to speak to him."

"Take us into the house!" Kumandan ordered angrily.

"As you command, I obey, *sahib*."

The aged little man led the way to the front door, then stood respectfully aside as Kumandan and Boudiaff entered the residence. Sura and Gamassy stayed on the alert outside, with the bodyguard still attached to the AK-47.

The home was comfortably furnished, with thick carpets and a few landscape photographs on the walls. The furniture was modern, and a color television set was on in one corner of the parlor. Evidently, with his master gone, Jab had been goofing off. The little man became frightened when Kumandan charged through the door into the bedroom. The servant cringed at the sounds of drawers being pulled out and items being thrown around the room. Now Boudiaff began going through things in the living room, making a mess of the place as he searched every nook and cranny.

Kumandan emerged from the bedroom, walking up to Jab, who now shook in fear. "Listen to me, *ikhtyar*! You tell me where he has gone, and I will not tolerate any lies on your part."

"I swear on the holy Koran that I do not know, *sahib*."

Kumandan punched him hard in the face, sending him flying over a nearby easy chair. The oldster bounced off the wall before hitting the floor. When he didn't move, Boudiaff went over and knelt down to examine the oldster. "His neck is broken, Kumandan. He is dead."

"Then we shall leave him here. If Bashir comes back he'll be greeted by the stench of a rotting corpse rather than an obedient and eager servant. Let us go!"

The two went back outside, and the four Arabs repeated

the routine for getting in the car. Kumandan looked in the backseat at Boudiaff. "As soon as we get back to headquarters I want you to send out an alarm to all our cells. Tell them to drop all their activities and start a manhunt for Shakeel Bashir."

"Your will be done," Boudiaff said.

THE WEST BANK
JUNUB-MARKAZ AREA
1400 HOURS LOCAL
1200 HOURS ZULU

Joe Saada had taken a roundabout route since leaving the safehouse at Musalmar. The Nijmi Engineering van was well-known in the area and was identified with its owner. That made a precarious situation even worse. Any Arab turncoat informers for the Mossad who saw it would be able to tell the Israelis of its locations and the times it was in their vicinity. Joe began going through various checkpoints to give the appearance of different directions of travel to make it impossible for anyone to figure out their real destination.

Shakeel Bashir was now wearing a kaffiyeh and a large pair of extra-dark sunglasses. This gave him the appearance of literally hundreds of Arab men, making positive identification impossible unless he was stripped of the accoutrements. He also had brought legally issued papers he had gotten from a bribed official in the Palestinian government that bore one of his many aliases used with Barq-min-Islam.

The four Unit operators' Canadian passports and other ID were also fail-safe, since only a well-trained and experienced document expert with the right instruments would be able to figure out they were counterfeit. Joe Saada, of course, was already well covered in that area of concern.

The only time a problem occurred during the entire trip was at an isolated roadblock in an area that Joe had never visited before. It was out in the open countryside that consisted of nothing but empty scrub brush. The road was a narrow dirt affair, with potholes and deep ruts from donkey carts, small trucks, and automobiles.

The sight of a rather well-constructed permanent roadblock complete with a small building seemed strange out in an area so remote. As the van drew up to the location, three Palestinian policemen stepped from the frame structure. One stood directly to the front, while another took a position off to one side, where he had a direct view of the vehicle. The third policeman posted himself to the rear.

The front man, wearing the three-starred epaulets of a captain, walked up to the driver's side, speaking in Arabic to Joe Saada. "Your papers and driver's license," the officer demanded. The fact that he didn't employ the word "*tfaddal*"—Arabic for "please"—was a sure sign he had plenty of authority backing him up. He took his time checking the documents. When he finished he didn't hand them back. "What is your destination?"

"We are exploring the area to look for a suitable place to construct a village for refugees," Joe answered. "We are an engineering company under contract to the Palestinian Authority."

"I can read the signs on your doors," the captain said curtly. Bashir was sitting next to Joe in the front seat, and his papers were examined next. The policeman took three full minutes, and then kept them. Then he spoke to Joe. "Open the side door."

"Of course," Joe said. "The four men there are Canadian. They do not speak Arabic."

"Tell them to give me their papers," the captain ordered.

Joe complied, and the operators handed over the documents. Jonas took what appeared to be a casual look at the scenery through the windows, but he was actually sizing up the number and location of riflemen around the van. This would be tricky in case of trouble, even though the Unit operators could reach inside their jackets and pull out the pistols in the matter of an instant. He started to utter some firing assignments, but stopped when the thought occurred to him that the policeman might very well speak and understand English. Everyone outwardly appeared to be calm, but the tension was almost like an electric charge in the vehicle.

Joe decided to make some small talk to see if he could break the ice and put the captain in a friendlier mood. "I was quite surprised to see a roadblock so far out here in the wilderness."

The captain made no reply. Instead he gave all four sets of the Canadian papers a thorough perusal. Then he tossed all the documents into the interior of the van in one quick, impatient motion.

"*Kammil*—go!" the captain commanded.

Joe pushed the switch to slide the side door shut, and drove away. Mack Gerhardt glanced out the rear window. "What the hell was that all about?"

"I'm not sure," Joe replied. "They're evidently out here to catch somebody flat-footed. I suppose it's as much to grab criminals as for security reasons."

"Man!" Jonas exclaimed. "Things are getting worse and worse on this mission."

"Boss, you're a pessimist," Mack said.

"Gee, I wonder why," Jonas shot back sarcastically. "We've killed a Mossad agent, meaning the whole godamn outfit is looking for us, and as of this moment we haven't got a safe way to haul ass out of here."

"Remember the old saying, boss," Mack said. "If it's easy, it ain't worth doing."

Jonas looked at him, his face showing his astonishment. "Sometimes I think you're completely out of your freaking mind."

"It helps when I'm hanging out with you guys," Mack fired back.

Hanaa Maamon was a thirty-year-old Arab woman with a plain face and a plump body that came more from a sedentary lifestyle than overeating. She wore a special built-up shoe and brace on her left foot and leg, the result of a childhood bout with polio. She was a member of Alif-hedal's armed section, called al-Askarin, and lived permanently at their base camp. But because of her handicap, she wasn't a fighter; instead she served as the group's adjutant and quartermaster, taking care of all the administrative and logistical tasks necessary to keep al-Askarin functioning.

At that particular moment she was driving an old Israeli army jeep down the road from the camp, dragging a hitch and rake behind the vehicle. Her companion was Jaleela Qazi, the beautiful young member of Alifhedal who was now well into her training as a fighter in the al-Askarin. At that moment she was on special duty, carrying an AK-47 assault rifle as security for Hanaa.

As the two women bounced in the jeep on the way down from the camp to the main road, the rake's teeth bit into the ground, removing marks in the soil such as tire ruts, footprints, and other signs of traffic. This was one of Hanaa's favorite chores, allowing her to get out of the headquarters shack for some fresh air once a day.

She reached the road within fifteen minutes, then came to a halt by an olive tree that was the survivor of what had once been a prosperous grove before the Palestine annexation. This was the location where al-Askarin people left the thoroughfare to make their way up to the camp. The tree was important because there was a place in its roots for a letter drop, where orders and messages could be concealed for Hanaa to pick up during her short drives. There was a powerful radio back in the camp that was capable of bouncing signals off satellites to reach any location in the entire world, but this letter drop was something special and necessary, because it was much more secure than transmissions.

Hanaa eased herself off the seat of the jeep to the ground and limped over to the tree. She reached down into the roots at the small hole dug there. Her fingers found an aluminum tube and she pulled it out. After unscrewing the top, she checked the interior, finding it empty. No message had been left that day. She put the lid back on and replaced the tube in its hiding place and went back to the jeep.

"No exciting information today, eh?" Jaleela remarked.

"Oh, well," Hanaa said. "Sometimes no news is good news."

Hanaa made a quick U-turn, then drove back up toward the base camp.

Chapter Six

The Mitsubishi pickup truck, though battered with dents and rust spots, had a well-running engine that hummed along with a sound close to that of a new vehicle. The driver, a happy-go-lucky fellow by the name of Inaam Maktum, whistled contentedly as he pulled up to the police roadblock. The captain in command stepped out of the station building with his riflemen, and they all walked up to the truck showing friendly smiles.

"Hello, Inaam," the captain said.

"Hey, there, Khaleefa," the driver responded as he waved to the others. "I brought you a load of food to take back to the camp. We do not want you starving out here, you know."

"More field rations, I would wager," Khaleefa Nasser said.

"I am afraid so, my friend, but I have a special surprise," Inaam said. "You will find two cages of chickens in the cargo. Sixteen fat hens ready for the oven. Now, what do you think of that?"

"You are a wonderful man, Inaam!" Khaleefa exclaimed as the riflemen cheered. "That means *kishk bil firaekh* for supper tonight."

"I'll pull around to the other side of the building and we can move the load to your truck."

"Go right ahead," Khaleefa said. He pointed to one of his men. "Stay in the road and keep a lookout. If another vehicle approaches give a sharp whistle."

Inaam gunned the engine and turned off the road to drive around to the spot where the other vehicle was parked. When he braked to a stop he got out and went around to the back. Khaleefa and the other two men were already pulling the cages of chickens off and transferring them to their own truck. It was Israeli army surplus, as were all the vehicles of Alifhedal's al-Askarin detachment. This one was an M-325 cargo and personnel carrier, a versatile model that could be equipped with various body configurations to convert it into a truck, van, or command car.

Inaam tried to lend a hand to the chore, but the others were too pleased with the chickens to make him work. "You take it easy, friend Inaam. We owe you a favor for the unexpected treat."

Inaam grinned and lit a cigarette as he watched them concentrating on the task. "I brought some magazines too," he told them. "And some boxes of cookies and bread from Israel. Really good stuff. You fellows are going to get fat."

One of the riflemen spit. "We will never get fat with that Egyptian in charge of training. The bastard loves to run. I tried to get assigned to the roadblock permanently, but Field Commander Aziz turned me down."

"I am the only one with that privilege," Khaleefa said.

"Well, I suppose that makes sense," the rifleman allowed. "You used to be a policeman, so you know how to run a checkpoint."

Inaam laughed. "Talent always pays off, eh?"

When the job was done, Inaam turned back toward his truck. "I must go, my friends. I have a message to drop off at the olive tree for Hanaa; then I must complete my run. *Maal salama!*"

Within a minute he was back on the road, heading for the letter drop.

AL-ASKARIN BASE CAMP
MAIN BUILDING
2100 HOURS LOCAL
1900 HOURS ZULU

The entire detachment was gathered in the briefing room for the special meeting that had been called by the leader Bahaadur Aziz. Some sat on chairs, while others, like Jaleela Qazi and a couple of her girlfriends, preferred the floor while leaning against the wall. There was discipline in this fighting arm of Alifhedal, but not much formality or spit and polish. The outfit was more like a family, with a lot of offspring supervised by a stern but affectionate big brother.

Hanaa Maamon was sitting at the table in front of the room with her pen and notebook to take the minutes of the meeting. Two men stood to her front: Bahaadur Aziz and his deputy, Peer Zeroual, who was a former paratrooper in the Egyptian army. Zeroual also served as the training officer, and would not settle for less than each member performing to his exact standards. He cut them no slack.

"*Sukut*—silence!" Zeroual barked.

All the small talk immediately ceased, and every eye was turned to the front of the room as Aziz stepped forward to speak. He looked around at the crowd of three dozen people. "I trust everyone is here."

Hanaa, from her place at the table, said, "We are all present, Bahaadur."

"Very good," Aziz said. "I called this meeting because a most important alert notice came to us at the letter drop this afternoon. Our contacts from several sources have sent in reports that confirm that a member of Barq-min-Islam has defected and is in the hands of either Canadians or Americans. As of this moment there is no confirmation one way or the other, except there is a strong suspicion that agents from the USA are involved. The defector is someone we know quite well, Shakeel Bashir. Our intelligence bureau has a great desire to get him into our custody. However, the Mossad is also after him for their own reasons. And they are in hot pursuit of the North Americans who grabbed him." He looked at the missive and carefully read a bit more before continuing. "Also, they say the party with Bashir is made up of an Arab, one African, and three Europeans. The latter would be the Canadians or Americans, and the African could well be a citizen of either of those countries as well."

Khaleefa Nasser, the pseudo–police captain who ran the roadblock, quickly rose from his chair. "A van with six men answering that description came through our checkpoint two days ago in the middle of the afternoon. Four had Canadian papers, and an Arab carried documents from Jordan. But there was one more Arab who appeared to be Palestinian."

"Of course," Aziz said. "That would be Bashir, the defector. Did they say where they were going?"

Nasser shook his head. "No. The Arab driving told me they were searching for a suitable spot to build a new refugee camp." He thought for a quick moment. "Ah! One more quick thing: There was a sign on the side of the vehicle. It said, 'Nijmi Engineering.'"

Now Jaleela Qazi scrambled to her feet. "I know the firm. It is owned by the Saada family in Amman. They are friends of my parents. I visited their house many times while I was growing up."

Aziz's interest was piqued. "Why do you think they would be driving a Barq-min-Islam defector around the countryside?"

"I do not know," Jaleela answered. "All the company employees are civil engineers. However, there is one named Yusuf, and he was born in the USA. His parents emigrated there and are permanent residents. Yusuf moved to Amman after graduating from college in America, and works for the firm as a project manager."

"This is a most important development," Aziz said. "Thank you for the information, Jaleela. I will dispatch that intelligence to our upper echelon for study and evaluation." He turned his attention to Nasser. "I want you to remain on alert for those men. If they went through the roadblock out here in the wilderness they are undoubtedly on the run. In my opinion the Mossad is hot on their heels. I would not be surprised if they came back this way. They might even be CIA if they are Americans, and thanks to Jaleela we know for sure that one is from the USA."

"I shall need extra men if they show up again," Nasser said. "Those fellows looked pretty tough to me."

"I will double your squad," Aziz said.

MUKHAYYAM-SHARQI REFUGEE CAMP

Anders Halverson was a Norwegian who had been working in the refugee programs of the United Nations for nearly a decade. The thirty-two-year-old was tall, with blond hair and blue eyes, in the Nordic tradition. When he first signed on with the international organization he had been confident and optimistic about the work he was going to do. He pictured himself bringing succor and comfort to distressed, frightened people who had been displaced from their homes because of circumstances beyond their control. That much was true, but the hardest lesson he learned was that all the situations that created refugees abounded with the cruelest, most evil human beings on the face of the earth. At first Halverson tried to keep a neutral stance in situations where rape, mutilation, murder, and starvation abounded, never once expressing his outrage. But after assignment to the Middle East, where he dealt with several violent, atrocity-ridden situations by numerous bands of local militia, he had to admit to himself that these deplorable conditions were caused by persons with agendas of power grabbing and genocide. That was when the bitter Norwegian began to take sides.

His frustration and sadness were noted by several people both in and out of the UN in the West Bank, and after some subtle and surreptitious interviews that he had not realized were taking place, his name was forwarded to Joe Saada of the CIA as a possible agent.

Joe made contact with Anders, and a friendship developed that eventually evolved into an arrangement in which the UN worker became an operative for Joe and the Jordan Station. He was assigned the code name "Lazlo."

As Lazlo's work became more complex and widespread, he recruited his own subagent among the inhabitants of the refugee camp. This was a young Arab bachelor by the name of Izhaar Badran, who worked for Lazlo as he wandered throughout Mukayyam-Sharqi. During these innocent-looking strolls, Badran gathered bits of information through listening to conversations and observing the

various activities that went on in the camp. The arrangement worked out well, and Lazlo's reports enabled Joe to
keep track of no fewer than three terrorist groups who were
active not only in the West Bank but the Gaza Strip too.

28 SEPTEMBER
1000 HOURS LOCAL
0800 HOURS ZULU

Lazlo strode through the camp with his customary clipboard. He made monthly walking inspections that were a
regular part of his assigned duties. During those occasions
he checked mostly for cleanliness, garbage pickup, and
health and safety among the populace. His methodology
was to visit different residents on a random basis, going
inside the small dwellings to see how the families were
getting along. He was particularly alert for the presence of
contagious diseases, such as typhoid, that could halve the
camp population in less than a month.

On this day he stopped by Izhaar's little hut and rapped
on the door. The familiar voice of the inhabitant called out
for him to come in, and Lazlo entered. The Arab had relatively comfortable one-room accommodations. Like others
he had to use a communal latrine for nature's calls and
showering, but his own residence had a nice bed, a table,
and chairs. There was also an old but comfortable sofa,
along with a table holding a television set. A small propane
stove was available for heating and cooking. The kitchen
lacked a refrigerator, but some home-built shelves held
canned goods and nonperishables for Izhaar's consumption.
Thanks to the money passed to him by Lazlo, he could af-
ford to eat out at least once a week at a local café in the
nearby town of Musalmar.

Lazlo accepted a cup of tea and an invitation to take a

seat at the table. After a sip and the usual cordial exchanges necessary in Arab society, the UN man got down to work. "Have you heard anything about a defector from Barq-min-Islam?"

"There has been some talk of one," Izhaar replied. "I made some understated inquiries, but no one seemed to have any definite information. And that includes a couple of fellows I know who are mujahideen and recruiters for the militants."

"That is what I expected," Lazlo said. He finished his coffee and stood up. "Keep your ears open. If any information—no matter how trivial—comes up on the situation, let me know immediately."

"I shall tend to the matter," Izhaar promised.

Lazlo left the hut to get on with his inspection tour.

FORT GRIFFITH, MISSOURI
POST AIRFIELD
1000 HOURS LOCAL
1500 HOURS ZULU

Colonel Tom Ryan stood by the small terminal building watching the military Cessna 401 jet aircraft make its approach to the runway. He had driven over in his POV per verbal orders of the passenger, who was coming in at that very moment. When a general officer came to a post for a visit and didn't demand any fanfare, such as an honor guard, it could mean only one thing: Something unpleasant was going down that had real possibilities of ending a career or two.

After touchdown the plane taxied completely past the usual parking area and came right up to the terminal. Ryan walked toward it, reaching the door just as it opened and the crew chief dropped the ladder. After scampering down it, the airman stood and saluted. With that taken care of, Brigadier General Stan Beckons debarked and stepped onto the concrete. He was a member of the Judge Advocate General's Corps assigned to the Joint Chiefs of Staff presidential advisory board. He walked rapidly toward Ryan, returned his salute, and asked, "Where's your car, Tom?"

"Right over here, sir," Ryan replied, noticing that the general had no luggage with him. The two went to the 2005 Honda Accord and got in. Ryan asked, "Where are we going, sir?"

"To your office."

"Yes, sir!"

The colonel drove off the field and turned onto the road leading straight to the 303rd Logistical Study Unit. General Beckons made no conversation, and Ryan took the hint, keeping quiet. They drove through the Unit's gate and the guard saluted, then gave a startled look when he noticed a brigadier general in the passenger seat.

Beckons led the way into the building, hurrying down the hall past a couple of startled Unit operators on their way out to the range. Ryan allowed the general to precede him into the office. Beckons took over the colonel's desk, and Ryan settled in a chair to the front.

Beckons frowned. "Do you have any—"

He was interrupted by the sudden appearance of Sergeant Kayla Medwar, who had a large mug of coffee in each hand. The female staff NCO smiled at the visitor. "Welcome back to Fort Griffith, sir."

"By God, Sergeant Medwar, I swear to Christ you're a mind reader!" Beckons boomed with pleasure as he took the mug offered him.

"Well, sir, you've been here several times," Kayla replied as she handed the second large cup to her boss. "If I'm needed, I'll be in commo."

"Thanks," Ryan said. He turned to the general, waiting expectantly.

Beckons took two huge swallows from the mug, then banged it to the desktop. "You're going back with me to Washington, Tom."

"Yes, sir!"

"You are just about to be subpoenaed by no less an ass-hole than Senator Herbert Kinkaid."

"Oh, man! Not again," Ryan moaned. "I hate it when that old bastard glares at me through those thick spectacles. They make his eyeballs look as big as saucers." Now he knew why a general had been dispatched to pick up a colo-nel. This situation could be described as sensitive, threaten-ing, and consequential far beyond Fort Griffith.

"I don't know what this is all about or what started it, but you're gonna be sitting in front of that godamn commit-tee getting grilled about everything from who killed Cock Robin to having to prove the Roman soldier who stuck his spear in Jesus on the cross was not a member of the Unit." He suddenly grinned. "He wasn't, was he?"

"No, sir," Ryan said with a chuckle. "I don't think the guy was parachute qualified."

"Go home!" Beckons said. "Get changed! Get packed! Get back here! We gotta fly halfway across this magnificent country and get ready for all this crapola."

"On my way, sir!" Ryan said, rendering a sharp salute.

CHAPTER SEVEN

TEL AVIV, ISRAEL
MOSSAD HEADQUARTERS
29 SEPTEMBER
0900 HOURS LOCAL
0700 HOURS ZULU

Agent David Mofaz entered the headquarters building, going past the elevators through a door that led to a vestibule with stairs. He went up the narrow staircase that led from the first floor up to an out-of-the-way nook on the third. When he reached the landing he had only to walk a few paces toward a room without a door. He could see Kalman Mandler, director of special projects, sitting at his desk inside. Mofaz went up to the doorjamb, stopped, and rapped on it.

Mandler looked up. "*Bokehr tov*, David. How are you?"

"Frustrated," Mofaz said. "I suppose you heard what happened to Dekal Benski."

"Yes," Mandler said. "What a pity to die at the hands of people from a friendly nation."

"I must admit he started it," Mofaz said. "The fool went for his gun while we were facing armed men who had us covered with their own weapons. A tragic shoot-out was inevitable under the circumstances. We were lucky he was the only casualty."

"Did any of the Americans get hit?"

Mofaz shook his head. "No. And I am not sure how I feel about that."

"The report I read said that there was some misunderstanding regarding the defector," Mandler said.

"I cannot comprehend the situation at all. In all my years of service I have never seen orders or instructions so misconstrued. And that is obviously what has happened."

"It is very strange," Mandler agreed. "You were told the defector would be turned over to you, but the Americans claimed they had been ordered to bring him back to the States, true?"

"That is exactly what happened," Mofaz replied. "I do not know what is going to come about from this incident. It may have been some cursed bureaucrat on either the American side or our side who confused the issue."

"Well, I have some news," Mandler said. "That is why I sent for you. We have been in contact with a CIA controller by the name of Norman DeWitt in America. The intent of the call was to inform him of the shooting, and his reaction was quite unexpected."

Mofaz frowned in puzzlement. "That almost sounds ominous."

"What he told us most definitely was," Mandler said. "According to him, the men you faced are out-of-control renegades."

"Then perhaps they decided on their own not to hand the defector to us," Mofaz opined. "There is always the possibility they wanted to sell him back to Barq-min-Islam."

"They are even suspected of committing war crimes

during many of their previous operations," Mandler informed him.

"Then they are doubly dangerous, Kalman," Mofaz said. "Those fellows shot fast and accurately. Real professionals. Are they CIA?"

"When asked about their organization, DeWitt would not say anything except that they are members of the American military."

Mofaz was silent for a moment; then he spoke softly, saying, "Special Forces."

"Excuse me?"

"I said, 'Special Forces,'" Mofaz replied. "They could not belong to any other group."

"You are probably right, David," Mandler said. "So the next thing I have to say to you is not going to brighten your day."

"Which is?"

"You are to get a handpicked team together and go after those Americans," the director said. "Your assignment is to kill on sight. I realize this goes to the extreme, but DeWitt's revelations of that team leave us no other choice. We cannot have a gang of madmen running around the West Bank. It would not take them long to get into Israel proper, or the Gaza Strip. So you must hunt them down and eliminate them."

Mofaz grinned a little. "May I have some time to make out my will?"

"I am glad to see you are taking this mission most seriously," Mandler remarked gravely. "If you were overconfident you would not come back."

"How many agents will I be allowed?"

"A dozen," Mandler said. "And we had to pull a couple of men off other cases to get that many."

"I appreciate that," Mofaz said. "All we need to do now is find out where the Americans have relocated. I have an informer in the Palestinian police who can help us with that. He is a captain."

"I suggest you call in *all* your assets, and do it quickly!"

"That I will do. *Luhitraout*, Kalman. It was nice seeing you again," Mofaz said, standing up.

"Same here, David. *Mazel tov*."

Mofaz went back to the landing to descend the narrow stairs.

CIA CONTROL CENTER
SOMEWHERE IN VIRGINIA
1015 HOURS LOCAL
1515 HOURS ZULU

Norman DeWitt and Delmar Munger were in the former's office. DeWitt stood at the window looking out, while Munger sat in the chair in front of the desk. DeWitt turned around. "This is not what I expected."

"That little shoot-out was a bit of a surprise," Munger agreed.

"We are in deep yogurt, my friend," DeWitt said. "And there is a possibility of dire consequences. I don't know why we even considered the possibility that Blane would willingly turn over the defector if his orders were to the contrary."

"I figured there might be an argument," Munger said. "But I never would have thought such an incident would end with a dead Jew and the rest running."

"That is going to be heavy on the sensitive side," DeWitt said. "Ryan's boys are not a bunch of incompetent buffoons. If they're determined to get something done, they have a propensity for completing the mission."

"Well, hell, Norman!" Munger exclaimed. "It's that eagerness that has caused so many problems. Especially when the rest of the intelligence community is kept in the dark about whom they answer to. As you well know, there has been serious discussion about the possibility that the Unit is pulling a big bluff and actually acting on its own." He paused meaningfully. "Y'know, you're absolutely correct. This situation could blow up in our faces."

"You can bet your ass it could!" DeWitt said. "The best thing we can do is to keep the pressure on Senator Kinkaid to go after the Unit."

"He's a crazy-ass left-wing nut, to the point of being a Stalinist," Munger said. "But the old geezer is smart. He must be shrewd if he can keep getting reelected in spite of his radical past."

"Yeah," DeWitt agreed. "And it's that radicalism that causes him to play dirty tricks to get what he wants. So let's you and I make sure that he dedicates himself to destroying the Unit."

Munger nodded. "Okay. And we also have to help the Israelis as much as we can at the same time."

"Between those two factions—a radical senator and the Mossad—I think this thing is going to work out for us," DeWitt said, walking to his desk and sitting down. "As a matter of fact, I may have set up something even better, as far as we're concerned. I informed my contact over in Tel Aviv that Blane and his guys are completely out of control."

Munger sat up straighter. "Jesus, Norman! They're gonna go after 'em with extreme prejudice."

"Like I said: That'll be better for you and me."

SHARQMED, WEST BANK
CITY DUMP
1900 HOURS LOCAL
1700 HOURS ZULU

David Mofaz sat in his little Fiat, staring out over the unpleasant scene of the waste site before him. There was no organized trash collecting in the area, and the citizens brought their refuse out themselves to that location. Over the years it had turned into a festering, reeking pile of rotting matter that at times included dead animals. And now and then human remains were dumped in the area by militants and criminals who had settled some scores. Mofaz thought he couldn't imagine a worse fate than to be killed, then heaved on top of a mound of Arab trash.

An engine noise caught his attention, and he turned his head to look with envy at the Mercedes that pulled up beside him. There were obviously distinct advantages to working in a culture that provided an opportunity to take bribes. Captain Khursheed Jaafari of the Palestinian police stepped out of the expensive sedan and walked over to get in the smaller car.

"*Masail kher*," Mofaz greeted him in Arabic.

"*Erev tov*," Jaafari returned in Hebrew. It was a little joke between them to express greetings in the other's language. "What can I do for you, David? You seem in a hurry."

"I am," Mofaz replied. "I am trying to locate the destination of some individuals moving around the West Bank."

Jaafari took out his notebook. "Descriptions, please."

"Six adult males," Mofaz said. "Two are Arabs, one is African and three are European. The African and Europeans are rugged-looking fellows with the appearance of thugs."

"They sound dangerous," Jaafari remarked as he wrote down the information. "Would they have anything to do with that shooting in the suburbs on the twenty-fourth?"

"What shooting?" Mofaz asked.

Jaafari chuckled. "I thought so! You were involved, eh?" He closed up the notebook. "I will begin perusing all reports sent in from checkpoints throughout the West Bank and the Gaza Strip. Anything else?"

"That's all for the moment."

Jaafari opened the car door. "*Luhiraot*, David."

"*Maal salama*, Khursheed."

WASHINGTON, D.C.
THE SENATE BUILDING
30 SEPTEMBER
0900 HOURS LOCAL
1400 HOURS ZULU

Colonel Tom Ryan and Brigadier General Stan Beckons sat down at the witness table after being sworn in by the clerk of the Senate Committee on Intelligence and Special Operations. The session was being held in a secure area of the building with Capitol police in the hall outside the door. The chairman, Senator Herbert Kinkaid, sat in his chair in the center of the committee's tall bench that allowed him to look down on those people scheduled to give testimony. He was flanked by senators Tom Wilson and Edna Gardner, both experienced in all matters of investigations and inquiries into special operations.

Since he had already called the meeting to order, Senator Kinkaid launched straight into the business of the day by addressing the general. "You were not subpoenaed to be here today. Am I to assume you are Colonel Ryan's legal counsel?"

"That is correct, Senator," Beckons answered. "We have been before this committee in the past, and it was established that due to national security there are certain things to which Colonel Ryan cannot testify. He is, in fact, under direct orders not to discuss those subjects. He also has constitutional rights not to be forced to make statements that might provide evidence against him."

The senator's eyes swung over to Ryan. "Colonel Ryan,

what are your present duties as an officer in the United States Army?"

"I am the commanding officer of the Three-oh-third Logistical Study Unit at Fort Griffith, Missouri," Ryan replied.

"And how does a logistical study unit occupy its time?"

"Well, Senator, such a unit pretty well does as it is named. It studies logistical procedures of all sorts in an effort to improve the methods of purchasing supplies for the army, as well as which items of supply are the most desirable. It also gives attention to the way the flow of matériel gets to the troops that need them."

"Is that the sort of unit you are in, Colonel?"

"I am in a logistical study unit, yes, sir."

"Mmm," Kinkaid mused, his eyes looking even larger than usual through the heavy lenses of his spectacles. "Didn't I just a minute ago see my clerk swear you in?"

"Yes, Senator."

"Then why are you committing perjury by lying to this committee?"

Beckons started earning his money. "I object to that question, Senator. That's like asking somebody if he stopped beating his wife. You are, in fact, violating the colonel's rights under the Fifth Amendment of the United States Constitution."

"Well, General, I'll withdraw that question," Kinkaid said. He looked once again at Ryan. "I have not served in the military myself, Colonel, but over the years I have been exposed to officers of all our nation's armed forces and have learned to identify various insignia they wear. As I gaze on you, I note what is called a master parachutist badge. And there is that combat infantry badge. And you have two arcs above that patch on your left sleeve. What words are embroidered on them?"

"'Special Forces' and 'Ranger,' Senator," Ryan replied.

"It seems strange to me that an officer with your

qualifications would have an assignment to logistical studies," the senator said. "However, I'll have some more questions for you later. Right now I will offer my colleagues sitting beside me the opportunity to pose their own inquiries." He nodded to the lady on his left. "You have the floor, Senator. Two questions only, if you please, madam."

The middle-aged lady, although a tough politico, had the look of a contented suburban grandmother. She studied some notes in front of her before speaking. "Colonel Ryan, are you involved in special operations?"

"I respectfully take advantage of my rights granted by the Fifth Amendment of the United States Constitution, ma'am."

"I see," Senator Gardner said. "Are any of the men under your command involved in special operations?"

"I respectfully take advantage of my rights granted by the Fifth Amendment of the United States Constitution, ma'am."

Now Senator Kinkaid indicated Senator Wilson with a sweep of his hand. "Two questions, Senator."

Wilson was an African-American who had served in Vietnam as an infantryman in the army. "Colonel Ryan, will you recite your chain of command for this committee? From the bottom echelon all the way to the top."

"I respectfully take advantage of my rights granted by the Fifth Amendment of the United States Constitution, sir."

General Beckons interjected, "The colonel is also under direct orders not to discuss that subject, Senator."

"All right," Wilson said. He thought for a moment, then asked, "Is the Three-oh-third Logistical Study Unit a Special Forces detachment?"

"I respectfully take advantage of my rights granted by the Fifth Amendment of the United States Constitution, sir."

"And that involves another direct order given the colonel," General Beckons added.

Senator Herbert Kinkaid was obviously controlling his temper when he began speaking again. "We are getting nowhere, and I think we all need about twenty-four hours to reconsider things. So, Colonel Ryan, you are going to appear here again tomorrow morning to answer questions put to you by this committee. And I plan on pursuing this notion about you being given orders not to describe your duties in the United States Army. Additionally, I also plan on getting much deeper into the matter of whom you report to. And if there are any more refusals to reply to such inquiries, I shall order your arrest for contempt of Congress." He banged his gavel on the bench. "This session is adjourned until nine o'clock tomorrow morning."

Ryan and Beckons exchanged glances, then stood up as the committee left the chamber.

CHAPTER EIGHT

MUSALMAR, WEST BANK
1 OCTOBER
1115 HOURS LOCAL
0915 HOURS ZULU

The old bus came to a stop that was announced by grinding brakes, shuddering shocks, and the rattle of its ancient chassis. The driver pushed the lever to open the door for the passengers to disembark. The people scrambling off the vehicle were all from the Mukyahham-Sharqi refugee camp who had come to a marketplace at the edge of the city. Most had paid the price of a single Israeli shekel for the short trip, but they did not plan to do any shopping at the bazaar. Instead they wished to sell miscellaneous trinkets or knickknacks for a little cash to augment the bland UN rations issued to them weekly.

One passenger, however, had come to the site for an entirely different reason. This camp dweller had no problem with his diet or having spending money. Izhaar Badran earned a good amount of hard cash from his reports to the agent Lazlo, and he came into Musalmar once a week to eat at a small outdoor café located at the edge of the crude bazaar. Now, amid the sounds of noisy haggling Arabs, he took a seat at a table, and the owner-waiter of the establishment came out to seek his pleasure. Badran ordered a serving of *firak shakasiya*, which was boiled chicken served with rice and a sauce made up of walnuts, chili pepper, and bread. But the eating place, because of certain shortages, had no walnuts for the sauce. Such inconveniences were not unusual in the West Bank, and Badran felt no great disappointment, since there was plenty of rice. Cups of rich, thick *ahwa torki*, a Turkish coffee, were also available for him, because he was a regular customer and a big tipper.

Badran was served the coffee first, and he sipped it slowly as he watched passersby going past the café as they went from one seller's booth to another. A familiar man caught his eye, and he watched as the individual casually approached. The man sat down, and the owner-waiter quickly appeared with another cup of coffee. Badran nodded to his companion. "How are you, Captain Jaafari?"

"I fare well, thanks to Allah," Jaafari replied. "And how go things with you, Lieutenant Badran?"

Badran sighed. "I grow wearier by the day of this wretched assignment at Mukhayyam-Sharqi."

Jaafari chuckled. "As I recall, you volunteered for it."

Badran grinned. "So I did. I had visited many refugee camps in the past, but I let the misery and deficiencies go past any consideration. At the time, I did not realize that someday I would be living such an existence."

"Ah! But I would argue that you are not truly living the life of a refugee," Jaafari said. "After all, there is an end in sight for you, and you are earning extra money. You have a home and family in Sharqmed."

"My patience is waning rapidly," Badran said. "Could we not have our meetings in a better class of eating establishment?"

Jaafari shook his head. "That would blow your cover in an instant. One of your refugee neighbors would eventually see you. Or perhaps a relative or friend, eh? They think you are going through advanced police training in Jordan, do they not?"

"You have made your point, Captain."

The owner-waiter appeared with the plate of *firak shakasiya*, placing the generous serving in front of Badran, then quickly withdrew, knowing that the other man would not be ordering anything. It had also been made clear to the restaurateur that he was not to remain in close vicinity of the pair except to wait on them.

Badran pushed the food around the plate listlessly with his fork. "I have reached a point where I feel I must recommend the arrest of Lazlo. My suspicions of him have expanded to the point where I have determined he is not working for the Israelis, as we first suspected."

"If not the Israelis then who?"

"The Americans," Badran replied. He took a mouthful of the chicken, then chewed and swallowed. "I think the CIA."

"That thought had occurred to me as well," Jaafari said. "His interests seem to be in subjects that the Mossad would already be well aware of. I imagine they have anywhere from three to six informants inside that miserable camp anyway." He picked up his cup of coffee, but set it down without drinking. "Has there been anything in particular that you have noticed about Lazlo's conduct that would link him with the CIA?"

"Indeed," Badran said. "I was in the camp office a little more than a week ago, and I heard Lazlo speaking with another UN worker. The fellow was warning him that the camp director was concerned about the amount of gasoline

Lazlo was consuming every month. That meant he was driving much more than would normally be done in his job. So he was obviously spending extra time beyond what he would do as a mere informant for the Mossad."

"I see what you're getting at, Lieutenant," Jaafari said. "Do you think he is actually doing operational tasks for the CIA?"

"I am convinced of it," Badran said. "That is why I am recommending that this operation be brought to a close and that Lazlo be arrested as soon as possible."

"That can be done, of course," Jaafari said. "But you will have to remain in the camp for at least another month. We cannot have him arrested and disappear from sight, then allow you to suddenly vanish as well. If that happened, you would be compromised and could never be placed on undercover work again."

"I understand."

"I will see that he is brought in to headquarters for interrogation," Jaafari said, pulling out his notebook. "What is his real name?"

"Anders Halverson. He is a Norwegian."

WASHINGTON, D.C.
THE SENATE BUILDING
0900 HOURS LOCAL
1400 HOURS ZULU

Colonel Tom Ryan and Brigadier General Stan Beckons had gone through a trio of interior checkpoints before reaching the door leading into the hearing room of Senator Herbert Kinkaid's Committee on Intelligence and Special Operations. Each time they stopped, the pair had to display their IDs and go through a metal detector. Now cleared and permitted to continue to their destination, the army officers walked into the hearing room, going directly to the witness table. The three members of the committee were not yet present, and the bench where they normally sat was empty save for glasses and pitchers of water.

Ryan and Beckons settled down as the general opened his briefcase to pull out some papers that had a list of answers to expected questions. A couple of minutes passed before a Capitol policeman came through a door at the front of the room. "All rise."

The two army officers obediently stood up as the elderly Senator Kinkaid led in his committee, made up of senators Tom Wilson and Edna Gardner. The chairman took his seat and rapped on the table with his gavel. "This session of the Committee on Intelligence and Special Operations is called to order." He looked pointedly at Beckons through his heavy, thick lenses. "Are you prepared for today's business, General Beckons?"

"We are, Senator," Beckons replied.

"Very well," Kinkaid said. "I want to remind Colonel Ryan that he is still sworn in and is thus liable to charges of perjury at any time should he commit the offense. Do you understand, Colonel?"

"Yes, Senator."

"All right, then," Kinkaid said. "Our last session was less than satisfactory. Questions were dodged by referring to the Fifth Amendment of the United States Constitution in a manner that made it impossible to conduct the committee's business. That is not going to be tolerated today. Not in the slightest! Now I am going to put a question to you, Colonel Ryan, and I demand that you answer it fully and truthfully to the best of your abilities. Is that clear?"

"Yes, Senator."

Kinkaid cleared his throat, then asked, "Colonel Ryan, are you at this time involved in special operations of the United States Army?"

"I respectfully refuse to answer that question," Ryan said. "I am taking advantage of my rights granted by the Fifth Amendment of the United States Constitution. And also because I am under direct orders from my assigned superiors not to answer questions regarding my current military status or duties."

Kinkaid sat in silence, gazing at the decorated combat veteran. After a deep breath he said, "I am holding you in contempt of Congress and order you to be placed under arrest and put in confinement in the Federal Detention Center at Elizabeth, Virginia." He paused again for long moments. "In the spirit of fair play and justice, I offer you one more chance. Will you answer my question, Colonel?"

"No, Senator."

"You are hereby remanded to federal custody for contempt of Congress."

With that final remark two Capitol guards came through the door and walked up to the colonel. One was a sergeant and he spoke politely but firmly. "Put your hands behind you, sir."

Beckons lost his temper. "You don't have to put handcuffs on him, for chrissake! He is a field-grade officer of the United States Army!"

"Official procedure, sir," the sergeant said. He snapped on the cuffs, and Ryan was led from the chamber out into the hall.

Beckons turned to face the three senators. "This is one of the most outrageous things I have ever seen in all the years I've been stationed here in Washington."

Kinkaid spoke in a tone of superiority and confidence. "When Colonel Ryan is willing to respond to the questions put to him by this committee, he will be released from custody." He smiled at the general. "This session is adjourned."

Beckons angrily shoved the papers back in his briefcase as the three politicians left the room.

Captain Khursheed Jaafari drove his Mercedes up beside David Mofaz's diminutive Fiat. He got out and walked over to the much cheaper automobile, opened the door, and got in. After each greeted the other in his own language, Mofaz offered a cigarette to his Palestinian informant.

Jaafari grinned in delight. "American! By all that is holy, David, I pray that we Palestinians develop better relations with the USA so that we may also enjoy their cigarettes."

"And liquor as well, right, Khursheed?" Mofaz asked with a grin.

"Oh, David!" Jaafari said in feigned shock. "I am a devout Muslim; thus I never imbibe alcohol."

Mofaz laughed. "Just like the Saudi Arabians, eh? Do you not know that scotch and soda is the favorite drink of the royal family?"

"And you and I have both eaten pork," Jaafari said.

"And fornicated with women not our wives."

Jaafari chuckled in agreement. "And fornicated with women not our wives."

"It is better than pork, is it not?" Mofaz asked.

"Most assuredly," Jaafari said with a wink. He cleared his throat. "I have some information that may be of great use to you."

"Does it involve the fugitives I seek?"

Jaafari nodded affirmatively. "Our central command has received several reports involving a group of men answering your description going through various checkpoints. There are two Arabs, an African, and three Europeans."

"Is there any way to confirm their current whereabouts?"

"I am afraid not," Jaafari said. "The only thing I was able to determine for certain is that they entered the city of Sharqmed and have not left. It is safe to assume they are still there."

"Is there any local address, or perhaps a sighting of them someplace within the city?"

"Not a single word of such intelligence," Jaafari replied. "But I have given strict instructions that if they are located, I am to be notified at once, no matter what the time of day. I also ordered that they *not* be taken into custody."

Mofaz was silent for a moment. "In that case, I will put the city under surveillance neighborhood by neighborhood. As long as they remain in Sharqmed we will eventually track them down."

Jaafari opened the door. "Good luck to you, David. *Luhitraot.*"

"*Maal salama*, Khursheed."

MUKHAYYAM-SHARQI REFUGEE CAMP, WEST BANK
2100 HOURS LOCAL
1900 HOURS ZULU

The Palestinian police van pulled up to the front gate of the camp, having to slow down only slightly, as the gate was quickly opened to admit them. The vehicle continued into the interior of the refugee center until reaching the main building. Four large, hard-core individuals got out and went into the structure, where a UN staff member was minding the desk. This was a young Frenchwoman who looked up, startled, at the Arab visitors.

"What can I do for you, *messieurs*?"

"We wish to speak with one of your people by the name of Anders Halverson," the first policeman said.

"May I inquire as to why you wish to speak to him?" the Frenchwoman asked.

"No," the first policeman said.

The young woman was obviously nervous, sensing that these were Palestinian authorities even though they hadn't identified themselves as such. But she spoke up in as firm a voice as she could muster. "Members of the United Nations staff are under special consideration."

Now the second policeman stepped up. "Send somebody to fetch Halverson. Or we will do the job ourselves." Then he added in a threatening tone, "Say nothing about us being here!"

The Frenchwoman hesitated, then picked up an interior phone. "Fritz? *Allez chercher* Anders, *si'l vous plaît.* Tell him to come to the office."

"Inform him to do so quickly!" the first policeman snapped.

"*Vite*," the young woman added. Then she hung up the phone as the third and fourth policemen went outside.

Ten minutes later Anders "Lazlo" Halverson strolled through the camp, munching on the late-evening sandwich he had fixed for himself. As he approached the office, he noticed the unmarked van but thought nothing of it. Lazlo, however, did not see the two large men who stood in the shadows of the building. He walked up to the door and was immediately seized and thrown to the ground, his sandwich flying away to fall into the dirt. One of the men knelt on his neck as the other strapped a plastic retainer around the Norwegian's wrists.

The first and second policemen stepped from the building as Lazlo was hauled to his feet. The cop who had bound the prisoner's wrists gave him a hard punch to the jaw; then all four wrestled him to the van, throwing him inside.

Less than a half minute later, the vehicle went back through the gate.

CHAPTER NINE

The Del Fontaine Restaurant was the most exclusive eating place in the nation's capital city, and the least known to the general public. The plush dining establishment was located conveniently close to the Beltway, offering easy access to its exclusive clientele. Dining was by reservation only, and even then there was no guarantee of a table. The caller's name had a lot to do with being granted admission into the luxurious interior for an evening of haute cuisine.

In spite of its sumptuousness, the facade around the entrance door was plain and unadorned. A heavy portal offered entry to the interior, where no-nonsense doormen were stationed during their shifts. The rather large gentlemen who served in that capacity were not clothed in fancy uniforms. Their attire was somber business suits, and they stood their posts with a list of reservations for the evenings they were on duty. Those persons entering the facility had to be dressed appropriately and seem the type who could order off the expensive menu. People refused entrance who protested the firm rejection were extremely surprised when officers of the Washington Police Department seemed suddenly to appear from nowhere. The cops would politely inform the undesirables that they had a choice of leaving quietly or being taken into immediate custody as trespassers and disturbers of the peace.

This was the Del Fontaine Restaurant of Washington D.C.

3 OCTOBER
2000 HOURS LOCAL
4 OCTOBER
0100 HOURS ZULU

The woman paid off the cabbie, then walked from the curb to Del Fontaine's front door. The doorman on duty gave her a friendly but respectful smile, admitting her into the foyer with a polite, "How do you do this evening, Ms. Donahue?"

Maggie Donahue, a feature columnist for the *Washington Beacon* newspaper, had a no-nonsense look about her. She was not vain about her appearance, caring nothing about the gray that streaked her light brown hair, or the fact that she was on the plumpish side. Her makeup was limited to a bit of lipstick and that was it. She walked from the foyer into the restaurant proper.

The maître d', a tuxedo-clad dandy with a dignified sort of snippiness, greeted her with a bow. "I shall take you to your table, Ms. Donahue. The gentleman awaits you."

"Thank you, Throckmorton," Maggie said. She met many people in the Del Fontaine who gave her exclusive stories anonymously but with absolute reliability. These were Washington insiders, who had access to information that most journalists would give their right arms to know.

As Maggie followed Throckmorton farther to the rear of the dining room, she quickly figured out she was going to get a real scoop that evening. They were headed for the most restricted area of the fashionable establishment.

She trailed after Throckmorton to the proper table. The maître d' pulled out a chair for her as John Fredericks stood up and offered his hand. "Hello, Maggie, my dear." He was a thin man in his early forties who was dressed conservatively in what would be called the proper Washington political fashion of an expensive but nondescript suit.

"Well, John!" Maggie said, surprised. "I haven't seen you for a while. And how is Senator Kinkaid getting along?"

"The old gentleman holds his own, as usual," Fredericks said. After Throckmorton withdrew, Fredericks sat down opposite her at the table.

Within a moment a waiter appeared to leave menus and take their drink orders. Maggie requested a glass of Jack Daniel's neat, and Fredericks called for a refill of his vodka martini. The two engaged in innocuous conversation about mutual acquaintances as well as some of the gossip going around town. They were served their cocktails, gave their orders, and continued the small talk until after the salads arrived. At that point Maggie buttered a cracker, took a bite, and spoke with her mouth full. "What the hell's going on, John?"

"I have a 'leak,'" he said. The type of news leak that he referred to was not the tattletale type. This was an unofficial exposé done with the implicit approval of an involved person of importance. And John Fredericks was an aide to Senator Herbert Kinkaid, and made sure whatever his boss wanted in the media got there.

Maggie chuckled. "Okay. So what does the senator want in the *Beacon*?"

"He's going after Colonel Ryan and the Unit once again," Fredericks announced.

Maggie stopped eating. "Aha! Now, that's the kind of scoop I like to get my teeth into."

"The senator has charged Ryan with contempt of Congress for refusing to answer questions. He began the session following the KISS principle to get the ball rolling as quickly as possible."

"All right," Maggie said. "This has happened before. Ryan always pleads the Fifth or refuses to answer because of direct orders issued to him by a person or persons unknown. We've been through this song and dance before."

"True," Fredericks said. "But this time the good colonel has been arrested."

At this point the waiter arrived with their main courses. He sensed an important conversation was in progress, and he wasted no time in putting the plates on the table and making a quick withdrawal.

Maggie began cutting her porterhouse. "Now, what was that you said?"

"I said that the senator ordered the arrest of Colonel Tom Ryan."

Maggie dropped her knife and fork. "You are kidding me!"

Fredericks shook his head. "As of this moment Ryan is confined in the Federal Detention Center at Elizabeth, Virginia."

"Is there a possibility of an interview?"

"I'm afraid not," Fredericks said. "All this is highly classified. After the colonel was cuffed—"

"He was handcuffed?" Maggie exclaimed.

"Just like your local liquor store holdup man. And after he was handcuffed, he was taken out a side entrance of the Senate Building to a waiting van."

"What brought on this latest situation?" Maggie asked,

confused. "The senator has never had the balls to actually throw Ryan in the slammer. What made him so confident that he went that far this time?"

"The reasons behind this latest hearing are because of information surreptitiously passed on to the senator by some men high up in intelligence."

"Oh, my God! That sounds like there is some real evidence available."

"Oh, yeah," Fredericks said. "But digging deep enough to locate any actual evidentiary matter will be difficult." He stopped speaking and smiled, then added, "Unless . . ."

"Unless this situation becomes public," Maggie said, finishing his sentence. She smiled and fed herself a hunk of the steak. "Like being put in an article to appear on the front page of the *Washington Beacon*, huh?"

"Exactly. The whole of Washington will be talking about it within twelve hours. The next day there should be mention of it on national television. Nothing can stop us from getting Ryan and his gang after that. But it must start with the *Washington Beacon*."

"It will be done," Maggie said. She cut off another hunk of the steak. "This was broiled to perfection. How's your baked chicken?"

"Superlative!" Fredericks replied. "What else would you expect at the Del Fontaine?"

SHARQMED, WEST BANK
PALESTINIAN POLICE HEADQUARTERS
0400 HOURS LOCAL
0200 HOURS ZULU

Captain Khursheed Jaafari and Lieutenant Izhaar Badran were close to exhaustion after conducting almost six straight hours of interrogation. Only the pitiful condition of the object of their attention kept them working at the task. The prisoner had reached a point where he was sure to break at any time.

Anders "Lazlo" Halverson sat on the cold cement floor of the interrogation room, stark naked. His hands were above his head, confined by manacles that were attached to chains bolted to the wall. He was unconscious, moaning audibly in his distress at the treatment he had been receiving.

Jaafari placed the cattle prod on Lazlo's thigh and pressed down to activate the electric shock. The Norwegian did not move, even though the tool left another circular burn on his leg to match the dozens of others. Badran knelt down and laid two fingers on the side of the prisoner's neck. "His pulse is still regular."

"We are going to have to carefully and frequently monitor his condition at this point," Jaafari said. "We do not want him to die on us. At least, not until we learn the intelligence we are seeking."

The chamber door clanked as it was opened, and Lieutenant Colonel Taariq Gohar walked in. Both Badran and Jaafari snapped to attention as their commander looked down at the unconscious man. "How is it going?"

"We are getting close, *Muqaddam*," Jaafari answered. "He has passed out on us."

"Try to make it as quick as possible," Colonel Gohar said. "The UN personnel at Mukhayyam-Sharqi are making inquiries." He looked at the bruises, burns, and contusions on Lazlo's body and face. "It would appear you have reached the limit of the physical applications."

"Yes, sir," Jaafari answered. "He can take no more. When he awakes, he will be ready for a gentler approach. We will reason with him with kind words and praise."

"Just remember to give him somewhat honorable and sensible reasons for cooperating," Gohar said. "He will be very susceptible in his dazed state, and will accept almost any rationale in order to avoid the renewal of pain." He gave Lazlo another glance. "Carry on."

The two officers snapped to attention as the colonel left the chamber. Badran sighed. "By the love of Allah, I am so tired."

Jaafari grinned. "Think of this poor bastard. Nobody has shoved a prod up your arse, Lieutenant."

At that point Lazlo groaned and turned his head. Then his eyes opened and he stared at the two Palestinian cops in bewildered terror. Badran pulled a key from his pocket and knelt beside the Norwegian, unlocking the manacles. Lazlo's hands fell to his lap, and he winced at the pain caused in his shoulder joints.

"Is that more comfortable, Anders?" Badran asked in a kindly tone of voice.

Lazlo nodded.

"Now, look, old boy," Jaafari said. "You've proven your courage. My God! I have never seen anyone last as long as you."

"Nor have I," Badran said. "You are a very brave man, Anders. Nobody could ask more of you."

"Indeed," Jaafari said in agreement. "So now it is time to be sensible and end all this horrible unpleasantness. And you certainly have the power to. You've shown your physical courage to us; now show your intellectual prowess."

Lazlo licked his dry lips and scratched his nose, taking deep breaths.

"So, Anders, would you not like to see Norway again?" Badran asked. "All you have to do is answer our questions, and we'll take you from here. You can clean yourself up in a nice hot shower. And after a delicious breakfast you can call the refugee camp to send someone to pick you up."

"You can go home," Jaafari said. "You will see your

family again. Would that not be a pleasure? And think of their joy in seeing you once more."

Lazlo raised his eyes and looked at them, but said nothing.

"We do not wish to hurt you anymore, my friend," Badran said. "Especially when it is not necessary. Anybody with any sort of logical mind would advise you to begin cooperating with us."

"You have much to gain," Jaafari emphasized. "You have been brave for so long now; thus it is time for you to be rational and reasonable."

Badran spoke in a soft voice. "Who is the man to whom you passed on the intelligence I gave you about activities in the refugee camp?"

Lazlo took three quick breaths, then said, "His name is Yusuf Saada."

"And to whom does Yusuf Saada report?" Jaafari asked.

"He is an American of Arab ancestry," Lazlo said. "Saada is CIA."

"Ah!" Jaafari exclaimed. "See how easy that was? No difficulty involved at all. Now tell us the location of the safehouse in Sharqmed."

Badran was confused, and he glanced over at Jaafari. "What safehouse in Sharqmed?" He didn't understand why there was a change in the line of questioning. This had nothing to do with why they'd had Lazlo arrested.

"It is another matter," Jaafari snapped at the junior police officer. This was the information for David Mofaz of the Mossad. "You are not cleared for it." He turned back to the prisoner. "Where is the safehouse in Sharqmed?"

Lazlo raised his hands in a gesture of futility. "The only safehouse I know of is in Musalmar."

"You must tell us about the one in Sharqmed," Jaafari insisted.

"I know of no safehouse in Sharqmed."

Jaafari snatched the cattle prod from Badran and jammed it into Lazlo's testicles. The resultant screams echoed off the walls of the interrogation chamber.

AL-ASKARIN BASE CAMP
FIRING RANGE
0600 HOURS LOCAL
0400 HOURS ZULU

Jaleela Qazi was in the prone position, aiming the AK-47 at the silhouette target three hundred meters to her front. The beautiful young Arab woman concentrated on everything she had been taught the day before during the preliminary rifle instruction given by Peer Zeroual, the Egyptian ex-paratrooper who was in charge of training the al-Askarin fighters. Jaleela made sure the front and rear sights were aligned, placed the front sight on the silhouette's chest, and took a steadying breath. Then she slowly tightened her grip on the trigger until the weapon fired.

"Good shot, Jaleela!" Hanaa Maamon, who was standing behind her, shouted out. She leaned against the jeep to ease the pressure on her crippled leg.

Zeroual put his binoculars to his eyes. "Yes! If the target had been a man, that would have killed him."

Jaleela smiled in delight, then settled down for the second shot.

The training in the camp was relentless, merciless, and continuous under the Egyptian's command. Zeroual was a former sergeant in Egypt's 1st Parachute Brigade and had ten years of service in the country's army. As a tough professional soldier who came from a peasant background, he'd found that his attempts to become an officer were stymied by his lack of proper education. Although he could read and write, Zeroual did so at a very low level. However, he was ambitious for a commission, and began a program of self-education by reading secondhand books he purchased at a small shop in a town near his garrison.

As his learning continued, the volumes he devoured became increasingly more intellectual, adding markedly to his vocabulary. Ironically, with this *increase* in knowledge, his faith in everything he had been taught as a boy *decreased*. The sergeant was unaware that many of the books he purchased at the little store were not written by adherents to the traditions and mores of the Middle East. This was particularly true of religion, and he began to question certain aspects of Islam that seemed to him outdated in the modern world. Further study brought him to the realization that both his nation and its army had serious shortcomings that he had never recognized before.

Within a couple of years of these self-imposed lessons, Peer Zeroual was completely disillusioned, and hungered to discuss his findings with others. But when he approached a young lieutenant with a couple of innocent questions regarding the morals of the Koran and the way the Egyptian army was run, he was reprimanded and threatened with punishment.

It was later, after he was sent as a recruiter to Cairo, that Zeroual finally discovered some people he could talk to. They were students who hung out at a café near the recruiting office where he worked. He took his afternoon breaks in the establishment, enjoying sitting by himself and smoking hookah water pipes while listening to the conversations and arguments of the scholars. His growing intellect was stimulated by the exchanges, and one day he actually entered into a discussion with a group. At first, because he was a soldier, the young intellectuals were suspicious of him. But Zeroual's openness and guileless way of expressing himself allayed their uneasy feelings.

After weeks of almost daily discussions, the paratrooper became quite friendly with a man named Omar Hafez, who was a communications major at Cairo University. Hafez was graduating and had gotten a position in Jordan as a TV commentator. He was going to travel to his new job within a few days. Hafez recognized something very special in the Egyptian sergeant: He was a trained soldier, yet displayed an obviously fast-developing and liberal attitude of judgment in regard to politics and religion. Hafez, who was later to recruit Jaleela Qazi into Alifhedal, subtly turned Zeroual toward the organization. The end result was that the sergeant deserted the army and went to Jordan with Hafez to join the fighting arm, al-Askarin.

Now, in the West Bank, Peer Zeroual prepared the more zealous members of the organization for the coming war to establish a true Arab democracy. It was a cause to which he would totally devote himself while inspiring—or driving—others to participate in the great crusade to bring the Middle East into the twenty-first century.

Peer Zeroual double-timed beside the column of trainees who ran in time to his shouted cadence. They held their AK-47 assault rifles over their heads, perspiration soaking their uniforms in the heat of the day. The firing-range exercise had gone better than expected, and the Egyptian's training methods, while stern and demanding, were getting excellent results. Jaleela and her young comrades in arms, though beginning to tire, continued to run with a fierce determination on the road between the firing range and the camp barracks.

Zeroual, gazing approvingly at his subordinates as they trotted in time to his tempo, looked forward to the discussions in the recreation hall that evening.

CHAPTER TEN

Two Palestinian boys, one twelve and the other ten, made their way across the trash and garbage, twirling their slingshots. The homemade devices consisted of a leather pouch and a thin cord that was whirled a few times before one of the cords was released. This would send a projectile flying across an empty space at an amazing rate of speed to do considerable damage to the selected target. Most of the time the lads used slingshots to hurl rocks at Israeli soldiers and vehicles, but this day their targets were rats that dwelt within the rotting refuse of the dump. It was a great game, and the kids were sharpshooters with their simple weaponry that went back to biblical times; such as the fateful day when the giant Goliath was taken down by the slingshot of a young Hebrew lad named David.

So far they had slain sixteen of the rodents, with the smaller boy ahead in the game ten to six. The older smarted under the humiliation of having the younger doing better, and he was determined not only to even the score, but to go far beyond his companion's count. He spotted two rats together on top of some cardboard boxes, and he moved swiftly and silently to get into range. He loosed two rocks in rapid succession. "I got them both!" he crowed.

His smaller friend disagreed. "One got away. I saw him! He scampered over the top of the boxes over there."

"He did not!" the other said, running to where he had slung the rocks.

Both boys scrambled forward and worked their way up to the apex of the trash, then stopped. The corpse of a naked man lay where it had been tossed to land faceup. The body was bruised, with numerous burns, and the crushed side of the skull indicated that a heavy blunt instrument had been the cause of death, rather than the smaller injuries. The kids were not particularly shocked; they had seen many dead human beings during the short time of their existence in the West Bank. Gunshots and shrapnel deaths were common, but this dead man was the first they had ever seen who had died from torture. They gazed with interest at the sight, then turned away to verify whether the older had gotten both rats or not.

Anders "Lazlo" Halverson's interrogation was over.

TEL AVIV, ISRAEL
MOSSAD HEADQUARTERS
1130 HOURS LOCAL
0930 HOURS ZULU

David Mofaz walked off the third floor landing directly to the bailiwick of Kalman Mandler, the director of special projects. Mofaz took advantage of the fact that there was no door on the office, and went directly in to take a seat in front of the director's desk.

"*Boker tov*," Mofaz said. "Sorry to be late, but I was out meeting my police contact when your message arrived."

"No problem," Mandler said in English, using the American expression that had been picked up and was used all over the world. Then he slipped back into Hebrew. "How is your work going?"

Mofaz shrugged. "Well, we have narrowed down the fugitives' location to a safehouse in Sharqmed, but we have no address. This was found out during the interrogation of a Norwegian UN worker. My Palestine police captain gave me the information."

"Ah!" Mandler said. "That must be the fellow the UN reported missing. They stated that the Palestinian police showed up and took him away." He chuckled. "Naturally we are being held responsible and they are expecting us to get him released."

"I do not think that is going to happen," Mofaz said. "They discovered he was working for the CIA. They will not be freeing him under any circumstances. I would not give a shekel for his chances. It's a pity . . . a real pity."

"You are right," Mandler agreed. "The poor fellow is doomed. I suppose he was working for Joe Saada, eh?"

"That was what I was informed," Mofaz said. "But he did not know the location of that other safehouse I just mentioned. I'm sure he was telling the truth. A man can stand up under torture for just a limited amount of time unless he's completely insane. I wish he had known where the place is."

Mandler smiled and slid a piece of paper across the desk to Mofaz. "This might be a bit of help to you."

Mofaz scanned the words written on it. It was not exactly an address, since house numbers and street names were rare in certain areas of the West Bank. But the location of the house was described by the neighborhood, a certain clothing store at a certain intersection, and the description of the fifth house down on the north side.

Mofaz looked up. "What is this?"

"That, dear David, is the safehouse that you seek."

Mofaz grinned with delight. "How did you get this?"

"From the chief director," Mandler replied. "Evidently the Americans you seek had radioed the CIA Control Center to report their situation and location. That controller, by the name of Norman DeWitt, received the transmission, then sent a message to us with the information."

Mofaz got to his feet. "The quarry has been run to ground. Will you excuse me, please, Kalman? I do have an urgent matter to tend to."

Mandler laughed loudly, calling out to his departing friend, "I shall expect a full report."

Mofaz waved over his shoulder as he headed for the stairs to round up his assault team.

WASHINGTON, D.C.
0700 HOURS LOCAL
1200 HOURS ZULU

The day's morning edition of the *Washington Beacon* hit the streets with the following article on page one.

ARMY SPECIAL FORCES COMMANDER CHARGED WITH CONTEMPT OF CONGRESS

By Maggie Donahue

This reporter has learned from confidential and reliable sources that Colonel Thomas Ryan, the commander of the notorious Special Forces detachment known as the Unit has been found in contempt of Congress after an appearance in front of Senator

Herbert Kinkaid's Committee on Intelligence and Special Operations. This hearing was highly classified and hidden from public view.

During the proceedings the colonel repeatedly refused to answer questions put to him by committee members, even after stern warnings from the senator. When he continued his defiant attitude, he was arrested, handcuffed, and carted off to the Federal Detention Center in Elizabeth, Virginia.

Reports of gross misconduct and war crimes committed by the Unit had prompted the committee to subpoena Ryan to answer questions regarding those charges. He pleaded the Fifth Amendment—a common tactic of mafiosos when hauled into court—and would not respond to any queries regarding past behavior of his men in the field; nor would he reveal the higher echelons to whom he reported and from whom he received orders.

Simply stated, Ryan and the Unit are an out-of-control rogue Special Forces organization that carries on clandestine missions in all parts of the world. There have been confirmed reports of summary executions of prisoners, mistreatment of civilians, and even theft and looting on a grand scale by the Unit. Without a normal chain of command, as conventional military forces have, there is no one to hold them accountable for their criminal misdeeds. Meanwhile, they hide behind a murky set of laws and regulations that heretofore have been unchallengeable. The Unit, which is no better than the Nazi SS of Adolf Hitler's era, is a threat to the freedom of all Americans. The members must be jailed for their crimes and this organization disbanded.

Let us hope that the first step in attaining these goals has begun with the detention of Colonel Thomas Ryan, U.S. Army.

Peer Zeroual was almost hoarse from bawling orders
and criticism at the struggling trainees he was running
through fire-and-maneuver exercises across the scrub brush
of the training area.

Jaleela Qazi, along with her comrades, struggled
through the live-firing exercise of alternating attacks and
withdrawals on the simulated battlefield. The sixteen trainees, four women and twelve men, had been divided into
two fire teams. They began with an assault in which the
Alif Team, to which Jaleela belonged, and the Beb Team
were assaulting a simulated machine-gun nest on the top of
a gently sloping hill. It began with the Alif Team storming
toward the objective while the Beb Team laid down covering fire. When the Alifs reached a spot designated by
Zeroual, they hit the dirt and began laying down their own
covering fire in their turn. Now the Bebs jumped to their
feet and advanced to a point beyond the Alifs. The roles
were reversed again and the drill continued until both teams
stormed the hill and "destroyed" the enemy position.

This was tough work under any circumstances, but Zeroual
made it even more trying by having everyone wear full field
gear, including some Russian-surplus steel helmets that had
been brought over from Syria by Alifhedal's logistical committee. Jaleela knew she must look ridiculous with the heavy
pack, combat vest, and the big helmet on her head. Additionally she was dressed in a camouflage uniform that was a size
too large, along with combat boots. She wondered what
those American boys back at Columbia University who had
admired her beauty would think if they could see her now.

The attack phase of the training was run a dozen times

before Zeroual was satisfied. He called a halt to the proceedings, and the relief felt by the trainees was brief when
he launched them into doing the same thing in a withdrawal
maneuver. They were so tired at that point that they stumbled clumsily through the exercise, retreating in an uncoor-
dinated and sloppy manner. Zeroual was so infuriated that
spittle flew from his lips when he bellowed at them. He
kept up the pressure until a correct withdrawal had been
performed a half dozen times.

With that done, he introduced them to the counterattack in
which they had to retake the hill after being pushed off it.
But before he started, he had a canteen inspection. His number one rule during the training day was that they would be
allowed only one canteen of water, since it was not summer.
Each person was required to pull their water bottle from its
carrier and hand it to Zeroual. He hefted it in his hand to
judge how much water had been consumed. He said nothing
to some of the trainees, but those who drank too much were
not so lucky. They were sent running up to the top of the hill
and back, holding their assault rifles over their heads.

When the punishment runs were completed, the coun-
terattacking began. Jaleela, panting and near exhaustion,
began to yearn dearly for her old job on *Hurriya Arabi*,
Alifhedal's newspaper.

ELIZABETH, VIRGINIA
FEDERAL DETENTION CENTER

Two members of the center's guard staff were real hard-
cases. Officer Mickey Dempsey and Officer Terry Nolan
were particularly disliked by the inmates. They made unannounced searches of cells for contrived reasons; wrote up
prisoners for offenses that would normally be handled by
simple reprimands; rejoiced in preferring charges that

would be brought before the institution's disciplinary board; used any excuse to disallow use of the canteen; and, worst of all, interfered with visitors to the inmates as much as possible.

When Colonel Tom Ryan in his spit-shined jump boots and class-A uniform with medals and insignia was brought into receiving in handcuffs, Dempsey and Nolan thought they had died and gone to heaven. Both had served in the U.S. Army as MPs back in the 1980s and were now forty-something fat boys. Old resentments of commissioned officers boiled anew beneath the lard, and they went to a fellow guard in the lodging assignments section to make sure that Ryan was put on their cell block.

Ryan was damn good and torqued about being locked up. But there was nothing about it that caused him any undue worry. He had begun many a SERE training exercise as a simulated prisoner of war, during which he endured interrogations, physical punishments, and demeaning treatment from some badasses who were real professionals.

The induction process into the detention center was a piece of cake. He was stripped and searched, then made to replace his uniform with a red jumpsuit and cloth slippers. After going through the signing-in process that included fingerprinting and getting a mug shot made, he was issued his bedding and taken to cell block three where officers Dempsey and Nolan were waiting for him in gleeful anticipation.

1300 HOURS LOCAL
1800 HOURS ZULU

Colonel Tom Ryan lay on the bunk in his cell, staring up at the ceiling. He had finished his lunch of a bologna sandwich (no mayonnaise or other dressing, just two slices of bread and the meat), a small cup of cherry Jell-O, a banana, and a very dry chocolate brownie for dessert. Since he had been classified as a special prisoner he was confined to the cell twenty-three hours a day, with one hour outside in the yard for exercise. He was also scheduled for one shower a week, but he had been confined only three days and had missed shower day.

His "special" status meant that Ryan did not eat in the dining hall. Food was brought to him on a chow cart, and an inmate orderly would place it on a small shelf in his cell door. After eating, he replaced the tray for pickup. Now, as he relaxed, letting his food digest, he mulled over the fix he was in. He had already had a run-in with a couple of the guards, a Mr. Dempsey and a Mr. Nolan. The first day he had gotten a write-up for having a trashy cell. It seemed the sight of a candy wrapper in one corner had offended the sensibilities of *messieurs* Dempsey and Nolan. Never mind that it was left by the previous occupant; Ryan was held responsible. As a punishment, he lost his canteen privileges, which he didn't know he'd had anyway. But at least that was the only penalty the first day. But that could be accounted for by the fact that he hadn't been processed into the system until mid-afternoon.

On the second day he received a write-up for insubordination when he didn't get off his bunk quickly enough when Mr. Nolan stopped in front of his cell. Later that same day, Mr. Dempsey wrote him up for loitering in the exercise yard when he was supposed to be back inside the block. Evidently, when the whistle was blown, he hadn't responded fast enough to satisfy Dempsey's high standards.

Now, after midday, Ryan was wondering what had gone wrong. He evidently had been a model prisoner since wake-up call that morning. He grinned to himself when a sudden clank caught his attention. He looked up to see his lunch tray on the floor, and both Dempsey and Nolan laughing at him. It was obvious they had pushed it off the shelf.

"Hey, look here, Mr. Dempsey," Nolan said. "The colonel has throwed his tray on the floor of his cell."

"Tsk! Tsk!" Dempsey said. "What I think the colonel needs is an attitude adjustment. He's a heinous criminal out of control; don't you think so, Mr. Nolan?"

Nolan opened the door and they entered the cell. Ryan stayed on his bunk, looking at them in silence.

"You're supposed to stand up when a member of the guard staff enters your cell," Dempsey said. "You been told that already."

Ryan got up slowly, facing them. Still he said nothing, a calm expression on his face.

"Turn around and face the wall," Nolan ordered. "And put your nose up against it with your hands behind you, Colonel."

Ryan calmly did as he was told, and Dempsey walked up and tapped him on the back of the head just hard enough to push his nose into the wall. Ryan spun around so quickly the two fat men couldn't react. The colonel drove the heel of his hand into Dempsey's face, sending him backpedaling to the cell door. Nolan watched his buddy bounce off the bars and slide to the floor.

Then it was his turn.

Ryan lashed out with a kick to the guard's kneecap, then stepped forward and smashed the man hard with the side of his closed fist. Now both custodians lay side by side in blissful unconsciousness.

Ten minutes later a team of five guards came double-timing down the cell block and found the colonel waiting for them back on his bunk, contemplating the steel ceiling overhead. The quintet swarmed all over him and got him on the floor. The prisoner was handcuffed and shackled, then dragged to his feet and marched toward the exit.

Colonel Tom Ryan, U.S. Army, was already on his way to the hole and he hadn't been in jail for quite seventy-two hours yet.

CHAPTER ELEVEN

NEW YORK CITY
ANCS STUDIOS
4 OCTOBER
1900 HOURS LOCAL
2400 HOURS ZULU

The program called *Hal Brassey Interviews* was the most popular talk show on the American News Cable System's evening broadcasts. Brassey was a portly, middle-aged bald guy with a cheerful demeanor that belied his professional instincts to get deep into the latest news stories when interviewing the main players. On this particular night his guest was Maggie Donahue of the *Washington Beacon*. Her story on the U.S. Army Special Forces outfit known as the Unit had stirred up a hornet's nest among the media, politicians, and other public figures.

Several talk show hosts had tried desperately to get Maggie on their programs, but the feisty lady of the fourth estate was not inclined to discuss her professional activities with people she considered "showbiz" rather than real news reporters. This forced the glitzy pseudojournalists to call on their regular bevy of pundits—mostly retired U.S. Army lieutenant colonels—to appear on their programs and expound their various hypotheses, opinions, and predictions regarding the Unit and its commander, Colonel Tom Ryan. The results were the usual repetitious, unremarkable commentary spouted by those with little intimate knowledge or familiarity with the subject at hand.

Brassey's set was a simple affair of an unadorned table and two straight chairs. A gray curtain hung on the far side of the furniture to keep down the reflections of bright studio lights, yet showed the interviewer and interviewee plainly. Brassey had a clipboard holding a list of potential questions as well as a pencil to jot down notes during the dialogue. He insisted that his guests bring nothing, which gave him something of an advantage if one became unhappy with the way the line of questions was going.

Now, with opening credits and introductions made, Hal Brassey and Maggie Donahue faced each other over that bare table. "Welcome back to the show, Maggie. It's been too long."

"I agree, Hal," Maggie said with a grin of delight. "I was very pleased to have received your invitation." Brassey always seemed to bring out the best in her, and she was flattered by the attention.

"The first question I want to ask is something you are not going to answer," Brassey said.

"You want to know my source," Maggie said. "And you're absolutely right. I'm not gonna answer that, Hal."

He chuckled. "Okay, no surprise there. So let's start this way. In your recent article in the *Beacon*, you displayed outright hostility toward this special operations group called the Unit. And you were particularly vicious toward its commander, Colonel Tom Ryan. Why?"

"I like those words, Hal. 'Hostility' and 'vicious.' They describe my attitude exactly toward those Neo-Nazis."

"That's a harsh accusation, Maggie. There are a lot of people who find your attacks on these American soldiers egregious, particularly in light of the threats against our nation in today's world."

"The only people who disapprove of my reporting are those who do not know the real story behind the Unit. Colonel Ryan and his men are taking advantage of the dangers the USA faces by giving the false impression that they are altruistic, dedicated men putting their lives on the line for the American people. They are, in fact, a gang of war criminals who are running amok across the globe, murdering, looting, kidnapping, and extorting money on a scale that makes the Mafia look like Boy Scouts."

Brassey looked at his clipboard and made a check mark on the paper. "That seems impossible, Maggie. How can a single detachment of soldiers conduct nefarious operations on such a grand scale?"

"They're not doing it by themselves, Hal," Maggie informed him. "They have what is called in the military a chain of command. This traces the level of leadership from the lowest-ranking soldier right up to the highest-ranking commander. The chain of command of the Unit is a deeply hidden secret. Nobody knows who is in charge or calls the shots." She stifled a grin, saying, "Pardon the pun."

"It is forgiven," Bassey said. "Please continue."

"And nobody knows the extent of their budget. Nobody knows their legal—or illegal—status. This is like a cloak of invisibility. And we are lucky that Senator Herbert Kinkaid and his Senate Committee on Intelligence and Special Operations have the moral courage to go after these hoodlums in uniform. And putting Colonel Ryan in jail is a momentous and meaningful first step toward pulling off that insidious cloak of invisibility and revealing the Unit for exactly what it is."

"Well, Maggie, Senator Kinkaid is noted for his leftist tendencies," Brassey commented. "It occurs to me that he might have a personal agenda in going after these soldiers for political rather than moral reasons."

"The only agenda the senator has is to protect the civil liberties of American citizens and to curb the criminal excesses of those out-of-control fascists," Maggie snapped. "And the blame goes all the way up within the government and the military."

"In a way you are indicting the President of the United States," Brassey commented. "After all, he is the commander in chief."

"Hal," Maggie said, leaning forward, "the president denies the existence of the Unit, which means even he can't penetrate their curtain of falsehoods and secrecy! And you just wait until the Unit turns its criminal activities from foreign countries to the USA. That is when their supporters and fellow travelers are going to come busting out into the open. When that happens there will be an armed insurrection that will undermine everything this country stands for. You can kiss the Constitution, the Bill of Rights, and all our other guarantees of freedom good-bye."

"Strong words, Maggie."

"I just received news earlier this evening that Colonel Ryan has been thrown into solitary confinement for attacking guards at the Federal Detention Center, where he is being held. The man has nothing to fear! And if you don't think the Unit is planning a raid on that place to free their leader, then you're a dreamer and an optimist."

Brassey gazed at her for a moment, not quite sure what to think. After a deep breath, he referred to his clipboard and continued the interview.

SHARQMED, WEST BANK
5 OCTOBER
0330 HOURS LOCAL
0130 HOURS ZULU

The rumble of heavy transport in the streets awoke the people of Sharqmed, causing instant alarm. Such sounds meant only one thing: the Israeli army. What in hell were the *yahudin* up to now? they asked themselves.

Those who rushed to their windows could see a heavily armed military convoy moving steadily through their neighborhood. The most imposing vehicles were the two Merkava tanks, their long-rifled guns pointing menacingly ahead. Although not up to par with other main battle tanks, these armored wagons had proven hundreds of times that they were perfectly suited for shooting up Palestinian towns. A quartet of armored personnel carriers brought up the rear of the column, while the middle was occupied by three Fiat sedans looking out of place among the other vehicles.

As the Israelis continued on their way and the sounds of engines decreased, the Arab observers breathed much easier. There would be no fighting in their immediate districts, such as shelling, small-arms fire, or houses being pulled down. Some other unfortunate Palestinians would be the object of that violent attention.

Mack Gerhardt was on duty in the living room of the safe-house, seated in an easy chair after making the rounds of windows to study the walled-in yard that surrounded the building. The place was a one-story affair that cut the chance of good observation to nil. It was impossible to see what went on on the other side of the cement barrier that bordered the yard.

The residential neighborhood was quiet in the early morning hours, as it had been since their arrival. One thing the residents of the West Bank did well was mind their own business. This was an environment where ignorance was almost as good a cover and concealment as a deep field fortification. Mack checked his watch, noting that he had another half hour before Bob Brown relieved him. Maybe today they would receive some information on how this situation was going to be ironed out. It would be great to get back to Fort Griffith.

A slight rumble sounded, then faded away. A moment later it came back again and persisted, growing more pronounced. When loud squeaks and clanks became clearly discernible, Mack leaped from the chair and rushed to the room where the other Unit operators were sleeping.

"Rise and shine!" Mack shouted, using the old cliché for waking up sleepyheads.

Jonas Blane sat up in an instant. "What's going on?"

"The Israeli army is on its way, boss," Mack said. "Listen!"

By then Bob and Carlito Grey were also wide-awake. Carlito got to his feet. "What the hell are they doing, sending an armored division after us?"

Joe Saada came in from the room he shared with Shakeel Bashir. "The time of reckoning with the Israelis has come upon us, guys."

"I know this is a useless question," Jonas said as he hurriedly dressed. "But do you happen to have any antitank weaponry handy?"

"The only thing we have are the M-fours we picked up at the safehouse in Musalmar," Joe replied. "And any armor-piercing rounds of five-point-fifty-six is not going to do any more than put a scratch on the hull of a tank."

Joe listened for a moment. "They're surrounding the neighborhood. We're cut off."

Mack draped a couple of bandoliers over his shoulder, grinning sardonically at Joe. "Maybe your idea of surrendering to them Mossad dudes wasn't so bad after all."

Joe glanced meaningfully at Jonas. "I think it would be a good idea to take that into consideration."

"I'm not giving up this early in the game," Jonas said. "The CIA wants Bashir back in the States, and we're gonna deliver him there."

Shakeel Bashir came into the room fully dressed. "The sounds outside are most familiar to me. The Israelis have discovered our location. They will show no mercy. And not to others who live in this vicinity also. Everything those soldiers must do will be whatever they want, no matter what happens to somebody else. Blowing up the neighborhood and killing everybody that lives here will not give them worry."

Mack asked, "Do you want to be turned over to the Mossad?"

"Better them than the Barq-min-Islam," Bashir said. "I think it better I live in an Israeli prison than suffer from my Muslim brothers."

"Everybody get to your assigned fighting positions!" Jonas snapped angrily. "Let's see how this is going to play out."

The defense inside the house was pitifully thin. Mack, Bob, Carlito, and Joe each manned one side of the dwelling. Bashir arranged a sofa and easy chair as cover in the middle of the room as Jonas personally checked each man. "Make sure you have a good field of fire," he ordered. "Any assault is going to have to be mounted over the walls, and unless they come swarming like hornets, well-placed shots can break up the attacks. They won't be able to lay down covering fire without exposing themselves."

A couple of minutes passed, and the only sounds in the house were those of occasional deep breaths or bumping noises as positions were shifted slightly. Carlito was tapping his foot in time with a tune going through his head, and Mack was whistling *Ring of Fire* under his breath.

"Attention!" The electronically magnified voice came from the direction of the front door. "You are surrounded by infantry and tanks. There is no escape. We will accept your surrender and turn you over to the proper authorities. Do not resist. You will have five minutes to respond."

Everybody automatically glanced at their watches, then gave Jonas quick looks before turning back to their fields of fire. Jonas said nothing, only walking in a slow circle with his eyes peering through the windows. Dry lips were licked and quick breaths taken to relieve the tension of the passing minutes.

"Sixty seconds!" the voice reported. "There will be no further appeal made to you.

"Forty-five seconds! Thirty seconds! Fifteen seconds! Ten . . . nine . . . eight . . . seven . . . six . . . five . . . four . . . three . . . two . . . one . . . zero!"

"Get ready," Jonas warned.

But instead of an attack, there was the loud detonation of a tank's 105-millimeter rifled gun. The shell slammed into the outside wall around the yard, sending a large hunk of masonry flying through the front window. It continued to the living room wall, where it crashed completely through to the kitchen and knocked the refrigerator into the stove.

Now Joe Saada came to life. "Follow me!"

No one asked any questions as they ran after him. Jonas had pulled Bashir from his furniture fort, pushing him forward as the whole group followed Joe to the basement door. He led the way down the stairs to a shelf filled with canned goods. He grabbed a large flashlight off a can of pineapples, then took a firm grip on one of the shelf braces and pulled. The shelf swung open just enough to expose an opening in the wall beyond. He stood back and ordered the others to enter the exit. As soon as all were through, he followed, then pulled the shelf back into position.

"Where the hell are we?" Mack demanded to know in the dark. His question was followed by the detonation of the tank firing again, the next round bringing the sound of more crashing inside the house.

"I'm glad we ain't up there," Carlito remarked.

Joe turned on the flashlight, revealing a long, damp tunnel. Once more he yelled, "Follow me!"

"I hope we have some particular destination," Jonas stated.

"This passageway leads to a large drainage canal two blocks away," Joe said over his shoulder.

The six men moved quickly over the slimy floor, being careful not to slip and fall. A dim light shone ahead, and when they reached the spot, they had to make a sharp right turn. There to their direct front was an iron grate over an opening. Jonas was about to ask how long it would take to cut through the device when Joe kicked it hard. It fell outward into a storm drain that had several inches of water in it. The group crowded into the stream of dirty water.

Joe led them down to an opening where a metal ladder was bolted to the wall. They scrambled up and out, finding a residential neighborhood much like the one they had left. After going down a block and reaching an alley, the group turned into a narrow lane. There was brush at the end of the pathway that blocked the view. After crashing through the vegetation, they found themselves in an olive grove.

Now Joe stopped. He panted and grinned. "Surprise!"

"Yeah," Bob said. "That was a surprise, all right!"

Some more heavy booms sounded a couple of blocks away, followed by an outbreak of rapid small-arms fire. "C'mon," Joe said. "We have to clear out of this area ASAP. They'll be storming the safehouse in another couple of minutes." He resumed running, with the others still following.

Jonas trotted up alongside him. "Are there any vehicles involved in this escape?"

"Sorry," Joe said. "We'll have to steal something."

Jonas chuckled. "Hey, no problem. Carlito can hot-wire anything on wheels."

David Mofaz led the way into the safehouse with his twelve agents behind him. They moved slowly, expecting to find dead, wounded, and perhaps one or two people still willing to fight. But there was nothing but blown-out walls, pulverized furniture, and mortar dust floating around the room. Then one of the men pointed to a door that was still on its hinges. Mofaz pulled a grenade off his vest and walked up to it. When he jerked it open, he saw it led downstairs to a basement. He tossed in the grenade and jumped back.

The explosion burst violently, slinging crackling shrapnel around. Mofaz charged down the steps, firing bursts with his Uzi. The men behind him were on his heels. When they reached the bottom, they found no signs of humans either dead or alive.

"Is there an attic?" one of the agents asked.

Mofaz ascended the steps in quick, angry strides. When he reached the living room, he pointed the Uzi at the ceiling and fired again. This time the others joined in, maintaining the fusillade until all magazines were empty. The ceiling sagged from the damage, and a quick look showed there was no attic. They had simply shot up the ceiling and blown holes in the roof.

Now the army major in charge of the troops came into the house with a couple of sergeants. "All dead?" the officer asked.

Mofaz looked at him with a furious frown, then ordered his men back outside to their sedans.

CHAPTER TWELVE

The mob of newsmen had been waiting at the back entrance of the Senate Building since 0430 hours. Most were TV reporters and cameramen from the networks, cable news, and local affiliates, but a few were still photographers from various print media, with a sprinkling of paparazzi freelancers who hoped to get some shots of the notorious Colonel Tom Ryan.

Ryan had been the subject of much speculation nationwide, with some calling him a dedicated patriot, while others shrieked that a real-life neo-Nazi and his fanatic storm troopers were running unchecked across the world, and it was only a matter of time before they would take up where Hitler left off. Subjects such as gay marriage, abortion, and even illegal immigration had been pushed off the front to the back burners of the public's interest.

When the van from the Federal Detention Center approached the scene, the Capitol police, reinforced by the D.C. Police Department, physically forced an opening in the crowd. At first the newspeople resisted, but the cops' tempers flared, and batons were used to push and pummel the newshounds until they fell back. When the vehicle came to a stop, flashbulbs popped and TV cameras recorded the figure of Colonel Ryan wearing an orange jumpsuit and his army jump boots as he was let out of the van. Ryan was handcuffed and his ankles shackled, forcing him to take short steps as a cordon of cops acted as his escort. The reporters immediately began yelling questions.

"Colonel Ryan, are you a Nazi?"

"Do you have stockpiles of weapons?"

"Is there going to be a fascist revolution in this country?"

"How many men are in your army?"

"Are there dirty bombs in your arsenal?"

"Are you part of an international right-wing conspiracy?"

Ryan kept his head high, staring straight ahead as he was hustled through the crowd toward the door. The reporters trotted after the officer and the cops, still shouting questions until the prisoner and his escort entered the building and disappeared from view.

Suddenly a voice yelled, "Senator Kinkaid is around at the front!"

Ryan was quickly forgotten, and the newspeople rushed toward the street, turning to the steps leading to the building's entrance. Senator Herbert Kinkaid, instead of avoiding them, stood waiting as they stormed forward. His aide, John Fredericks, had positioned himself next to the old man in a defensive posture.

The senator signaled for quiet as the journalists gathered

around him, and the crowd quickly settled down. "I have time to answer a few questions. But make them brief. Obviously this is neither the time nor the place for a detailed discussion. And please keep in mind that the proceedings involving Colonel Ryan are classified. That means I am unable to reveal all the information I have."

A young woman quickly hollered, "Are you aware of a leak in your organization, Senator?"

Kinkaid shook his head. "I am mystified as to how Maggie Donahue of the *Beacon* obtained the information she put in her article."

"Do you deny her allegations?"

"No comment," the senator said.

"Do you have strong, conclusive evidence against Colonel Ryan and the Unit?" a TV reporter asked, thrusting his microphone toward the politician.

"I cannot discuss that at this time," Kinkaid said. "All I can tell you is that we are in the process of obtaining the truth."

"Will there be arrests of more soldiers from the Unit?"

"If necessary I will haul the whole bunch into my hearing room and drag the truth out of them," Kinkaid declared. "Justice will be served, my friends; justice *will* be served!"

"Has Colonel Ryan confessed to any crimes?"

"I think it is most apparent that he has not," Kinkaid replied. "In fact, he has refused to answer any questions put to him. And that is why he is a federal prisoner." He raised his hat. "I must go, ladies and gentlemen; thank you for your interest."

Fredericks took his boss's arm and led him up the steps and into the front door. When they stepped inside the foyer they found senators Tom Wilson and Edna Gardner waiting for them. The African-American veteran of the Vietnam War sported a miniature combat infantryman's badge on the lapel of his coat. He and Senator Gardner fell into step with Kinkaid as Fredericks respectfully walked a few paces behind.

Wilson asked, "How far are you taking this thing, Herbert?"

"As far as I can," Kinkaid replied.

"I think we've reached that point," Gardner interjected. "Colonel Ryan isn't going to answer any questions today. He'll not do it on any other future occasions either. Having him appear is a waste of time and taxpayer money."

"He'll break sooner or later," Kinkaid opined.

"He's not going to give in," Wilson insisted. "He is both obeying orders and taking the protection afforded him by the Fifth Amendment. This committee cannot punish him. You may have him in custody, but that's not going to last much longer. He cannot be held indefinitely under the circumstances. We're not going to get one damn thing from these sessions that we can take to the Justice Department."

"Do you want to give up, Tom?"

"I want to stop wasting time," Wilson said. "I'm not sure what your agenda is, beyond making trouble."

"You can resign from the committee, if you wish," Kinkaid said. "And that goes for you too, Edna."

"This is an important committee in light of global terrorism," Gardner said. "I serve on it because I think its mission is vital to national security."

"Humph! Then *don't* resign!"

Wilson and Gardner came to a stop, watching Senator Kinkaid and John Fredericks continue down the hall.

"All rise!"

Colonel Tom Ryan and Brigadier General Stan Beckons stood up as Kinkaid led in senators Tom Wilson and Edna Gardner. Members of their personal staffs followed and courteously waited until the committee members settled down at the bench.

Kinkaid rapped his gavel. "I hereby call to order this session of the Senate Committee on Intelligence and Special Operations."

"Senator," Beckons said.

"Yes, General?"

"I object to Colonel Ryan's being disallowed from wearing his uniform," the general said. "He was paraded in front of the press like a common criminal."

"I have gone so far as to have his handcuffs and shackles removed in this hearing room," Kinkaid said. "That is the limit of my charity." John Fredericks came in through the back door and handed a sheet of paper to the senator. After reading it, Kinkaid glared at Ryan through his thick lenses. "I have just been informed about a television interview given by Maggie Donahue. She stated that you have been less than a model prisoner at the detention center, Colonel Ryan. According to this memo from the warden, you assaulted two of his staff."

"I knocked 'em on their asses, Senator," Ryan said calmly.

"I don't think you realize the seriousness of such an action," the senator said. "You could be facing felony charges, Colonel. Perhaps you had better get used to wearing orange jumpsuits."

General Beckons blurted, "That is uncalled for, sir! You don't even know the circumstances of the incident."

Kinkaid smiled and shrugged. "Just an observation, General. No offense intended." He sorted through some papers for a moment before speaking again, turning toward his committee members. "Do either of you have statements or questions you wish to bring forward?"

"I have none," Senator Tom Wilson replied.

Senator Edna Gardner stated, "I will not be participating."

"Very well," Kinkaid said, and he turned to the witness. "Colonel Ryan, during this morning's session I intend to address three topics. These involve war crimes that were committed in the Democratic Republic of the Congo and the French Republic. Has your—excuse the expression—'*logistical study unit*' conducted any operations in Africa lately?"

"I am under direct orders not to discuss such matters," Ryan said.

"I see," Kinkaid said unruffled. "There was a massacre of innocent villagers at a place called"—he hesitated— "Mwitukijiji. These unfortunate victims were shot down in cold blood. My sources tell me that was done by members of your '*logistical study unit*.' Is that true?"

Beckons leaned over and whispered in Ryan's ear. The colonel nodded, then stated, "I have seen no after-action reports pertaining to such an incident."

"No paperwork trail to follow, eh?" Kinkaid said sarcastically. "I am also in possession of further information that states that prisoners of war were summarily executed and buried in a mass grave. This horrible crime was committed in the vicinity of the first. Was this done by your '*logistical study unit*'?"

"No after-action reports have been made regarding such an incident," Ryan replied.

"And now we leave Africa," Kinkaid said, "and travel to *la belle France*. Two citizens of that country were assassinated in cold blood. Again I must ask you if your '*logistical study unit*' was involved."

"I refer to direct orders that have been passed down to me through my chain of command," Ryan said. "I cannot answer that question."

Kinkaid now had the incidents read into the records of the hearings. He had accomplished all he wished to that morning. He turned to his committee members. "Protocol requires me to ask once again if my distinguished colleagues have any inquiries they wish to direct to Colonel Ryan. No? Very well. This session is adjourned."

Ryan stood up as the restraints were replaced on him by the Capitol policemen.

THE WEST BANK
6 OCTOBER
0430 HOURS LOCAL
0230 HOURS ZULU

SERE was difficult and dangerous under any conditions. The circumstances that the Unit operators and their companions, Joe Saada and Shakeel Bashir, were in made it ten times worse than normal. They were completely cut off, with no communications or safe haven available; proper equipment such as night-vision goggles and binoculars were lacking; their attire was civilian and completely unsuited for the field; and they were underarmed with M4A1 carbines and a small supply of ammunition. Worst of all, they had no canteens of water. And added to all this, Israeli Apache helicopters, obviously hunting for them, were flying search patterns across the West Bank.

Jonas Blane and Joe were on point of the small column, since the CIA agent was familiar with the terrain. Bob Brown and Bashir made up the center of the formation, while Mack Gerhardt and Carlito Grey brought up the rear. They had spent the nearly twenty-four hours since escaping from the safehouse moving continually through the countryside. Jonas allowed only the briefest of breaks as they skirted built-up areas, sticking to terrain and flora that provided the most cover and concealment. It became obvious that the search choppers had no infrared capabilities for picking up body heat, and that took off much of the pressure. And even if they did have IR, it would not have identified friend from foe. The aircraft were noisy and the *chop-chop* sounds of the engines gave plenty of warning for the fugitives to get under cover.

Now they followed a deep gully in the scrub brush as the false dawn eased up out of the east. The cuts and creases in the earthen walls provided shadows and areas of concealment. Jonas glanced rearward and noted that everyone was badly fatigued. Shakeel Bashir was the worst off, almost staggering from exhaustion. When they reached a spot where an overhang offered an excellent hiding place, the Unit leader called a halt. The group moved into the protection and settled down.

Bashir's appearance began to alarm the others, now that they could see him better. His breath was shallow and his face pale as he leaned against the side of what was actually a shallow cave. Jonas began to think the man might be heading for a heart attack. He spoke to him, asking, "How are you feeling, Bashir?"

Bashir gave him a heavy-lidded gaze. "I have thirsty."

Mack nodded his head in agreement. "We're gonna have to do something meaningful pretty soon, boss."

"I can't argue with that," Jonas said. "Here's a question from Field Operations One-oh-one. What do you do when you're not sure of exactly where you might be or what you should do?"

"I know!" Carlito said, holding up his hand like an excited schoolboy. "Send out a reconnaissance patrol."

"Right," Jonas said. "And thanks for volunteering. I want you and Bob to make your way up this gully and see how far it goes. Then find out what's beyond it. Don't take any unnecessary chances."

Carlito and Bob quickly got to their feet and moved out, turning in the direction the group had originally been traveling. Jonas switched his eyes to Joe Saada. "Do you have any contingency plans or procedures to take care of situations like this?"

"Sorry, Jonas," Joe said. "But we never figured anyone out of the Jordan Station would be wandering in the wilderness, cut off and lost in the West Bank. We're in the intelligence business more than special operations."

Bashir frowned. "Why did you not surrendered when the Jews gave you the chance?"

"I tell you what," Jonas said irritably. "If you want to give yourself up, go ahead. I won't stop you." When Bashir didn't move, he continued. "You might just run into some of those old buddies of yours, eh?"

Bashir turned away, sinking back into silence. Mack idly tapped his hand on the stock of his M4A1, while Joe Saada wisely closed his eyes to nap.

A slight sound came from outside the overhang, and Mack immediately moved up, ready for trouble. He peered down the gully for a couple of seconds, then turned back. "Bob and Carlito are coming this way."

When the two-man patrol arrived, Carlito did the honors of presenting the report. "This gully flattens out a bit after a couple of hundred meters, but still gives pretty good cover. But we couldn't go all the way down, 'cause we ran into a chain-link fence that blocked the way."

Now Bob chimed in. "But there was a wide enough gap between it and the ground that we could crawl under. It looks like erosion from a recent rain. Anyhow, we went about fifty meters and saw a camp of some sort. There were some armed guys hanging around, and we spotted some vehicles and frame buildings."

"A flag was on the roof of one," Carlito said. "It was black with crossed spears in white on it."

Suddenly Bashir scampered forward on his hands and knees, his eyes alight with happiness. "I know what they are. A new group of mujahideen called al-Harbin Mukkaddas. In English it means 'the Holy Lances.'"

"Yes," Joe said. "They are relatively new, and as far as we know have not participated in any active operations."

"That is true!" Bashir exclaimed. "The al-Harbin are understrength but well equipped."

"Could be," Bob said. "Me and Carlito counted maybe a half dozen of 'em."

"I can tell you something else," Joe said. "That camp is in an extremely isolated area. I have seen its location on a map."

"That is true!" Bashir exclaimed again.

Jonas nodded and tapped Carlito on the shoulder. "Trace the layout of the place in the dirt here."

Carlito was the first under the fence. He crawled forward twenty meters and halted. After a quick look around, he turned and signaled back to the others. Mack and Bob were the next to enter the compound. Bob went to the right and Mack the left to form up a prone skirmish line with Carlito.

Jonas and Joe followed, leaving Bashir behind. Joe, who had no intense military training, was to stick close to the Unit leader while adding to the firepower. Now that everyone was in position, Jonas let out a soft whistle. The group rose up as one man and walked slowly toward the objective of three buildings. Although a couple of the terrorists could be seen through a window of one cabin, no one was outside.

Suddenly a slim young man in a kaffiyeh stepped from a door. When he caught sight of the five men approaching, he simply stood and stared at them for a moment in surprise. Then the sudden awareness of what was actually happening leaped into his mind, and he jumped around to get back into the building.

Jonas's carbine spit out a four-round fire burst that knocked the guy through the door.

Now all the armed Unit operators began sending forth fusillades that blasted through the slats of the buildings, blowing out windows. One individual stupidly rushed outside to fire at the attackers, but was blown into a twisted heap in the volley of slugs directed at him.

All the buildings were now stormed and secured, and a close inspection of the site revealed there were no survivors. Jonas immediately organized a search of the place. One building was a combination supply room and armory. The interior was stacked with uniforms, field gear, and boots waiting to be issued. The arms racks were filled with Soviet AK-47 assault rifles with stacks of ammo boxes behind them.

Carlito and Mack, who had been sent around to the other side of the structures, came back with a report of a three light utility vehicles. These were Portuguese UMM Alters that could be used as command vehicles or weapons carriers. Each had accommodations for a driver and six passengers.

"We won't make pigs of ourselves," Jonas said. "Let's just take two of 'em."

"Did you find any commo?" Joe Saada asked.

Bob shook his head. "Not as much as a cell phone."

"Too bad," Joe remarked. "There is a special frequency that would prove helpful to us. But without a radio . . ." He left the sentence unfinished.

"We can't worry about that now," Jonas said. "Let's get to work."

Carlito and Bob were appointed drivers, and everyone turned to equipping themselves with military clothing, web gear, AK-47s, and as much ammunition as could be crammed into the vehicles. Unfortunately there were no night-vision devices, binoculars, maps, or compasses.

By then Shakeel Bashir had joined them, and he gave advice as to which clothing to take to give the best appearance of militants. He also strongly recommended that everyone don a kaffiyeh, as well as some large sunglasses he found in a box on a windowsill. There were also scarves to wrap around the bottom of faces to offer further concealment of their features.

With all that taken care of, the evaders loaded into the two vehicles and drove through the front gate, heading east.

CHAPTER THIRTEEN

SHARQMED, WEST BANK
BARQ-MIN-ISLAM HEADQUARTERS
6 OCTOBER
1400 HOURS LOCAL
1200 HOURS ZULU

Ishtiaq Naguib, aka Kumandan, had called a meeting of his two senior staff officers: Taqqee Boudiaff, intelligence and operations, and Chiraagh Fahmy, administration and supply.

Now, as the session opened, Kumandan sat at the table glowering at the two officers. "We discovered that Shakeel Bashir disappeared ten days ago. Our sources tell us that it is certain that he has yet to leave the West Bank. Yet our mujahideen scurry around, poking here and poking there, and have yet to find a single solitary clue as to where the traitor might be." He turned his glare at Taqqee Boudiaff. "Do you have any comments regarding this bungling idiocy?"

Boudiaff, rather than being nonplussed, showed a confident air. "A new development has arisen, Kumandan. I was informed of the situation less than an hour ago."

Kumandan's eyebrows raised. "You seem favorably impressed by this unforeseen information, Brother Boudiaff. What did you learn, and who passed it on to you?"

"Our old friend Captain Jaafari of the police," Boudiaff answered.

Chiraagh Fahmy was not favorably impressed. "I have absolutely no confidence in the man. There are many things about him that leave a bad taste in one's mouth."

Kumandan shrugged. "He is treacherous and mysterious, yet he has given us useful information in the past. Why would he suddenly wish to confuse us with misinformation?"

"I can think of no reason," Fahmy remarked with a shrug. "But what does he want in return?"

"That is a good point," Kumandan said. "It could be that he wishes for us to do all the work; then he can get his hands on Bashir and sell him to the Israelis."

Boudiaff shook his head. "He does not want Bashir. However, he does desire to have the traitor's companions in his custody. He says they are an Arab, an African, and three Europeans."

Fahmy did not like the arrangement. "We have a right to punish anyone who helps one of our own turn against us."

Kumandan frowned. "Of course we do. But we must consider what interest Jaafari might have in them, as well as the motives behind these circumstances."

"He would not say, Kumandan," Boudiaff replied. "But in exchange he will keep us informed as to when and where to strike in order to capture the entire group."

Kumandan was thoughtful for a few moments. "You know, I am convinced he is also working with the Jews."

"Probably," Boudiaff said. "That could mean he has access to the Mossad. With the information they can provide we can go directly to where Bashir and his friends are hiding while Jaafari delays the Israeli agents."

"Tell him his terms are acceptable," Kumandan announced.

"We have another matter to discuss, Kumandan," Taqqee Boudiaff said. "It has now been firmly established that the rumors of the existence of Alifhedal are true."

"And are they, in fact, Arab infidels?" Kumandan asked.

Boudiaff nodded affirmatively. "All are fallen Muslims."

"Then they must be dealt with as the Koran dictates," Kumandan said. "Kill them without mercy and let their souls burn in eternal hell."

"I can spare half a dozen men to begin searching them out," Boudiaff said.

"Waste no time in starting the operation," Kumandan ordered. "This is a sacred duty that must be fulfilled. They are as much our enemy as are the cursed Zionists."

"It will be done," Boudiaff replied. "And I have one more report. It is very puzzling, but has been verified. There was a raid on the training camp of al-Harbin Mukkaddas."

"That is madness!" Kumandan snapped. "Al-Harbin is only lately organized and has not reached full operational strength. Who could have attacked them?"

"That has yet to be determined," Boudiaff said. "But the information is confirmed that all six of the men at their camp were killed; then a good deal of the supplies and arms were looted from the warehouse and arsenal."

"That does not seem possible," Kumandan argued. "Who corroborated this report?"

"A friend of mine in Hamas," Boudiaff said.

"Perhaps Alifhedal committed this outrage," Fahmy suggested. "Arab against Arab, eh?"

Kumandan shook his head. "What is this world coming to?"

Olivia Brandon, Senator Kinkaid's sexy receptionist, sat at her place in the outer office, idly paging through a copy of *People* magazine. When she came to work that morning she was glad to see that the senator's executive secretary had not placed a list of daily callers on the desktop. That meant it would be a nice, slow day, without people barging into the office bothering her. Olivia would have plenty of time to catch up on reading the latest news of celebrities, doing her nails, and maybe calling up some friends for a chat. And she didn't have to use her cell phone, since there was a regular landline instrument on her desk.

Olivia glanced up, startled, when two men stepped in from the hall. She looked frantically for the daily caller list in case she had missed it, then pulled out the drawers to see if it had been inadvertently placed in one. But there was none. The receptionist regarded the unexpected visitors with a smile. "I think you're in the wrong place."

Both men had an official air about them. The taller, gray-haired man spoke politely. "Please inform Senator Kinkaid that Mr. Collier wishes to speak to him."

"All right," Olivia said. She pointed to the other man, asking, "And who is he?"

"Not to worry," Collier said. "I'll introduce him to the senator."

Olivia picked up the interoffice phone. "Herbie—I mean Senator Kinkaid—there is a man here named Collier."

Pause. "He has someone he wants you to meet." Pause. "That's what he said." She looked at Collier, scrutinizing him suspiciously. "He wants to know where you're from."

"Tell him I'm from the White House," Collier said. "The senator knows me."

Olivia spoke into the phone again. "The gentleman says you know he's from the White House." Then she spoke to Collier. "He says to go right in."

The two men walked through the door leading to the inner office, going down the corridor toward the senator's place of work. Harold Collier had the title of assistant chief of staff at the White House, but he was actually a clandestine intelligence representative. His job was to handle special security circumstances that were either sensitive, essential, or a combination of the two, thus requiring a touch of diplomacy and firmness. Mostly what he did was inform people that their conduct had upset the balance of things in certain areas of the U.S. government. When he reached the office, he rapped on the door and stepped inside.

Senator Herbert Kinkaid was not happy to see Collier, but he stood up and offered his hand with a smile. "How are you, Harold?"

"I'm fine, thank you, Senator," Collier said. "I'd like you to meet Ed Pullini. He's a deputy director of protocol for the CIA."

Kinkaid retook his seat with a strong feeling of apprehension. He knew that Collier was a hatchet man with some powerful backup. "Sit down, gentlemen. And what can I do for the White House and CIA today?"

"Certain parties have grown very concerned about these hearings you are having involving Colonel Thomas Ryan. They find the unauthorized publicity particularly upsetting. And when it became known that Colonel Ryan had been arrested and confined to the Federal Detention Center in Elizabeth, they were very much taken aback."

"Well, that is understandable," Senator Kinkaid said. "I received some very disturbing information regarding the colonel and the Three-oh-third Logistical Study Unit. It was enough that I felt it my duty to look into the matter."

Pullini was a heavyset man with the look of a prizefighter, in spite of his well-tailored suit. "Who provided that information to you?"

"I am not at liberty to say, Mr. Pullini."

Collier continued. "And why was the colonel put in jail?"

"I charged him with contempt of Congress," Kinkaid replied. "He refused to answer questions put to him."

"And his reasons?"

"He claimed the Fifth Amendment, of course," Kinkaid said. "All scoundrels do that. And he also stated that some mysterious entity high up in the military had forbidden him to answer any questions regarding his chain of command or the operational activities of his men."

"I believe we've been through this before, Senator," Collier said.

Kinkaid picked up a pencil and nervously tapped his desktop. "This time was different, Harold. We had specific information that Ryan and his men had been involved in war crimes committed in the Democratic Republic of the Congo. To wit, killing innocent villagers, illegally executing prisoners of war, and assassinating two French citizens in France."

Pullini shifted in his chair. "Were you planning on pressing those charges against the colonel and his command?"

"That is exactly what I intend to do," Kinkaid insisted. "These are rogue soldiers who think of themselves as some Praetorian Guard who are not required to answer to anybody, no matter how outrageous their conduct."

"What about this leak to the newspaper?" Collier

asked. "Maggie Donahue had quite an article. And there was also her appearance on *Hal Brassey Interviews* on the ANCS. She made some extremely strong statements and accusations."

"I know nothing of the leak," Kinkaid said. "I was also quite shocked to see what the *Beacon* had published. However, I was not able to discover the identity of the culprit."

Pullini pulled a notebook out of his pocket, flipping it open. "According to the CIA's investigations, outside of Colonel Ryan and General Beckons there are only five people who had knowledge of your committee's proceedings. There was you, Senator Tom Wilson, Senator Edna Gardner, your aide, John Fredericks, and your executive secretary, Phyllis Vance." He put the notebook back. "It shouldn't take us too long to find out which person or persons are responsible for revealing this classified information. And, of course, charges will be brought against them. The Homeland Security Act provides harsh punishment for such misconduct."

Much of Kinkaid's original political glibness of his youth had faded with age. The brusque statement by the CIA man caused it to wither entirely. He was speechless.

Harold Collier let a moment pass before speaking again. "It is neither wise nor prudent for you to continue with those hearings. You have wandered into an area that is a matter of national security. And to make things worse, you or someone close to you has divulged information that is now well-known to the public. And that means our enemies. If you insist on continuing your so-called investigation, there will be dire consequences for you and your staff."

Kinkaid remained silent as the two men stood up. They left the room without another word, and it was a couple of minutes before the senator could move. He reached out with a shaking hand, picking up the receiver from the phone. He punched his executive secretary's number on the speed dial. When she answered, Kinkaid cleared his throat, then said softly, "Phyllis, please call senators Wilson and Gardner. Inform them that the hearings regarding Colonel Ryan and the Unit are canceled. Permanently."

THE WEST BANK
7 OCTOBER
1400 HOURS LOCAL
1200 HOURS ZULU

The two command cars moved at a steady seventy-five kilometers per hour down the rural road, bouncing across the ruts. These vehicles were misnamed in a way, since they had a front cab as weapons carriers. Behind that was a regular truck bed with an enclosed capsule that could either be used for cargo or have seats installed for passengers. Before leaving the al-Harbin Mukkaddas camp after the raid, Jonas Blane had removed one of the rows of seats from each to make more room for the stolen ammunition and other gear.

Carlito Grey was driving the first, with Jonas in the passenger seat. Behind them sat Joe Saada and the defector, Shakeel Bashir. Back in the other vehicle the driver was Bob Brown, while Mack Gerhardt rode shotgun. The rear of this car was packed with even more stolen items than the other. Everyone was dressed as terrorists, with the prerequisite kaffiyehs, nondescript uniforms, pistol belts, bandoliers, and face masks of scarves.

They came to a blind curve with the view ahead blocked by a high bank of dirt with thick scrub brush along the top. As soon the obstacle was cleared, they spotted a Palestinian police checkpoint a scant half kilometer way. It was too late to stop, and Carlos glanced at Jonas for orders.

"Crash through!" Jonas snarled.

"Wait!" Bashir said from the rear. "Slow down and drive up, then stop."

"Are you crazy?" Joe asked, worried.

"Everything is okeydokey," Bashir assured him. "Let me for to do all the talk. Understand?"

"Do we have a choice?" Jonas asked under his breath. He glanced at Carlito. "You heard the man."

"Okay, boss."

Back in the second car, Bob and Mack wondered what was going on, but knew enough to follow the example being set for them.

Carlito pulled up to the crossbar blocking the road and braked to a stop. The policeman looked in the vehicle and said something in Arabic. Bashir immediately interrupted him, spewing out angry words at the man. The officer nodded, saluted, then turned to his partner with a signal to lift the barrier.

Both vehicles went through the roadblock, quickly getting back up to speed. Jonas turned in his seat, speaking to Bashir. "What did you say to that guy?"

"I am telling him that we are on our way to make a raid in Israel," Bashir said. "And if he is stopping us, he will be most very sorry. Does he be wanting to be pulled from his bed one dark night and took away?"

"Sounds good to me," Carlito said with a laugh.

The small convoy continued on its way out into the boondocks of the West Bank.

ELIZABETH, VIRGINIA
FEDERAL DETENTION CENTER

Officers Mickey Dempsey and Terry Nolan were two nervous Nellies. This uneasiness had come upon them late on October 5, during the evening news. Both had been at their respective homes, watching the scene where the detention van pulled up behind the Senate Building in Washington. Between sips of beer, they observed Colonel Tom Ryan getting out of the van in restraints while wearing the orange jumpsuit of prisoners. The commentary with the scenes described the officer as a Special Forces commander of a deadly crack detachment that performed dangerous missions in some of the wildest places on the face of the earth.

The next morning the two guards met in the staff locker room prior to beginning the day's work. Dempsey spoke to Nolan in a trembling voice. "Did you see the news last night?"

"You mean about Ryan? Yeah, I seen it," came the nervous reply.

"We been harassing a real bad guy, Terry," Dempsey said. "You can bet your ass he's gonna sic them killers of his on us."

"God!" Nolan wailed. "What are we gonna do, Mickey?"

"We gotta undo what we did; that's what we're gonna do. Maybe if we're real nice to him he'll let bygones be bygones."

"Whaddaya got in mind, Mickey?"

"Just follow my lead," Dempsey counseled him.

0645 HOURS LOCAL
1145 HOURS ZULU

The cell block hummed with the noise of prisoners getting ready to start another day of confinement. The two guards, Dempsey and Nolan, walked down the row of cells slowly, as if they were on the way to their own executions. When they reached Colonel Tom Ryan's cell, they stopped, with Nolan hanging back behind his buddy.

Dempsey smiled widely. "Good morning, Colonel. Leaving us today, are you?"

Ryan had already gathered up the few things he had collected during his short stay and put them in a small cardboard box to carry them out. He didn't answer the question and he didn't get off his bunk.

"How'd you like your breakfast?" Dempsey inquired politely. "Me and Nolan seen to it that you got a great big helping of oatmeal and two extry pieces of toast."

Ryan remained silent.

"Uh," Dempsey went on hesitantly, "we kind of, y'know, kind of got off on the wrong foot when you first came in here. And we're sorry about that, Colonel, sir. We shouldn't have acted the way we did."

Ryan made no reply, only giving the guard a steely-eyed glare.

Nolan stepped forward in a panic. "Me and Dempsey are veterans, Colonel! We served in the MPs together. Army, y'know? We was in from 'eighty to 'eighty-three."

"Fort Riley, Kansas," Dempsey added.

"We came in early this morning and went to the clothing room," Nolan added. "We shined your boots and Brassoed your brass."

"You'll look real sharp when you leave, sir."

"If there's any way we can make up for what we done, you just say the word," Nolan said, trying to sound cheerful. "Why, we'll do anything you want us to do."

"Even mow your lawn," Dempsey said. "Ha! Ha!"

Ryan knew the two had heard of his reputation and were now scared to death that an assassination team of Green Berets would be hunting them down. He stood up slowly and walked up to the bars. When he spoke, his voice was low and menacing. "I'll be seeing you boys." Then he went back into a silent mode.

The guards looked at him, looked at each other, looked

up and down the cell block, then made a rapid departure for the exit.

0900 HOURS LOCAL
1400 HOURS ZULU

Brigadier General Stan Beckons stood beside the army sedan, leaning against it with his arms crossed. The chauffeur, a bit awed at driving a general, stood by the driver's door at a strict position of parade rest. When Colonel Tom Ryan came out of the detention building he was dressed in his class-A uniform with the jump boots that Dempsey and Nolan had shined. Beckons waved at him with a grin and went up to shake hands. The driver immediately opened the back door of the vehicle.

The two officers got inside and Ryan set his box on the floor. The driver hurriedly took a seat behind the wheel. The automobile went up to the front gate and came to a stop. Ryan handed over his release slip to the guard on duty, and the barrier swung open. The vehicle went through it, turning onto the street that led to the freeway.

"How're you feeling, Tom?"

Ryan shrugged. "Actually, it was pretty easy. A lot cushier than a SERE prison camp." He chuckled. "There're two fat-ass ex-MP guards in there who evidently thought they made things rough for me."

Beckons understood. "Now they're afraid the big, bad Special Forces guy is gonna come and get 'em, right? Of course you told 'em 'no hard feelings.' "

"Are you kidding?" Ryan remarked. "I didn't want to spoil the romance of our farewell."

CHAPTER FOURTEEN

The Unit operators with Joe Saada and Shakeel Bashir were back driving through the scrub-brush country they had traversed before in Joe's engineering van. Everyone was secure in their new role as dedicated terrorists heading for a mission objective. The conduct of the police at the last checkpoint gave good evidence that the Palestinian authorities had no desire to actively interfere with any operations directed against the Israelis. They preferred getting the raiders through their areas as quickly as possible to avoid any sort of trouble, such as being linked to them.

As the two command cars traveled at a steady forty-five kilometers per hour through the barren countryside, Jonas Blane and Joe held an impromptu planning conference. The

CIA agent had been in deep thought since leaving the terrorist camp, and expressed some opinions and advice that he had. "We have two choices, basically," Joe explained from the backseat. "We can make an attempt to get across the Jordanian border and head for my office in Amman."

"Mmm," Jonas mused. "What do you estimate the risk of that option is?"

"Well, things could be a bit awkward," Joe said. "Even though this vehicle is unmarked and we have our identity papers, any Jordanian police or military stopping us would be curious as hell about these uniforms and the equipment."

"Well," Jonas said, "the first thing we'll have to do either before or right after entering Jordan is to dump these kaffiyehs, along with the weapons, ammo, and field gear." He turned his eyes to Bashir. "What sorts of ID do you have with you?"

Bashir put his hand into one of the side pockets of his trousers and pulled out a small bundle held together with a rubber band. After going through the documents, he pulled one out. "It is here that I am having a Jordanian passport."

"Great!" Joe said. "And I suggest you throw all the rest away. No matter what we do, your Jordanian identity will work fine. We can worry about getting you back to the States later on."

"All right," Bashir said. He rolled down the window to toss out the papers.

"Hold it!" Jonas said. He tapped Carlito on the shoulder. "Pull over."

When the vehicle was stopped, Jonas got out and went around to the back and retrieved an entrenching tool from the field gear. Next he got the papers from Bashir. Bob Brown leaned out the window of the second command car. "What's happening, boss?"

"I've got some documents to hide," Jonas answered. He quickly scooped out a two-foot-deep hole in the soft, sandy soil. After dropping Bashir's extra IDs into the small excavation, he covered them up and stamped down on the dirt. A quick sweeping of the hiding place with some dead brush to disguise the spot finished the job. He hopped back into the vehicle, nodding to Carlito to drive on.

"I have one more suggestion," Joe said. "It's a lot more dangerous, but will get us to the Mediterranean Sea, where American warships are located."

"What's so dangerous about it?" Jonas asked.

"It involves crossing Israel and sneaking across the border into the Gaza Strip," Joe explained. "When we reach the sea, we'll have to steal a boat and—"

"Never mind," Jonas said, interrupting. "We'll take our chances in Jordan. Getting across Israel is almost impossible, and if we do and gain entry into the Gaza Strip, we'd be back playing hide-and-seek with the Palestinians."

"Then Jordon it is," Joe said in agreement.

The two-vehicle convoy continued eastward.

1630 HOURS LOCAL
1430 HOURS ZULU

"Hey, boss!" Carlito said, pointing through the windshield. "Another police checkpoint."

Joe looked down the road. "That's the same one we went through in the van a couple of weeks back."

"Yeah," Jonas said. "As long as we have these kaffiyehs and the scarves they shouldn't recognize us."

Bashir sat up straighter. "I am ready for to tell them we are on mission. They will be glad to be getting us out of their hairs."

The convoy slowed and came to a halt. The same police captain who had stopped them before walked up to the vehicles. Bashir leaned forward and spoke forcefully in Arabic. But instead of responding like the cops at the last checkpoint, this one simply peered in the first car for a few moments. Then he went back to the second to give Bob and Mack a look-see. Suddenly he whistled loudly and shrilly.

A dozen riflemen appeared from around the small station house. They quickly surrounded both vehicles, and the captain aimed his pistol at Carlito's head. He gestured the drivers and passengers to get out of the cars.

"Do as he says," Jonas said. "There's no way in hell we're gonna break loose from here."

Within a half minute all six men stood in a single line with their hands up. The captain, who was Kaleefa Nasser of Alifhedal's al-Askarin combat detachment, smiled as he pointed to each of the prisoners one by one. *"Itnen Arabin! Wahid Ifriki! Talata Urubawin!"*

Joe, speaking softly out of the side of his mouth to Jonas, said, "He just counted two Arabs, one African, and three Europeans."

Jonas nodded his understanding, whispering back, "They've been watching out for us. They know we're the guys who came through here before."

Less than ten minutes later a jeep and weapons carrier, both surplus Israeli equipment, pulled up. The prisoners were crowded into the second vehicle with a couple of guards, while three others hopped into the jeep. The other nineteen pulled themselves up into the cargo area of another truck parked behind the station house. Nasser and his two "policemen" waved as the group drove back down the thoroughfare from the direction the captives had come. When they reached the lone olive tree, they turned off and headed for the hinterlands along a bumpy track that passed for a road.

The captives were ordered off the vehicle and taken into a frame building. Their guards instructed them to lower their hands. Plastic restraints were placed on their wrists, and the six men had to sit on the floor with their backs against the wall. Mack amused himself by winking at the shy Arab girls of the camp.

Since the detachment commander, Bahaadur Aziz, was away at a special meeting at Alifhedal's general staff in Lebanon, the Egyptian Peer Zeroual was in temporary command. He came in to examine the captives, bringing Jaleela Qazi with him to act as translator. One of the guards handed the prisoners' papers over to Zeroual, who immediately passed them to Jaleela. Jaleela perused the passports for a couple of minutes. "Who is Yusuf Saada?" she asked in English.

"I am Yusuf Saada," Joe answered.

"Your family owns Nijmi Engineering, does it not?"

"Yes."

Next she looked at Bashir, asking, "And you are Anjum Jammeh, a citizen of Jordan?"

Joe interjected, "He is an employee of my engineering firm."

Zeroual, even though he couldn't understand what Joe said, stepped forward and kicked him hard. "You do not speak until spoken to!"

The Unit operators exchanged meaningful glances among themselves in silent warnings that the guy was going to end up being a big problem. Carlito, however, had been instantly mesmerized by the translator. He even smiled at her, noting that she didn't seem to know how to respond to him.

Now Jaleela looked at the Canadian passports. She pointed to Mack. "Where are you from?"

"Ottawa," he replied.

"And what do you do there?"

"I'm an engineer," Mack replied. "My buddies and I are all working for Nijmi Engineering on a special job."

Jaleela asked brief questions of Jonas, Carlito, and Bob. When she finished her short interrogations, she looked at them as if they were naughty boys. "You are not Canadians. I have an aunt and uncle in Montréal, and I have been up there many times while I was attending college in New York City. You four certainly do not have that accent." She smiled. "And not one of you used the word 'hey' in your answers."

"What is going on?" Zeroual asked.

Jaleela explained that the African and Europeans did not speak with Canadian accents, and she knew for sure they were Americans. Zeroual was tempted to start beating some answers out of the prisoners, but the fact that they were American made him hesitate. And it was also obvious that the so-called Jordanian employee of Saada's was the defector Bashir that everyone in Palestine seemed to be looking for.

Zeroual turned to the guards. "Take these six and lock them in the supply annex until further notice. We will have to look after them until we receive word of Aziz's return, or somebody else who will decide their fate."

The guards went to the prisoners and hauled them to their feet, then kicked and pushed them out the door.

WASHINGTON, D.C.
8 OCTOBER
0700 HOURS LOCAL
1200 HOURS ZULU

The day's morning edition of the *Washington Beacon* featured another front-page article by Maggie Donahue.

INVESTIGATION OF SPECIAL OPERATIONS COMMANDER MYSTERIOUSLY CANCELED

By Maggie Donahue

The hearings regarding Colonel Thomas Ryan and his notorious combat force known as the Unit have inexplicably been permanently terminated by Senator Herbert Kinkaid, chairman of the Senate's Committee on Intelligence and Special Operations.

Senator Kinkaid was not available for an interview when this reporter contacted his office. His executive secretary, Phyllis Vance, had no comment regarding the situation, other than to state that certain administrative and procedural protocols brought about the end of the investigation. "As far as the senator's committee is concerned, the matter is closed," Ms. Vance said. She added that there would be no further statements issued or interviews given by senators Kinkaid, Tom Wilson, or Edna Gardner.

This makes one wonder what powers brought about the end of an investigation into the war crimes of an out-of-control Special Forces officer and the hired thugs under his command. How are the killings of innocent civilians, summary executions of prisoners, and the cold-blooded assassinations of two French citizens swept under the rug? Who does this notorious Colonel Ryan answer to? Who conspires to

maintain these bandits in the service of the United
States of America?

These and other questions must be answered satis-
factorily to put an end to this flagrant disregard of
law and order. It is a disgrace to our nation and everything it stands for that professional soldiers are given
an implicit license to run amok, murdering and plun-
dering innocent and defenseless victims.

I promise all my loyal readers that I will not rest
until I have exposed every single bit of evidence regarding this cancer that is now eating away at the
heart and soul of the American way of life.

AL-ASKARIN BASE CAMP
10 OCTOBER
1100 HOURS LOCAL
0900 HOURS ZULU

None of the members of al-Askarin had ever met their
commander in chief. During this early organization and
training phase of the detachment, he had been busy tending
to a myriad of administrative and logistical chores necessary to establish a sound foundation from which to launch
active operations. This included continuing communications with Alifhedal's sponsors and supporters, who had to
maintain the strictest secrecy about their association with
the organization. Because of the sensitivity of his duties,
the man's name was completely unknown to those he
would eventually lead in combat. But on this day, they
were to meet him face-to-face, all because of the six men
now locked and guarded in the supply annex.

Although close-order drill had not been an important
part of al-Askarin's training schedule, Zeroual had instilled
enough marching instruction so that the members could

move around a drill field in an acceptable fashion. Now they were drawn up in three ranks with their AK-47s slung across their chests. Haleefa Nasser, down at the pretend checkpoint, had radioed up to report that the commander in chief was now on his way up to the camp.

Ten minutes later a Honda Odyssey van pulled up to the front of the headquarters building. When the right passenger door slid open, a tall, slim man with a beard trimmed short and neat stepped out. He was wearing a starched and ironed khaki uniform he had changed into from civilian clothing back at the checkpoint. Peer Zeroual rightly figured him as the guest of honor, and he stepped forward, rendering a sharp salute.

"Training Officer Zeroual reporting to the commander in chief!" he barked.

The man returned the salute, then gave the assembled fighters a fond look. "Good morning, comrades in arms," he said in a loud voice. "I am happy to finally meet you. My name is Behraam Taimur, and I have the honor of being the commander in chief of al-Askarin of Alifhedal. Your detachment commander, Aziz, is still very busy at headquarters and was not able to accompany me here. And that is fine, because I welcome this chance of finally getting to know all of you on an informal basis. But first I must deal with this matter of the six prisoners now in our custody." He turned to Zeroual. "Take me to the prisoners, Training Officer."

"Yes, sir!" Zeroual said. He pointed at the formation of young fighters. "Jaleela Qazi, come with us."

The young woman, surprised at the summons, quickly broke ranks and joined the two men as they strode across the camp to the supply annex. Taimur smiled at the young woman, speaking to her in perfect but accented English. "They tell me you are a graduate of Columbia. A degree in journalism, I was informed."

"Yes," Jaleela replied.

"You will be very helpful in our intelligence branch."

"I hope to remain here as a fighter."

"Most admirable," Taimur remarked. "I will see that your request is honored."

When they reached the supply annex, the guards did as Zeroual had instructed them earlier: They kept their AK-47s slung over their shoulders and displayed salutes to the commander in chief. Then the door was quickly opened, and Jaleela, Taimur, and Zeroual entered.

Jonas Blane and the others stood up. Taimur nodded to them with a smile, then asked, "Who is in charge?"

"I am," Jonas said.

"You have forged Canadian passports," Taimur said. "That has already been determined."

Jonas eyed him closely. "All right. I'll come clean. We're Americans."

Joe Saada now got to his feet, knowing that there would be no use trying to fool the guy. "I'm an American too."

"I see," Taimur said. "Of Arab ancestry, no?"

"Of Arab ancestry, yes."

Taimur swung his attention to the others. "I would like each of you to give me your names."

"That isn't necessary," Jonas said.

"The Geneva Convention allows you to give your names, dates of birth, and military service numbers," Taimur said.

"You are not a signatory to the Geneva Convention," Jonas pointed out.

"We will deal with this later," Taimur stated.

Bashir regarded Taimur in silence. The al-Askarin leader gazed back, asking, "And you are Jordanian, are you?"

"I am."

"No you're not," Taimur said. "You are Shakeel Bashir,

a defector from Barq-min-Islam. A lot of people are searching for you." He stepped back, looking silently at the six prisoners. "You are now in the hands of a secular Arab revolutionary group. Never mind the name. Never mind our aims. We are going to figure out what we are to do with you. If you are accommodating, we will treat you in a civilized manner. If you are argumentative or uncooperative, I can promise you an extremely calamitous outcome of your stay with us. Understand?"

He turned and walked to the door, knocking on it. The guards opened the portal, and Taimur walked out, with Jaleela and Zeroual following.

1300 HOURS LOCAL
1100 HOURS ZULU

Behraam Taimur had brought some food with him to feed the whole al-Askarin detachment. Two caterers, who Jaleela figured out were his servants, arranged a buffet, complete with cutlery and silverware. All this had been carefully and skillfully packed into the Odyssey van.

The meal consisted of *bitingan mikhalil*, eggplant stuffed with herbs and spices; *salatit gargir*, watercress salad; *kofta*, grilled minced meatballs; and for dessert *esh al saraya*, deep-fried rolls covered with syrup. Since Alifhedal people were secular and didn't observe the rules of Islam, Taimur also provided an assortment of red and white wines.

During the meal the commander in chief chatted easily with all the fighters and was especially solicitous to Hanaa Maamon, complimenting the polio victim's dedication to duty despite her handicap. As he spoke and joked, Jaleela recognized his accent and mannerisms as Lebanese. Taimur was quite possibly from a wealthy Christian merchant family, and obviously very well educated and urbane, possessing an ability to fit into any social setting, no matter the type of company.

When the meal was finished and the servants were busy cleaning and packing, Taimur took Jaleela and Zeroual into a separate room. After they were seated, the supreme leader of al-Askarin got down to business. "We are going to take Bashir into custody and transport him back to Jordan," he explained. "He has valuable information that will affect our future planning. Also, I have been informed by certain sources that the African-American is anxious to leave the Middle East with the man. We cannot permit such a thing."

Zeroual shrugged. "I see no problem with preventing that. Although it has occurred to me that all those Americans could be CIA."

"That is not what is so sensitive," Taimur said. "We also do not want them to get out of the West Bank, whether they are agents or not. They have already seen too much, and since we are not certain of their origins or who they work for, they are big risks to our organization."

Jaleela felt a flash of nervousness. "What will happen to them?"

Taimur smiled at her in a brotherly way. "You said you wanted to be a fighter. To be a fighter you must kill."

Jaleela swallowed hard. "You are going to kill them?"

"I do not enjoy taking such an extreme step, but it is necessary," Taimur said. "I am going to tell them we will insert them into our escape and evasion network, but that we must split them up. To avoid any problems with the African-American we will permit him to keep Bashir at his side. You are to accompany us to see that they do not become suspicious or alarmed. Be friendly and talkative with them." He glanced at the Egyptian. "You too. Show a spirit of camaraderie toward the prisoners."

"I understand," Zeroual said. "When we have them separated, then everyone with the exception of the defector will be executed."

Jaleela sat in silence as the two men continued to discuss the task ahead.

CHAPTER FIFTEEN

Jonas Blane, Mack Gerhardt, Bob Brown, and Carlito Grey were seated on folding chairs along with Joe Saada and Shakeel Bashir. To their direct front stood Commander in Chief Behraam Taimur and Jaleela Qazi. Peer Zeroual, holding an AK-47 assault rifle, had positioned himself at the door.

"I trust you are comfortable here," Taimur said. "We hope the mattresses and sleeping bags will allow you to rest well as long as you are our guests."

"That was an excellent lunch you provided us," Jonas said, wanting to keep the proceedings on an informal and friendly level. "Do you always eat like that?"

Taimur chuckled. "Actually I brought the food with me. I'm afraid that this evening's meal will be field rations. But I am sure you will not go hungry." He paused to judge his audience. They seemed attentive and at ease. "I have come here to give you some important information that should please you. As I said before, we are a secular Arabic organization. Additionally, it is our goal to establish democracies here in the Middle East and bring down all Islamic republics. We consider them archaic and cruel, and feel that the Arab people will not prosper in the twenty-first century as long as the mullahs are in charge of things."

"What is your attitude toward Israel?" Joe asked.

"We are Arabs," Taimur said. "And as Arabs we wish to see the total destruction of the Israeli nation. So do not think we are in strict accordance with all Western—or American—aims and goals. However, we also wish to see a similar fate for Islamic fundamentalist terrorist groups. Therefore, it is in our own best interests to see that Shakeel Bashir is taken to wherever it is you wish to relocate him. I am sure he will be able to help you with the objectives you share with us."

Jonas was skeptical. "I'm curious as to why you haven't submitted us to intense interrogation. Aren't you curious about who we are?"

Taimur laughed loudly. "Of course we are, my friend! But we have good reason to trust that this mission you are on is as beneficial to us as it is to you. Therefore, we are going to insert you into our escape-and-evasion net to see you safely to Jordan. From the direction of travel you followed when you drove up to our checkpoint, we assume that is where you wish to go." He paused and smiled. "That police checkpoint is not a real one. We use it to maintain surveillance on the road."

"I was wondering about that," Joe Saada said.

Jonas wasn't in the mood for small talk. "How long will it take to get us to Jordan in your net?"

"Three to five days," Taimur answered. "However, we'll have to split you up in order to accommodate you. It will be necessary that you are divided into three two-man teams. Jaleela, because of her fluency in English, will be traveling with one of your duos."

"Isn't there some way we can remain as a single group?" Jonas asked.

"I am afraid it would be impossible to get you through our organization in that manner," Taimur replied. "Our facilities and procedures are designed for one or two people at a time. Sorry. But we employ several routes in order that if one is discovered, the others are not compromised."

"That makes sense," Jonas allowed.

"I am glad you understand, my friend," Taimur said. "I assume that you personally wish to take Mr. Bashir with you."

"Yes," Jonas replied. He looked at the others. "Here's the order of battle. Joe and Mack. Bob and Carlito."

"Okay, boss," Mack said, answering for everybody.

"When does this start?" Jonas asked.

"The operation commences at twenty-two hundred hours tonight," Taimur replied. "The first will be you and Mr. Bashir. Then those two." He pointed to Joe and Mack. "And lastly those gentlemen." He indicated Bob and Carlito. "They will be accompanied by Jaleela." He walked toward the door. "I suggest you get some sleep. It will be a long night until you reach your first safehouses."

The soon-to-be evaders remained silent as their hosts left the room. After they departed, Carlito grinned. "That Jaleela is a hottie, ain't she?"

Jonas growled at him. "Don't start getting romantic, Romeo."

Jonas and company were back in their civilian clothes that had been taken from the two command cars. The other weapons and gear in the vehicles were to be confiscated by al-Askarin for their own use, leaving the Americans, Joe, and the defector unarmed.

A loud knock sounded on the annex door, and it was opened. Taimur stepped in with Jaleela, Zeroual, and Haleefa Nasser. All three were armed, and the men stayed at the entrance, obviously standing guard. Taimur was in a good mood. "I see everybody is ready. Then shall we start with Mr. Blane and Mr. Bashir. Training Officer Zeroual will accompany you."

Jonas and Bashir walked to the door, where a couple of the al-Askarin met them. After they left, the four remaining settled onto the folding chairs. Taimur gave them a friendly look. "You seem very calm and collected, gentlemen. I am going to assume you have been through this sort of thing before."

"It seems to be well organized," Mack remarked.

Jaleela took a chair and carried it over to a dark corner of the room. She sat down, leaning her AK-47 against the wall. She tried to fight the trembling that was beginning to affect her breathing. The young Arab woman closed her eyes and rationalized: *This is a war, and it is necessary to kill in a war. I volunteered to be a fighter, so I cannot lose my nerve here. Our goals of changing the Middle East will never be realized without having cold, calculating hearts and minds. Never falter! Never show mercy! Remain strong and resolute!*

She suddenly recalled the assassination in Pakistan of Benazir Bhutto. Was this the same thing? If they wanted Bashir the defector, why not take him and send the Americans away, even if they had seen the camp and people of al-Askarin? Killing them in cold blood would be murder, plain and simple; and she truly had a special affection for America and its people.

Then her mind settled as she recalled a Japanese maxim: *Duty is as heavy as a mountain, while death is as light as a feather.*

Jaleela took a deep, steadying breath, steeling herself for the ordeal she faced in the next few hours.

2300 HOURS LOCAL
2100 HOURS ZULU

Joe Saada and Mack Gerhardt were the next to leave when a driver appeared at the door. Nasser followed them out of the building to a waiting Toyota sedan. As soon as they left, Carlito stood up and walked over to where Jaleela was sitting. He smiled at her. "How are you doing?"

"Quite well, thank you," she replied in a quiet voice.

"You're pretty new at this, aren't you?" Carlito asked. "Don't be nervous. It seems you guys have this set up pretty slick."

"Yes," Jaleela said.

Bob came up to them with a grin. "Me and Carlito are pretty lucky. Our escort is really good-looking. And charming too."

"Thank you," Jaleela said.

Carlito looked at her closely. "Relax, honey bun. This is going to be a piece of cake. In a couple of days we'll all—"

"They're going to kill you!" Jaleela whispered desperately.

The two Unit operators went into professional mode as they knelt down beside the young woman. Carlito spoke in a calm, matter-of-fact manner. "Give us the full story."

Jaleela told them about the plot and how Bashir would prove valuable to Alifhedal in the fight against the Islamic extremists. "They are taking you to three separate safe-houses in Musalmar. There are men waiting for you there. After you are all sleeping, you'll be shot with pistols that have those quiet things on them."

"You mean silencers?" Bob asked.

"Yes! Silencers!"

"All right," Carlito said. "Do you know where all those places are?"

"Yes," Jaleela replied. "I have seen the map. Musalmar is not a big place and the houses are close to each other."

"Here's what we do," Bob said, taking over. As a ser-geant first class he outranked Staff Sergeant Carlito Grey. "We leave just like the others. Don't say anything or do anything. Follow your orders. Leave the rest to us." He nudged Carlito. "There's some wire on them boxes over there that'll make dandy garrotes."

"I'm way ahead of you, buddy," Carlito said, getting up and going over to the supply bin.

11 OCTOBER
0002 HOURS LOCAL
10 OCTOBER
2202 HOURS ZULU

The rap on the door, though expected, startled Carlito, Bob, and Jaleela. She got up from her chair with her AK-47 across her shoulder as the portal was opened by the guard outside. The driver stepped into the annex, nodding to the young woman. After they exchanged some words in Arabic, Jaleela turned to the Americans. "It is time for us to go."

The two Unit operators followed the driver and Jaleela out to the Toyota. The Americans got in the back while the chauffeur and young woman situated themselves on the front seats. The motor was already running, and the driver shifted into gear, turning around and heading for the track leading out to the olive tree by the road.

"Jaleela," Bob said, "when we come up to the headquarters building, tell him to stop."

She nodded her assent. At the right time, she said, "*Wakkif haun.*"

The man brought the car to a halt, slipping into park. He started to ask her the reason for stopping when the wire garrote was slipped over his head. Bob pulled tight, bracing his knees against the seat for more leverage, and leaned back as hard as he could. Even with the victim's desperate shaking and gurgling, it was over in less than a minute.

"What's going on?" Carlito asked, puzzled. "This wasn't supposed to happen here."

"I just had an idea," Bob said. "C'mon!" He got out and led them around the building to where the two command cars were parked. The weapons, ammo, and other gear had not been unloaded yet. "You won't have to hot-wire it, Carlito. The key is still in the ignition."

The trio quickly got inside, and Carlito switched on the key. The engine kicked over, and he drove it slowly away from the building. Within five minutes they reached the olive tree and turned east. After going past the empty checkpoint, Jaleela gave directions for how to reach the first safehouse in Musalmar.

"I just hope we ain't too late," Carlito said, pressing down on the accelerator.

MUSALMAR, WEST BANK
0200 HOURS LOCAL
2400 HOURS ZULU

The neighborhood was unlit as the command car pulled up to the curb by the gate leading into the safehouse yard.

Both Carlito and Bob tensed for action as they approached the wall. Bob whispered some instructions to Jaleela, and she walked up to the speakerphone on the gate. She picked up the receiver and waited for an answer. When someone in the interior of the house responded, she spoke in rapid Arabic, explaining that the Toyota had broken down about five kilometers back. The driver stayed with it and wanted someone to come give him a push. Then she hung up.

"All right," she said softly. "He's coming."

A couple of minutes passed; then they heard the sounds of the gate being unlocked and the hasp sliding back. The barrier swung open and Jaleela gestured for Bob and Carlito to go inside. The guy who admitted them stood calmly waiting to close the entry when Bob spun on his heel and drove his fist straight into his throat. After the victim had hit the cement, a vicious stamp on his Adam's apple finished the job.

The three scampered noiselessly down the driveway to the door, and entered the house. The other man inside was dozing in an easy chair, oblivious to what had been going on. His pistol was on the table beside him. It was a weird-looking Chinese Type 67 with a built-in silencer. It fired .32-caliber bullets with adjusted powder charges that aided in the silencing. Carlito picked it up and fired a round into the guy's head.

Bob stepped through a door, then walked down a narrow hall to an open entry. He glanced inside and saw Mack Gerhardt and Joe Saada each lying on a cot. "Hey!" Bob said. "Wake up."

Mack responded so fast and violently that he was on his feet in an instant. He blinked at the unexpected sight of his teammate. "What the hell?"

"This is a setup for offing us," Bob said. "Jaleela wised us up. Let's get out of here. I'll explain later."

Joe was now wide-awake, and he numbly went along.

When they went through the living room, they could see the dead guy half-on and half-off the chair. A stream of blood oozed heavily out of a head wound, soaking his shirt.

"Let's go!" Carlito urged them.

They went outside, passed the other corpse, and stepped through the gate. The sight of the command car was so surprising that Mack and Joe came to a complete stop.

"Get in!" Bob urged them impatiently. "We have one more call to make tonight."

It took only five minutes to reach the other safehouse. On the way, Bob explained that they would use the same ploy again, and tell them that the Toyota had broken down.

When they reached the street, Carlito let the vehicle coast to a stop. Then all five eased out of the car and approached the gate. Once more Jaleela got on the intercom. Then she hung up. "The guy is coming."

The sound of the door being opened was a low squeak, and Bob was ready to spring forward. But the man he saw startled him. "Boss!"

Jonas Blane looked at them in happy surprise. "For the love of God!" he whispered hoarsely. "Bashir translated the phone call for me."

"Jaleela wised us up," Carlito said. "We have Mack and Joe here too."

"I'll go back and fetch Bashir," Jonas said. He trotted down to the door and went back in the house. A moment later, the Unit team leader and the defector appeared, hurrying toward the gate.

After everyone was crammed into the command car, Mack turned to Jonas. "What happened, boss?"

"Things weren't adding up," Jonas said. "Then I guess those two idiots guarding us forgot that Bashir was an Arab. One of them let the truth slip out while they were talking to each other. I made the right moves to neutralize 'em, but I got to thinking that we had really gotten ourselves in deep." He winked over at Jaleela. "Then the inter-com rang and I heard an angel speaking."

"Boss," Bob said, "we've got weapons, ammo, and field gear in the back. They hadn't taken it out yet."

Jonas actually laughed out loud. "Things are looking up!"

Carlito, at the wheel, asked, "What do we do now, boss?"

"They'll expect us to make a run for Jordan," Jonas said. "We'll throw 'em off by heading west to the Medi-terranean Sea."

"Hey, boss," Mack said, "didn't you and Joe figure that was the most dangerous way out of here?"

"Beggars can't be choosers, my friend," Jonas said.

CHAPTER SIXTEEN

Captain Khursheed Jaafari was a contented man. Not only was his present position with the Palestinian police providing him with a more than ample income, but his financial prospects for the future had never been brighter.

Besides the usual bribes associated with his position, such as business licenses, construction permits, buy-offs from criminal elements, and other under-the-table transactions, he had multiple revenue arrangements with branches of Israeli intelligence: businessmen in Israel, the West Bank, and the Gaza Strip; and various Islamic militant groups. Jaafari's main commodity was information, and he distributed it generously, amply, and equally among his clients. He found it interesting when one piece of intelligence would benefit one set of patrons while being detrimental to the others. He could not wait to see who would come out on top of the resulting conflicts. Eight out of ten times it was the Israelis who seemed to be able to move faster and more effectively than their Arab enemies, even if they were the side at a disadvantage. The Jews seemed like cats to the Palestinian lawman: They were able to survive great plummets that seemed fatal, yet always landed on their feet, then quickly recovered and pounced viciously for the kill. The mujahideen seemed like scurrying rats, losing more than they gained.

Jaafari not only admired the Israelis' adaptability, but felt no animosity toward them because of the partitioning of Palestine. The Arab policeman, after due consideration, thought the change would improve the lives of his people, who had been stagnating for generations through corrupt and incompetent self-government. His foresight fully convinced him that his homeland would become an independent state in a way that would have been impossible without the establishment of the Jewish nation. When sovereignty was finally realized, foreign aid would come pouring in, with international agencies providing direct support and other incentives to build up the local economy.

Because of that very real probability, Jaafari was not squandering his extra income; instead he was holding it for big investments once Palestine joined the rest of the world. He had given the matter a lot of thought and consideration, finally reaching a decision that his fortune could be made by investing his funds the good old American way: through fast-food franchises. With the authority of his police position, he could make sure that competition was kept to an absolute minimum. There wouldn't be a hamburger, piece of chicken, basket of French fries, or a cup of latte coffee that could be sold from an establishment he didn't own.

Another plentiful and reliable source of money would be skateboard parks. A whole generation of Palestinian youth, now undernourished from sparse diets and lives of deprivation, would eventually have the money and energy to take

up the same sports American kids liked. They would fuel
their energy for skateboarding with junk-food calories offered by his eating places, and each time one of them
stuffed a greasy serving into his fat face or paid for admission to a park, all the profit would go into Jaafari's pockets.

It was like a game of chess in which he influenced the
moves of his opponents.

ISRAEL
LATITUDE 31° NORTH, LONGITUDE 34° EAST
1000 HOURS LOCAL
0800 HOURS ZULU

The command car had been pulled into a deep gully and
quickly covered with scrub brush. The camouflage pattern
of deep, medium, and light brown splotches painted on the
body added to the effect of keeping it invisible. The seven
evaders were gathered together in the shade afforded by the
gash in the terrain, and could now relax after the harrowing
breakout of the West Bank into Israel proper.

"We're not going to be able to use the vehicle beyond
this point," Jonas Blane said to his lounging companions.
"From here on it's a hike to the Mediterranean Sea. And
we're going to have to avoid built-up areas. That means a
lot of zigzagging."

Carlito Grey was studying a map of the area they had
found in the glove compartment. "Well, boss, we have a
couple of routes to choose from. There's Israel all the way,
or we could cut through the Gaza Strip if that looks advantageous."

"Don't forget a more southern route through the Sinai
desert of Egypt," Joe Saada pointed out.

"Whoa!" Mack Gerhardt said. "It's been a while since I
went through desert survival training."

"This map shows oases in that place," Carlito said. "At least, that's what I think these green palm-tree symbols mean."

Joe walked over for a look. "Yeah. But it's a long walk between 'em. And Egyptian army patrols are heavy in the area, not to mention tourism. Nobody can get in your way like a bunch of dippy vacationers wandering around stumbling into places they aren't wanted."

Jonas stretched to get the kinks out of his back. "As I recall, terrorists have attacked busloads of tourists in the area."

"That was a big mistake on their part," Joe pointed out. "The murders cut into profits that could be made by local merchants. Not a good public relations move. And that is why the national military is active as hell in the area."

Bob Brown grinned in his usual manner whenever things looked tough. "Let's see. We got Islamic terrorists, the Israeli Mossad, the Israeli army, and other folks looking for us. Would it make that much difference if the Egyptians jumped into the mix?"

"I'm putting the Sinai desert way down at the bottom of our options list," Jonas said.

Shakeel Bashir was detached and silent as he listened to the Americans talk. He glanced over at Jaleela Qazi, who sat patiently with her AK-47, seemingly unworried. He smiled to himself at her display of youthful optimism. In truth he felt pretty safe as long as they were in Israel. If they were captured by the army, he would be taken to a prison for interrogation. After he spilled his guts willingly and copiously, the Jews would see that he was treated right to set a good example for future defectors. He could end up in comfortable circumstances in Europe or even America.

Jonas spoke up, saying, "Well, folks, we're out here on our lonesome with no radios, binoculars, or compasses. I suggest we all make special note of where the sun sets.

That's the way to the sea." He looked at Joe. "How far do you think it is?"

"By the way the crow flies, I'd say somewhere around eighty kilometers," Joe answered. He closed his eyes and did the math in his head. "That'd be maybe forty-nine miles."

"A swift pace would get us there in fifteen or sixteen hours," Jonas opined. "But we ain't gonna be walking fast because of that zigzagging I mentioned. So here's the drill, troops. We'll move in roughly three- to five-mile stages toward our destination. A two-man recon team will go out while the others wait. Once they've determined the best route to the next point, they can come back and get the rest of us. When we're up to the point where they've scouted, the next team will take off."

"That's gonna be slow as molasses in the winter, boss," Mack remarked.

"In these circumstances that might prove to be a marked advantage," Jonas said. "We'll have to load up with ammo and those field rations in the back of the command car. It looks like we'll be eating one meal a day."

"What about water, boss?" Bob asked.

"The first thing is that we're lucky it's not summer," Jonas replied. "The second thing is that finding water will be a side issue for the guys on recon. Let's hope it doesn't turn into a big problem."

"What are we gonna do when we reach the Mediterranean?" Carlito asked.

Jonas winked at him. "Do you know how to swim?"

"We can do better than that, boss," Carlito said seriously.

"I'm sure we'll find some dandy opportunities," Jonas commented.

"By the way," Mack said, "I was checking the bandoliers while we were driving over here. I counted thirty.

Each holds six pockets with thirty-round magazines. That's a grand total of five thousand, four hundred bullets."

"While you were back there counting, what else did you figure out?" Jonas asked.

"We can each have a belt and harness with a carrying pouch on the back," Mack said.

"The rations can go in those," Jonas instructed.

Mack continued. "There was two dozen canteens and canteen carriers that hook onto the belts. That comes to three apiece, with three left over."

"Okay," Jonas said. "Bashir will take two of the extra and Joe one extra. Also, since we will each carry four bandoliers, Joe will also carry the extra two. Let's get this stuff divvied up."

"What about the entrenching tools?" Mack asked.

"One for everybody," Jonas decided. "There's always a chance we might have to go into a field fortification mode."

They went over to the command car and Mack got inside. He began tossing out the harnesses, bandoliers, entrenching tools, and canteens. Bob and Carlito put them into seven piles. They were all the same except the two for Bashir and Joe.

"The first recon team is gonna be Bob and Mack," Jonas said. "You two guys load up and move out." He glanced up toward the top of the gully. "Carlito and Jaleela, you guys are security topside. Let's go, people!"

Carlito had found a good place that offered both concealment and an excellent view of the surrounding countryside. He was pleased to note that Jaleela was trained well enough to pick an excellent spot that provided a satisfactory field of fire. The Unit operator settled down beside her for the duration of their guard duty.

Jaleela positioned the AK-47 where she could grab it quickly if need be. Carlito gave her a surreptitious glance, admiring her beauty as he placed his own weapon close at hand. Even in the boonie hat she displayed a sexual attractiveness. He cleared his throat. "Have you fired your weapon yet?"

"Yes," she replied. "I scored more hits than the others on the silhouette targets."

Carlito laughed. "Remind me not to make you mad at me."

She chuckled. "I have never shot another human being. I am beginning to wonder if I can."

"It's not easy, even for a veteran," he said. "Maybe not when you first squeeze the trigger, but later when you think about it, you sort of have mixed feelings no matter how much you rationalize."

"The commander in chief was so cold-blooded about wanting to kill you guys," Jaleela said. "I guess since I spent so much time in America, I just could not let them do it."

"Believe me, we're grateful for what you did, no matter the reason."

The couple fell into silence, their eyes scanning the horizon around them. They could hear soft conversation below between Jonas and Joe while Bashir remained silent.

Carlito took another admiring glance at his beautiful companion.

1400 HOURS LOCAL
1200 HOURS ZULU

Shakeel Bashir decided to see how much he was going to have to carry. After Jonas showed the defector the proper way to attach the canteens to the belt, he hooked on the four he had been assigned. Next he slipped into the harness and slung the bandoliers over his shoulders, picking up the AK-47 rifle that had been allotted him.

"This is much heavy," he complained.

"Stop bellyaching," Jonas said. "You're not going to do any of the reconnaissance duty. It's only fair that you carry an extra canteen. Joe is toting two extra bandoliers."

"I think it is best we go look for Israeli soldiers and surrender," Bashir said.

"My orders are to get you back to the States," Jonas said. "And that's where you're going."

"I change my mind. I stay here with Israelis."

Jonas eyed him thoughtfully, realizing that the guy might decide to sit down and refuse to move, hoping the Israelis would show up and take him into custody. Jonas walked over and took the AK-47 off the defector's shoulder, then flung it on the other side of the car. "If you get stubborn and decide it's best if you wait for the Mossad, you won't have a weapon with you."

Bashir smiled disdainfully. "What difference do that make?"

"What if your old pals in the Barq-min-Islam find you out here instead of the Jews? You wouldn't be able to defend yourself."

Bashir was shaken up. "Okay. I go with you. I promise. Give me back my gun."

"I won't give you back your weapon," Jonas said. "But I'll give you the two extra bandoliers that Joe is carrying. I've just taken about eight pounds off your load when I threw that AK-forty-seven away." He walked over and grabbed the ammo, bringing it back and hanging it around the Arab's neck. If you start lagging behind I'll give you a hard kick in the ass. Understand?"

"I understand," Bashir said. He took the gear off, dropping it in a pile.

Carlito's voice suddenly sounded from above. "Boss! Mack and Bob are coming in. I can see 'em about a kilometer out."

Fifteen minutes later Mack Gerhardt and Bob Brown walked at a slow but steady pace up to Jonas. They were tired, but seemed in fairly good moods. "We found some water, boss," Mack reported. "Five klicks out. A small stream with plenty of vegetation around the place. Good concealment."

"It's open country all the way," Bob added. "But nobody is gonna be able to sneak up on us because the visibility is practically unlimited. We'll just have to spot the bad guys before they spot us."

"We'll be taking chances with that water," Jonas said. "We got no purification tablets."

Mack shrugged. "Just one more risk among dozens."

"Yeah," Jonas said. "We'll make this a night movement."

2000 HOURS LOCAL
1800 HOURS ZULU

Since Bob and Mack had discovered their destination, they were put on point. Carlito and Joe went out as flankers, while Jonas, Jaleela, and Bashir stayed in the center. Jonas observed that Jaleela turned and covered the rear of the formation every ten or fifteen meters of travel. That showed she had gotten some pretty solid training by the Egyptian training officer of al-Askarin.

The night sky was cloudy, cutting down visibility to some extent, but it was still possible to observe the terrain a few hundred meters around their small column. Bashir trudged on with his head down, a bit uncomfortable with the extra canteens and bandoliers. But Jonas noted he was far from struggling, and his pace was steady.

They reached the objective a little after 2200 hours, and it was an ideal place, just as Mack and Bob had described it. A small, shallow stream flowed rapidly but silently over a sandy bottom as it wound through a copse of trees that grew along the banks. The undergrowth provided good concealment, and some of the trees were large enough to be climbed if it became necessary to peer out farther over the desert country.

The evaders settled down quietly as Jonas announced the guard roster. With that taken care of, he turned to Bashir. "Behave yourself, understand? If I lose my confidence in you, I'll not only tie you up at night, but make you walk with your hands bound behind your back during travel. Any questions?"

Bashir shook his head, and sank to the soft dirt along the stream.

CHAPTER SEVENTEEN

Commander in Chief Behraam Taimur and Field Commander Bahaadur Aziz looked down at the two bodies that were sprawled across the living room of the house. One had been shot, and the other showed a couple of wounds from a blunt instrument of some sort, either of which could have been fatal.

Training Officer Zeroual came into the room from the second floor, the expression on his face glum. "I have made a thorough search. There is nobody else present in the house."

"So!" Taimur hissed through his teeth. "The African and defector have escaped after killing the men who were supposed to have executed them."

"The two should not be too difficult to find, Commander in Chief," Aziz said. "They cannot get too far on foot."

Taimur started to reply when the sound of a car could be heard coming into the walled yard. A moment later Haleefa Nasser entered the house. "Both our comrades at the first safehouse are dead," he reported. "We found them sprawled in the entryway where they had been tossed. One had his throat crushed while the other was shot in the head. The captives are missing."

"That accounts for the Arab and the other American," Taimur said. "What about the other safehouse?"

"Our two fighters are unharmed," Nasser said. "They stated that no one showed up. We can assume that the prisoners to be taken there are gone, as are the others."

"Does that include the young woman Jaleela Qazi?" Zeroual asked.

Nasser shrugged. "There is no sign of her."

"Perhaps the Americans killed her," Aziz suggested.

"No," Taimur said. "She is alive. I should not have trusted her. It never occurred to me that she would betray us."

Zeroual was stunned. "I find that hard to believe, Commander in Chief. She was an excellent soldier and did well in her training. No matter how difficult I made it, Jaleela never faltered. I am proud to say that it is my opinion that she gave her life for Arab democracy."

"There is also the driver who was with her," Aziz reminded them. "Perhaps he is the traitor. She could be lying dead someplace by his hand. He could have driven them all to freedom."

"Let us get out to the camp and see what we can discover there," Taimur said. "I do not want to risk making contact by radio. These unhappy occurrences could be the result of a well-planned scheme directed by outsiders and carried out by a traitor in our midst. If we are under any sort of surveillance, any transmissions we make could be monitored."

AL-ASKARIN BASE CAMP
0800 HOURS LOCAL
0600 HOURS ZULU

As soon as the Odyssey van pulled up, Hanaa Maamon limped up to it as fast as she could. When Taimur got out, she reported to him in a strained voice. "Commander in Chief! We found the driver Abdul's body at the side of the building. He had a wire around his neck, and the vehicle the Americans came in is missing."

"Now we know what happened to them," Taimur said bitterly. "All six of our prisoners have escaped, and there is a possibility that Jaleela Qazi assisted them in their scheme."

"Oh, no, Commander in Chief!" Hanaa cried. "That would never happen. Jaleela is loyal to our cause."

The trainees were all armed and standing around the headquarters building, obviously distressed. Now Zeroual was out of the van in an instant, and he rushed up to them, shouting, "What is the matter with you? You know better than to do nothing! Go to your defensive positions, as you were taught!" The fighters suddenly regained their senses, splitting up to go to their predetermined posts.

Hanaa led the commander in chief, Aziz, and Zeroual into the building, where the dead driver, Abdul, had been laid out on a table. Someone had removed the garrote and tossed it to the floor. Taimur gave the body a quick glance, then turned to Hanaa. "And there has been nothing seen of the young woman Jaleela?"

"We searched all around the camp for her, Commander in Chief," Hanaa answered. "But we could find no sign of her. Maybe the Americans took her as a hostage."

"Did not anyone hear a disturbance?" Aziz asked.

Hanaa shook her head. "Not a single sound, Field Commander."

"Damn! Damn!" Taimur exclaimed in fury. "Those foreigners have to be devils to do all this in silence."

Zeroual was in agreement. "Do you suppose they are Mossad agents in disguise?"

"No," Taimur said. "They are American, no doubt of that. I recognized the accent, as did Jaleela. I think they are CIA or Special Forces. And it was important for them to get the defector out of here and back to the USA." He thought a moment. "We are going to need some help with this problem. They are undoubtedly heading for Jordan, so there is not much time." He pointed to Nasser. "You must drive me to Jerusalem!"

JERUSALEM, ISRAEL
AKHDAR FRUIT AND VEGETABLE COMPANY

Aaron Jabit was an Arab-Israeli who ran a very successful fruit-and-vegetable company that bought the harvests from various kibbutzim and sold the crops in the Gaza Strip and the West Bank. The Palestinians preferred the food grown by the Israelis because of the marked superiority to that produced by their own countrymen. The Arab farmers lacked the agricultural skills of crop selection, irrigation, rotation, and fertilization employed by the Jewish farmers, thus their yields were smaller and of a far lesser quality.

Jabir, besides exporting the produce to the Palestinians, was also a charter member of Alifhedal.

Haleefa Nasser pulled the van into a visitor's parking space in front of the Akhdar Fruit and Vegetable Company's main building. Behraam Taimur, now dressed in casual clothing, left the vehicle and went through the front door to a reception desk. The private security guard on duty recognized him and buzzed him through the door to the rear of the station. Taimur went into the interior and up a flight of stairs to where the office of Aaron Jabir was located. It took only a moment to be admitted into the boss's presence.

Jabir was a short, pleasant man with a neatly trimmed mustache. His bald head, which he shaved every morning, was shiny in the overhead fluorescent lights. He had been advised of Taimur's arrival as soon as the van turned into the lot from the street.

Taimur sat down without being invited. "We have a big problem, Aaron. The defector and his escorts have escaped."

Now Jabir's pleasant expression turned into a frown. "How did that happen?"

"Those Americans with him pulled it off in a step-by-step procedure," Taimur explained. "After they had been inserted piecemeal into our escape-and-evasion net, they simply rolled up to where the defector was, eliminating the personnel of each safehouse as they came to them. We lost five valuable men, and perhaps one of the women from al-Askarin."

"It sounds as if they had been warned they would be executed," Jabir said.

"Yes," Taimur agreed. "And I have strong suspicions about the woman Jaleela Qazi."

"I have heard of her experiences in America," Jabir said. "And you think she is involved in the plot?"

"I fear so," Taimur said. "They left the bodies of those they killed scattered about like discarded trash. But we found nothing of the woman."

"Mmm," Jabir said thoughtfully. "Perhaps they kept her for a plaything for a while before killing her."

"I do not think so. Those Americans were serious professionals. They were able to garrote one of the drivers inside the camp without making a disturbance. I do not think they would risk their mission to satisfy their lusts for a woman's body."

"All right," Jabir said. "I have contacts in both the Palestinian police and Israeli intelligence. I will pass the information on to them. As long as the fugitives remain in Israel, the West Bank, or the Gaza Strip they will be unable to evade capture or death for long." He reached for his phone. "Excuse me, please. I have much to do in a very short time."

Taimur got to his feet without speaking and left the office.

WASHINGTON, D.C.
THE SENATE BUILDING
SENATOR KINKAID'S OFFICE
1000 HOURS LOCAL
1500 HOURS ZULU

Norman DeWitt and Delmar Munger stood in front of Senator Kinkaid's desk, looking down at the old politico. Somehow he appeared to have aged since they last saw him. The senator's shoulders were hunched, and his face seemed more lined than ever. Even his eyes, magnified by the thick lenses of his glasses, seemed to have lost their usual fire and vigor. When he spoke it was as if it were a strain to make conversation. "There's not a hell of a lot I can do for you fellows."

"You left us in the lurch quite unexpectedly," DeWitt complained. "We set things up perfectly, and when you suddenly dropped your investigation of the Unit you left us holding that proverbial bag. If you had doubts about your ability to maintain the pressure on the Unit you should have told us."

"I had no choice," Kinkaid said. "Circumstances spun out of control."

Munger leaned forward. "This is putting us at one hell of a disadvantage, Senator. All we asked of you was to keep hammering at Colonel Ryan. You didn't need to convict him of anything. We're at a point now where we can't call in his dogs without having egg all over our faces."

"Delmar is making an understatement," DeWitt said. "This could well mean the end of our careers."

"It would be worse than simply losing our livelihoods!" Munger snapped. "We'd more than likely end up in federal prison."

"Each time one of you fellows speaks, things look worse and worse," Kinkaid said. "I'm no longer sure about your true intentions in this unhappy matter. I'm beginning to suspect that there was a deeper plot you made no mention of. I'm not going to be able to help you anymore. Big pressure was put on me. You must believe me, even though I can't go into the exact details."

Now DeWitt leaned forward, his hands on the desk. "We have big pressures too, Senator. And you gave us the impression that you were ready to go all the way in what was supposed to be the final strike against the Unit. Now all of a sudden you quit on us. If we get into trouble, it would mean things would be much worse for you than if you called Ryan back in for more hearings."

"By God!" Kinkaid squeaked loudly. "You don't seem to appreciate my position in all this. My committee has turned against me. Senators Wilson and Gardner might even bring me up before the Senate Ethics Committee if I continue this case. They were already complaining the last time I had Colonel Ryan dragged in when all those newspeople were outside with their cameras and their microphones and their questions. Senators Wilson and Gardner didn't even take part in the proceedings. That was hard for me to deal with; you'd better believe that. And General Beckons was starting to get feisty too. He sensed I had hit a dead end."

DeWitt started to speak, but changed his mind. He straightened up. "Thank you, Senator Kinkaid." He gestured to Munger, and led him to the door.

CIA CONTROL CENTER
SOMEWHERE IN VIRGINIA
1130 HOURS LOCAL
1630 HOURS ZULU

Norman DeWitt hung up the secure phone that linked his office with Colonel Tom Ryan's headquarters at Fort Griffith, Missouri. He glanced across his desk at a very glum Delmar Munger. Munger took a deep breath, then asked, "Well?"

"There has been no contact with Jonas Blane and company since they departed the Saint Louis airport for the Middle East."

"Perhaps that is not an omen of bad tidings where we are concerned," Munger suggested. "You remember that we instructed them to make no transmissions back to the Unit's headquarters."

"I find no comfort in that," DeWitt said. "Ryan started

getting pushy about wanting a sitrep on his guys. He says they've been gone far too long for the type of mission they're on. He flat out asked if something was wrong."

"I trust that you told him everything was okay," Munger said. "He can't put too much pressure on us, since all we have to say to him if he gets too nosy is that he has no need to know."

"By the way," DeWitt said, "I checked with our own message center, and they haven't heard a thing from Joe Saada since the fourth of October. That's been nine days."

"The fourth day was when the Mossad reported they had lost contact with them after they escaped from the safe-house at Sharqmed," Munger said thoughtfully. "That means they've been spending their time wandering around the countryside evading capture."

"And that is what they do best, Delmar!" DeWitt said angrily. "I wouldn't be a bit surprised if Blane and those bandits aren't on the French Riviera sipping wine with that godamn defector! They've probably put off transmitting their location because they're having such a godamn good time!"

"Calm down and stop exaggerating," Munger scolded. "No matter where they end up, Joe Saada will eventually have to contact our commo center here. Once they've done that, we can sic the Mossad back on them. There's not one solitary godamn place they can go to get away from a bunch of pissed-off Israelis."

"We have to be sure they're killed," DeWitt said. "There is no question of their survival." He stood up and turned to look out his office window. "If only that old bastard Kinkaid hadn't caved in. I'd give anything to find out who scared him off."

"Forget about the senator," Munger said. "Our big problem is seeing that those Unit operators are killed and their bodies hidden somewhere over in the Middle East. That's how the Mossad will handle a situation like that. Poof! Out of sight, out of mind."

"All we can do is hope," DeWitt said in a strained voice.

"Want to go out for some lunch?" Munger asked.

"I'm not hungry."

"Is it okay if I order in from the commissary?"

CHAPTER EIGHTEEN

Mack Gerhardt and Bob Brown lay among the scrub brush on a slight rise in the desert terrain. The pair was out on a reconnaissance patrol to determine what existed in the area where the group had taken refuge. They were each armed with an AK-47 assault rifle and one bandolier of six magazines, and each had a single canteen attached to their combination pistol belts and harnesses.

Jonas Blane had added grim instructions to their patrol orders before they left the temporary camp in the trees. In case of unavoidable hostilities with unfriendlies—no matter who they might be—the two Unit operators were to avoid returning to the bivouac at all costs until they were absolutely certain contact had been completely broken. If they were unable to break out of the firefight, they were to lead the attackers as far in the opposite direction of the command post as possible. This would mean certain death, since surrendering was not an option, and if one were wounded the other was not to leave him alive.

0600 HOURS LOCAL
0400 HOURS ZULU

Mack and Bob gazed at a dark spot on the horizon some five hundred meters to their direct front. "I'd give anything for a pair of binoculars," Mack said.

"I'm never going on any mission again without a pair of binoculars and night-vision goggles," Bob groused. "I don't care if it's an antipickpocket operation on Times Square."

"Naked eyeballs ain't a good way to look at faraway things," Mack agreed.

The best method to visually study a distant object without telescopic aid was to avoid staring directly at it for long moments. All this accomplished was fuzzy vision and a bad temper. It was necessary to take quick glimpses, then gently close the eyelids and repeat the process. After a half dozen times, they knew to look away and give the eyes a rest.

"I got it!" Bob suddenly said, looking down. "I picked up a high wire fence with some buildings behind it. I'll bet it's a kibbutz."

Mack frowned. "A kibbutz? Isn't that what you do when you watch a card game?"

"That's *kibitz*," Bob said with a chuckle. "A kibbutz is a farm settlement in Israel."

"Oh, yeah," Mack said, suddenly remembering. "Those places are strongholds, ain't they? They got to be ready for unexpected attacks twenty-four-seven, right?"

"Right. They're defensive positions as well as a place for the farmers and their families to live. I imagine security is tight around there, so we'd better let the boss know about it so he won't take us too close when we leave the area."

Mack pointed off to their left front. "There's knoll in that direction. Let's see if we can observe better from that point."

The pair of Unit operators bent over to keep as much of themselves off the horizon as possible, moving at a steady pace toward the site. When they reached what was no more than a poor excuse for a hill, they were a hundred meters closer. Once again they went into surveillance mode to determine exactly what lay to their front.

"They have vehicles," Mack said. "Looks like tractors, maybe. Some kind of trailers are hooked onto 'em."

"Could be plows or other farm implements," Bob opined. "Uh-oh!"

"What's up?"

Bob lowered his head and blinked his eyes. "I think I just saw a jeep with a heavy machine gun mounted on it."

Now Mack took a couple of quick glances. "Oh, yeah, baby! And it just rolled out of a gate in the fence."

"Make sure it ain't coming our way!"

Mack made another speedy observation. "Nope. It's turned to head down the fence line."

"Prob'ly a perimeter patrol," Bob surmised. "I bet they've got plowed-up soft areas to show footprints if infiltrators penetrate their defenses." Now he looked again. "Mmm! A freaking watchtower! And you can bet they got searchlights and automatic weapons up there."

"That jeep is sticking close to the fence," Mack said. "That means there's probably land mines out farther from the route it's taking."

Bob rolled over on his back and looked up in the sky to

take the strain off his eyes. "I heartily recommend that we avoid that place."

"And I agree," Mack said. "Let's head back."

They got to their feet and, once again bent down, hurried away from the area, this time in the direction of the camp in the trees.

TEMPORARY BIVOUAC

Carlito Grey had arranged it so that he was once again out on an OP with Jaleela Qazi. That had become her permanent assignment, and Carlito had figured out a way he might spend a few hours on guard with her. He informed Jonas that he had twisted his ankle in the soft sand and needed a little time to recuperate from the minor injury. Thus it was Bob chosen to go scouting with Mack rather than Carlito earlier that morning. Now Carlito looked forward to what he hoped would be quality time with the beautiful Arab woman.

They sat together in the underbrush that grew in the copse. It was a comfortable spot, and they leaned against a tree, each on the side opposite the other. "Looks like it's gonna be a nice day," Carlito remarked.

"This is the best time of year in the Middle East," Jaleela commented. "This and the springtime."

A couple of minutes passed, and Carlito decided to get some more conversation started, rather than sit and make occasional remarks about the weather. "So your big dream is to be a journalist like Christiane Amanpour, huh?"

"That was before I joined Alifhedal and al-Askarin," Jaleela said. "But after all this latest brouhaha, I guess I shall get back to my journalistic ambitions."

"You better be careful where you go to get your news

stories," Carlito said. "Alifhedal might want to make trouble for you. I'm sure they're upset about us getting away, as well as losing the guys we took out."

"There is always that possibility," Jaleela agreed. "But if I do not reveal any information about them, there is a chance they will decide to forget all about me."

Carlito leaned over so he could see her. "That ain't gonna happen, Jaleela. They'll know you'll have been debriefed after we get back to the States."

She turned her head, slightly startled by how close his face was to hers. "Alifhedal are not fanatical Islamics, Carlito."

"They were gonna kill us, weren't they?"

The two gazed at each other, and natural forces kicked in. These were emotions and feelings that came to the fore during certain times when human beings were unconsciously stressed out because of potential effects on the survival of the species or other processes of the cosmos. It was so basic and primitive an experience that all the fineness of customary courtship customs were forgotten or ignored. These phenomena occurred during wartime or other periods of peril, such as when a departing soldier and his girlfriend suddenly decided to get married; or when a soldier and wife abruptly chose for her to get pregnant when they learned he was to be deployed overseas. It also happened in instances where men and women were comrades in arms, fighting side by side. Circumstances caused them to damn convention and develop intimate relationships while serving together on a battlefront.

This great driving force made Carlito lean forward and kiss Jaleela on the lips. She didn't resist, and within a quick moment she was pressing back against him. Both were unaware of what lay behind their emotions, or that they had slipped into that condition where physical attraction was the order of the day. The only thing the couple was aware of was that they had eased into romantic affection and sexual lust for each other.

Carlito leaned his AK-47 against the tree and came around to her side. Both were on their knees as they embraced, and the kissing continued breathlessly. They parted slightly, and Carlito placed his hand fondly on her face, whispering, "You're real special, Jaleela."

"So are you."

He glanced in the direction of the impromptu CP, where Jonas Blane, Joe Saada, and Shakeel Bashir were located. The last thing Carlito wanted was for the sergeant major to make an unexpected appearance. Then he decided, *To hell with it*, and tightened his embrace.

Jaleela, who had never been kissed by a man before, was eager to continue with this handsome young American she had learned to love so quickly. "Kiss me more, Carlito!"

He complied and they ended up in a long lip-lock that lasted fifteen seconds. When it was reluctantly ended, he took a deep breath and sighed. "If only we were someplace where we could be completely alone."

"It's nice here in the quiet of the trees," Jaleela said.

"We're gonna have a real hard time making love under these circumstances."

"Are we not making love now?"

"Uh, yeah," he said, realizing she was a virgin. "But there are deeper ways."

"I want you to teach me about them," Jaleela said eagerly.

"Oh, Jaleela, I really want to!"

A sudden rustling of brush sounded, and they broke apart. Carlito went back to his side of the tree and seized his AK-47 as he instinctively assumed a position of full alertness. Then he grinned as he realized how idiotic he must look. When no one appeared, he said, "False alarm."

"What are we supposed to do?" Jaleela asked, sensing that this romance had placed them in a somewhat problematic situation.

"I think we'd better keep our feelings to ourselves for the time being," Carlito replied. "Just follow my lead, okay?"

"Okay, Carlito."

1900 HOURS LOCAL
1700 HOURS ZULU

The illumination in the desert was more gloom than darkness at this time of the evening. Jonas Blane, with Carlito Grey behind him, walked upright with his AK-47 cradled in his arms, ready for instant response to any unpleasant situation that might arise. Carlito was also alert, scanning the terrain to his left and right as well as taking occasional looks on his six.

This was another of the reconnaissance patrols so necessary in the SERE operation. Jonas and Carlito had left the camp an hour earlier, and after a slow, careful trek had traversed some three kilometers of the desert. Both noticed that the farther west they went, the more uneven and rocky the terrain became. Neither was disappointed by the discovery. Only the most expert of trackers would be able to trail them.

Carlito hefted his weapon. "I keep looking out there for some mountains to suddenly appear on the horizon, boss."

"It ain't gonna happen," Jonas replied. "But rugged ground means excellent cover and concealment."

"Roger that!" Carlito replied with a grin.

After going fifteen hundred more meters, the earth they

trod became almost like a moonscape. The dips and rises increased, as did the size of the numerous rocks scattered throughout the area. A moment later, Jonas came to a halt. "Take a look at this, Carlito."

Carlito increased his pace and caught up to the team leader, stopping to see what he had discovered. It looked like some natural sort of a shallow trench that led slightly to the southwest. "Whadda we got here, boss?"

"A wadi," Jonas explained. "It's actually a streambed that's dry most of the time. But when one of those rare heavy rainfalls hits the desert, that hummer can turn into a raging river."

"It's been here a long time, huh?"

"I would imagine so," Jonas said. "If a Roman legion had been at this place at the right time of year they would have had to build one of their pontoon bridges to cross it. And maybe on one occasion or another they did."

"Well, the rainy season ain't here," Carlito commented. "So we won't be having that work detail."

"Let's see where it takes us," Jonas said.

They stepped off again, going into the wadi, which got a bit deeper until its banks were waist-high to the two Unit operators. It took forty-five minutes to reach a canyon, where it was obvious any flood in the wadi would have flowed. "Well, Carlito, we've found our next bivouac area to hole up in."

"It's better than where we are, but there's no water," Carlito said.

"When we bring the others with us, we'll make sure all the canteens are filled before we abandon our present home," Jonas remarked. "And since the area is underwater at times, we might be able to dig down deep enough to find some. If not, we won't be able to stay here long."

"Break time, boss?"

"Not a bad idea."

The two sat down, nestling into the soft soil between a couple of small boulders. Even though they were on the run and didn't know how they were going to extract themselves from what might be certain death or capture, they both felt at ease in the place. It was dark now, and the night seemed like a comfortable covering over the scene. Neither said anything for a couple of minutes; then Jonas asked, "How's that twisted ankle of yours doing?"

"Huh? Oh! Completely okay. Couldn't be better."

"Well, you weren't completely useless," Jonas said. "At least you could go to the OP with Jaleela."

"Yeah."

Jonas studied his subordinate closely before inquiring, "Is there something going on between you and that young lady?"

"Not as much as I'd like," Carlito replied.

"Romance on an operation isn't a good idea."

"Some things can't be helped, boss. They just happen."

"You should have known enough not to let your feelings get out of hand," Jonas said. "You learned about that in your training. As I recall there were some pretty good historical examples given for why romance isn't smart in combat."

"I know," Carlito admitted. "They taught us about the Israeli fighting forces when Palestine was partitioned. There were women mixed into the units with men." He hesitated, then added, "Some big problems popped up when a withdrawal had to be made and there were wounded females who couldn't be taken along."

"Suppose that happens to us?" Jonas asked. "Picture Jaleela shot up bad in a situation where we really had to haul ass fast and hard."

Carlito said nothing.

"Are you gonna shoot her?"

Still Carlito remained silent.

"All right then," Jonas said, getting to his feet. "Then *I'll* shoot her. Does that make you feel better?"

Carlito made no reply as they reversed their direction of travel to get back to the bivouac in the trees.

CHAPTER NINETEEN

Captain Khursheed Jaafari reported to police headquarters that morning to pick up his assignments for the day. These were eight-and-a-half-by-eleven-sheet forms that provided him with the who, what, and where of individuals and situations he was supposed to investigate. Since he had the proverbial "empty plate" as far as cases went, these would be brand-new ones with no previous activity. After a quick look at the tasks, he stuffed them into a manila folder. Before leaving the building for his day's work, he made the rounds, touching base with some of his fellow officers who were at their desks, checking records, or catching up on the latest announcements sent out as memorandums. The short exchanges between Jaafari and his colleagues were to catch up on the latest scuttlebutt and any unusual developments that might be of interest among the investigators.

When that was taken care of, Jaafari went out to the parking lot in the back and drove off in his Mercedes. After going a couple of blocks he pulled behind the public works building, went to a far corner of the parking lot, and stopped. At that point he pulled out his assignments and began quickly filling out the blank spaces for writing in the current status or final dispositions of the cases. He scribbled in such statements as, *Unable to locate witness*, *Situation resolved*, or *Will follow up leads*. With that done, he crammed the documents under the front seat and set off to take care of his real business for that day.

This was SOP for the Palestinian police. Nobody really cared about these insignificant and inconsequential situations of minor crimes or disagreements, and if the officers concerned turned in some sort of report, it covered everybody's asses. Any inquiries would be answered with, "Officer So-and-So is working that case, and reports he is making good progress. Check with us again in a month or so."

EAST JERUSALEM
KOCHAV BAR
1000 HOURS LOCAL
0800 HOURS ZULU

The Kochav Bar in East Jerusalem was a favorite watering hole of both Israeli and Arab businessmen. The large but plain establishment was owned by an American named Harry Leibowitz, who had dual American-Israeli citizenship and had been born in Brooklyn. After serving as a paratrooper in the American army during the period prior to the Vietnam War, he emigrated to Israel. Harry had left the military with a lot of uncertainties about what he really wanted out of life, and he thought he might find himself in the Jewish homeland.

When the 1967 War broke out, Harry felt compelled to volunteer for the Israeli Defense Force, and since he was now fluent in Hebrew and had served as a rifle squad leader in the 82nd Airborne Division, he was gladly accepted. Harry was assigned to the crack 202nd Parachute Brigade of the IDF, and participated in some of the heaviest fighting of that short war. During the attack on the Suez Canal, Harry was badly wounded and given a medical discharge. Now, limping a bit because of some shrapnel still in his left leg from an Egyptian HE shell, he ran the business of the bar with a brusque friendliness for all his customers, no matter their ethnic backgrounds.

The Israelis liked the bar as a good place to meet and set up deals, while the Arabs were attracted for the same reasons, with the additional appreciation that they could enjoy alcoholic beverages out of sight of their stricter, more religious brethren.

It was here that Captain Khursheed Jaafari had gone to meet with Aaron Jabit, the owner of the Akhdar Fruit and Vegetable Company. What Jabit didn't know was that Jaafari had three more appointments scheduled that day dealing with the same subject he and the Palestinian cop were going to discuss. The business under consideration involved those deadly strangers wandering around unchecked in their midst.

Jaafari found the Arab-Israeli sitting at the bar alone, sipping a vodka martini. Jabit turned when he sighted his guest in the mirror, and got off the bar stool. "I arranged for a booth," he said, leading the way over with a waiter following.

The Palestinian policeman ordered a scotch and soda, then reached out and took one of the American cigarettes his host offered him. "How is business, Aaron?"

"The same," Jabit replied. "As long as Palestinian stomachs can digest the kibbutz crops, I shall earn money."

The waiter dropped off the drink, then went to another table to check on refills. Jaafari took a sip, then licked his lips. "I should have ordered a lemon twist. But I forgot."

"You do not get many opportunities to enjoy a couple of cocktails, do you, Khursheed?"

"Only when I manage to visit Israel."

"I have a favor to ask of you," Jabit said with an abruptness not usual in Middle East negotiations. "It is one that must be done as quickly as possible."

"I trust it is not too difficult."

"There is a group of foreigners running loose in the West Bank," Jabit said. "We need to have them located. And, if possible, taken into custody for us."

Jaafari's face showed nothing of the surprise he felt about this inquiry into a subject he was familiar with. "This is most unusual. Should I assume this involves Alifhedal?"

"I know nothing of any group called Alifhedal," Jabit said.

"Of course not. Now, what about those people you want? Any idea where they might be?"

"They might be in Jordan or Israel," Jabit said. "In fact, I can give you only the barest suppositions of their location."

"If they are in this country I cannot help you," Jaafari said. "As you well know, the authority of the Palestinian police is limited to the West Bank and the Gaza Strip."

"I am well aware of that. However, I am sure you will be able to use certain contacts you have with the less desirable elements of Israeli and Jordanian society, as well as Islamic terrorist groups who infiltrate this nation to make raids. A good deal of money will be paid to have these people delivered to us."

Jaafari saw a two-pronged opportunity working in his favor. If he could use David Mofaz of the Mossad to lead him to the fugitives, he could turn over the information to

Jabit for an additional payment. At that point Alifhedal could battle it out with Jewish intelligence over who got their hands on the foreigners. But he could not let on to Jabit that he was aware the defector Bashir was part of the group. "Where were these foreigners when you last heard of them?"

"In the town of Musalmar," Jabit replied. "Unfortunately, from there they vanished into thin air."

"Where did you first make contact with them?"

"At a police checkpoint in the Junub-Markaz area," Jabit said. He didn't know that the roadblock he mentioned was the phony one put up by al-Askarin. Although he had heard of it through conversations with Bahaadur Aziz and Behraam Taimur, he assumed it was a real one.

Not surprisingly, Jaafari was a bit taken aback by the information about the site. He knew of no checkpoint out that far in the boondocks. However, he answered confidently, "I shall begin inquiries immediately. But may I be given enough time for another drink before I leave? This is a rare pleasure for me."

"Certainly. This time don't forget to ask for a twist."

Jaafari smiled, then raised a finger to signal the waiter.

SHARQMED, WEST BANK
CITY DUMP
1200 HOURS LOCAL
1000 HOURS ZULU

David Mofaz could see Jaafari's Mercedes in the rear-view mirror of the Fiat. He shook his head at the expensive sedan, as he always did when they met. This time the Mossad agent got of his car to climb into the policeman's POV. He settled into the passenger seat. "*Kayfa halif?*" he inquired in Arabic.

Jaafari answered in Hebrew, "*Tov muod*," indicating he was very well.

"Any news?" Mofaz asked.

"The only thing we know is that your quarry has faded away and is completely out of sight," Jaafari said. "All my contacts are baffled. But I do have some information that might interest you. You are familiar with Alifhedal, are you not?"

"Certainly," Mofas replied. "A secular group that is as dangerous to Israel as are the Islamic extremists."

"But they use no suicide bombers. One must be very religious in order to blow oneself to pieces in the name of Allah," Jaafari said. "It might interest you to know they are also searching for your targets."

"Has any particular reason been given you for their desire to know where the Americans and the defector might be?"

"I have a theory," Jaafari said. "It is my opinion they wish to sell the defector Bashir to the highest bidder."

"That might not necessarily be the Mossad," Mofaz said.

"I would be happy to keep you apprised of the price. I would hate to see a good friend like you lose out on something you want so much."

Now Mofaz knew there would be a bidding war among all who desired to take the defector into custody. Although he had no authorization to say so, he declared, "The Mossad will surpass the price any other group may be willing to pay."

"Suppose I was able to tell you who had them and where?" Jaafari said. "That would cut down the bidding."

"I can get you a firm price," Mofaz said.

"Do not think ill of me, my friend, but if I can get more from anyone else, I will cut you out." He shrugged. "It is business, nothing personal."

"Understood," Mofaz replied. He opened the door of the car and got out. "You know where to find me."

Jaafari started the engine and backed up. Then he turned and drove away from the dump. When Mofaz got back to his little car, he sat in silence without driving away. He had an intelligence agent's instincts that had been honed to absolute maximum sharpness over the two decades he had been an operative. He began considering what had gone down in the last few weeks.

After the attack on the safehouse on October 5, a special Mossad investigative unit had conducted a thorough search of the place. It took them two days to discover the tunnel the Americans had used to make their amazing escape. When Mofaz went down its length and came out two blocks away, he walked slowly around the neighborhood, trying to figure out how the getaway continued. Did a car meet them? That seemed impossible, because at the time Israeli army units had had the entire neighborhood sealed in. When he discovered the alleyway leading to the olive grove, he knew that had been the only way out.

On the day after the escape there had been the attack on the al-Harbin Mukkaddas camp. The ever reliable Jaafari had informed him that the supply room was looted of weaponry, ammo, and field gear. A Portuguese UMM Alters vehicle had also been stolen. The place wasn't burned down, as would happen if rival militants had been involved; nor was any equipment left over destroyed. There hadn't been time, and that made it obvious the Americans and the defector were the perpetrators.

A sudden and purely instinctive awareness rushed into Mofaz's consciousness, and he was going to act on it: The evaders had not headed east to Jordan, as would be expected. He would bet his pension that they had gone west, and were even then crossing the desert toward the Mediterranean Sea. Mofaz knew the exact people he could call on to track down the evaders. And once they had been located, he knew a way of getting at them that would not waste one drop of Mossad blood.

He started the engine and left the dump so fast his tires threw up a cloud of sandy dust.

SHARQMED, WEST BANK
BARQ-MIN-ISLAM HEADQUARTERS
1330 HOURS LOCAL
1130 HOURS ZULU

Kumandan Ishtiqq Naguib, Staff Officer Taqqee Boudiaff, and Staff Officer Chiraagh Fahmy sat at the table gazing at Captain Khursheed Jaafari. Kumandan was angry, but it was the type of resentment he could control. His voice was low as he stated, "You have some guts, do you not, Captain Jaafari?"

Jaafari displayed a pleasant smile. "I always do when I am sure of my position in certain matters, Kumandan. So, do we reach an agreement on an immediate payment, or do I walk out of here with the same sense of security I had when I walked in?"

Kumandan returned the smile, but it was not quite so pleasant; in fact, it was downright threatening. "Brother Jaafari, how do you know you will be allowed to leave here alive?"

"My commanding officer and all the officers in my squad are aware that I have come here. You must know that. No Palestinian policeman makes contact with a militant group without letting his comrades know exactly where he is and when he can be expected to return."

This was an outright bluff, and Kumandan suspected as

much. But he had to give Jaafari the benefit of the doubt. "Ten thousand euros is a lot of money to fork over on just your say-so," Kumandan remarked.

"It is not much when you consider what information I can provide you," Jaafari countered. "And I guarantee it will please you."

"What is it about?" Fahmy asked. "Have you information on the traitor Shakeel Bashir?"

"Oh, come, now, Brother Fahmy!" Jaafari exclaimed. "Do you think I will reveal anything until we have struck a bargain?" He thought a moment, then turned his eyes on Kumandan. "But let me say this much: I know where you must go to begin the journey leading toward the goal of which I speak. You would fail only through stupidity. And I do not think you stupid."

Kumandan snapped his fingers at Boudiaff. "Fetch ten thousand euros."

Boudiaff got to his feet, his glare at Jaafari showing his mistrust of the Palestinian policeman. He walked from the office, and the three men at the table sat in cold silence. Boudiaff was back in less than five minutes, and he tossed a banded stack of bills down in front of Jaafari. The captain counted them, then stuck them into his inside jacket pocket. "Go to the Junub-Markaz area," he said. "There is a road that goes across it."

"I know the place you are talking about," Kumandan said.

"It is in that area that you will discover a police checkpoint," Jaafari said. "It is not a real one, but is used by the infidel Alifhedal to stop traffic on the road for their own security reasons. Very near there you will find their camp. I am not sure of the exact location, but it can be found without a lot of effort. You will be able to attack and destroy it as well as kill everyone there."

Kumandan's eyes opened wide. This was something he

had been wanting for a long time. But he remained passive and sullen. "If we do not find them, we will hunt you down and kill you, Khursheed Jaafari."

"If you do not find them, I will give your money back," Jaafari said. "And here is a surprise bargain: After you have killed the infidels, you will probably find clues leading to where Bashir has been taken." He stood up. "If not, I may have information by then to set you on the right trail." With that said, he walked from the building.

Kumandan looked at his two staff officers. "Gather up a strike force. We will go find the infidels tomorrow and destroy them."

CHAPTER TWENTY

It was a little-known fact that an important part of Israel's border police was units made up of ethnic Bedouins. These people were Arabic nomads inhabiting the deserts ranging from the Atlantic coast of the Sahara through the Western, Sinai, and Negev deserts all the way across to the kingdom of Saudi Arabia. Their existence as a people went back to prehistoric times, and was tribal, with a patriarchal lineage made up of various loyalties that ran through clan and family ties. For the previous fifty years or so, these customary relationships had begun breaking up as the wandering people moved into settled areas, where employment opportunities offered jobs that provided a much more comfortable living than following their pastoral herds. Among these were the Negev Bedouins, a group who had found it convenient and beneficial to settle in Israel. They were accepted as full-fledged citizens in spite of their Muslim faith, and repaid their

adopted country with loyalty and compliance with national laws and standards.

These Bedouin-Israeli men met their military obliga-
tions over the decades by serving in Desert Patrol detach-
ments of the border police, and many had given their lives
in the service. Their duties were carried out mostly in the
vicinity of the perilous border along the Gaza Strip. They
were hardy outdoorsmen with exceptional tracking skills as
well as heightened senses of sight, hearing, and smell that
made them excellent in isolated OPs. These patrolmen were
able to hear night sounds that others could not perceive,
making it doubly difficult for even skilled infiltrators to
sneak through their areas of surveillance responsibilities.

As the twenty-first century dawned, these unique people
were a valued and respected part of the nation of Israel.

BEDOUIN DESERT PATROL CAMP
16 OCTOBER
0730 HOURS LOCAL
0530 HOURS ZULU

Major Arshad Zarimad, the commander of the local
Bedouin patrol detachment, sat at his desk in the headquarters tent, perusing the papers just presented to him by
David Mofaz of the Mossad. The agent, dressed in an unadorned IDF uniform, had arrived unannounced to visit the
isolated bivouac.

Zarimad read the documents carefully, then set them
down. He and Mofaz were old friends, having worked together many times in the desert country. The Bedouin
commanding officer stated, "This is most unusual, David."

"Believe me, I realize that," Mofaz said. "But it is of
paramount importance. And be assured that it has been
cleared with the highest echelons of Israeli intelligence."

"I have no doubt of that," the Bedouin said, looking at the papers again. "Let me get this straight: I am to take a team of trackers to the town of Sharqmed in the West Bank to pursue some evaders from there out to the desert leading toward the Mediterranean Sea or perhaps Gaza. You write here that there are five Americans and an Arab defector from Barq-min-Islam. And you do not have any idea where they departed the West Bank, eh?"

"I am afraid not," Mofaz said. "But they are traveling in one or more command cars." He reached into his briefcase and pulled out some photos. "These are the type of vehicles they took. They are Portuguese UMM Alters. They were taken from the al-Harbin Mukkaddas camp."

"I am familiar with the vehicles," Zarimad commented. "But al-Harbin is unknown to me."

"They are a new band that has not been in active operations," Mofaz informed him. "And from the way things have been going for them, they probably never will."

"So when we catch up with these friends of yours, what shall we do? Attack them? Capture them? Wipe them out?"

"None of the above," Mofaz said. "Just keep tailing them and let me know their location. Stick close to them until I give you the word to break contact, but do not let them catch sight of you. I have a plan of my own about who will be dealing with them in the final showdown."

Zarimad shrugged. "Why not let us handle it? What advantage is it to use others?"

Mofaz smiled mysteriously. "My aim is to kill two birds with one stone. All I require from you is to shadow them until the death blow can be dealt."

"As you wish!" Zarimad replied. "I shall personally pick some of my best men for the job and take command of the mission."

"I'll lead you to your starting point," Mofaz said. "I

have an idea of my own where they may have left the West Bank and entered Israel."

"I have every confidence in your instincts, David. You have performed more than one miracle that I have witnessed during difficult operations." He winked at his companion. "Are you sure you do not have Bedouin blood flowing through your veins?"

"*Sach kha'kol Ye'hu'di,*" Mofaz replied, feeling complimented. "Pure Jewish."

THE WEST BANK
JUNUB-MARKAZ AREA
0800 HOURS LOCAL
0600 HOURS ZULU

Three ordinary vehicles made up the convoy. The first was a light blue Fiat sedan driven by Barq-min-Islam's premier driver, twenty-year-old Sura Jettou. Kumandan's bodyguard, Mabood Gamassy, sat in the passenger seat, while Kumandan Naguib was in the back with his operations officer, Taqqee Boudiaff. Two Toyota pickup trucks with roll bars followed, each with a driver and section chief in the cab, while the back was occupied by a total of eight mujahideen. The two assault teams were armed with Soviet AK-47 assault rifles; four of these formidable firearms were equipped with GP-25 grenade launchers attached under the barrels. These were single-shot weapons using grenades shaped as chambers for the propellant. A pull on the launcher trigger fired off the forty-millimeter projectiles to a maximum range of 420 meters.

Jettou suddenly called out, "There is the police checkpoint ahead."

"Pull off to the side," Kumandan ordered. He jumped

out of the car when it came to a stop and waved at the trucks as they approached. "Take the roadblock!" he shouted.

The two trucks each went to opposite sides of the road, and the mujahideen leaped out to form two attack formations. They rapidly approached the site without taking the trouble of looking for cover or concealment. No incoming fire came from the small building, and it was taken in less than a minute.

Kumandan got back in the car, ordering it forward, and Jettou rolled up to the structure and stopped. Now both Kumandan and Boudiaff exited the small vehicle. The senior leader of the rifle sections approached them. "There is nothing inside, Kumandan," he reported. "None of the usual police record-keeping paperwork, and no sign the place has been occupied lately."

"Well!" Kumandan exclaimed with a grin, looking at Boudiaff. "It would appear that the noble Captain Jaafari has told us the truth. This is, indeed, a sham checkpoint."

"Now we must locate the infidels' camp," Boudiaff remarked.

"I will send out scouting parties," the senior leader said.

"Tell them to find the place, give it a thorough surveillance, then come straight back here," Kumandan ordered. "I plan on finishing up this task before returning to Sharqmed."

"It will be done," the senior leader replied.

0930 HOURS LOCAL
0730 HOURS ZULU

The recon patrols returned, and both the senior and junior leaders walked over to Kumandan to make their report. "It is not far," the senior said. "There is an olive tree off to the side of the road. All one must do is go to that point and go directly south. It is so obvious that it might as well be a signpost."

"What is the camp layout?" Boudiaff asked. Since he was the band's operations officer it was up to him to organize the attack.

"Four small buildings," the junior leader said, joining in the conversation. He knelt down and used the top of his ballpoint pen to trace the layout in the dirt. "There is a guard post here"—He made a small circle, then another a bit farther out.—"and another here."

"What about exits?"

"The place is open on all sides," the senior leader informed him. "There are no fortifications or barriers. We have the advantage of elevated positions between seventy-five and a hundred meters from the garrison."

"How many people did you see?" Kumandan asked.

The senior leader answered, "A half dozen outside who were having a lecture of some sort between the two largest buildings. All the structures are frame and will not stand up to heavy automatic firing or rifle grenades. I estimate that perhaps the same number of people could be out of sight inside them."

Boudiaff took a moment to study the markings in the dirt. "All right. The first section will take the west side. Position the grenade launchers on both ends of the skirmish lines. I will go with you." He turned his attention to the junior leader. "You do the same on the east side. We are not going to rush the place. As soon as everyone is in position, I will fire a shot." He pulled his Beretta 951 pistol from its holster. "When that happens you will fire directly into the camp. Pick two riflemen to rake the buildings with fusillades to inflict casualties inside. Also, have the grenade launchers focus their weapons on the same targets, and fire the projectiles through the windows. The rest of the men

will concentrate on exposed targets outside, such as that
bunch having a class in the fresh air. If anyone runs from
the buildings, use the rifles on them. When I think it is
proper, I will order you to close in and occupy the site."

Kumandan was impatient. "Any questions? Then move
out!"

AL-ASKARIN BASE CAMP
1000 HOURS LOCAL
0800 HOURS ZULU

Hanaa Maamon finished typing the training schedule
scribbled out for her by Training Officer Peer Zeroual. His
clumsy handwriting had been difficult to decipher, as always, but the polio-crippled staff clerk was able to change
it into a legible, neatly organized document on her word
processor. She called up the printer and sent the schedule
over to have twenty-five copies prepared for distribution,
all collated and stapled.

Suddenly a distant pistol shot cracked from outside. Almost immediately the window across from Hanaa's desk
shattered as a forty-millimeter rifle grenade crashed
through the glass. The projectile hit the wall just above her
head and exploded, sending out a blast of shredding shrapnel. Her right side was pulverized by the hunks of metal as
her skull imploded under the mass of steel that penetrated it
in less than a millisecond.

Just outside the headquarters, the Egyptian Zeroual was
standing by an easel with a 1:25,000 military map mounted
on it. His trainees were listening and taking notes as he
explained the grid magnetic angle to them. At the same
time that the grenade detonated inside the building, the
training officer was stitched by a four-round fire burst that
blew him into the side of the meeting hall to his direct rear.

He bounced off the building, collapsing to the ground as more incoming 7.62-millimeter rounds pulverized the trainees attending the lecture. All were hit, and those not killed outright were wounded badly enough that they were immediately hors de combat. Meanwhile a trio of additional grenades was fired into the other buildings.

Over at the supply annex the sounds of firing interrupted the work of two clerks taking an inventory of pistol belts. The unexpected uproar startled them, and the one with the tally sheet sat motionless while the young woman helping him quickly ran from the building. She was cut down immediately by incoming salvos, and the clerk still inside died in the steel shower of a grenade that came in through the door, hit the far wall, and ricocheted to the floor before exploding.

Others in the camp responded by grabbing their personal weapons, but without Zeroual's leadership they weren't quite sure what to do. Most ran to the windows to find targets of opportunity, but could see nothing to fire at. As soon as more grenades and fusillades ripped through windows and the frame sides of the buildings, they were cut down.

"*Inqata atlak*—cease firing!" Taqqee Boudiaff bellowed.

The last vestiges of echoes of the firing faded off into the distance. Now the Barq-min-Islam mujahideen left their fighting positions and cautiously approached the camp. The grenades had started several fires, and smoke bellowed up as flames flickered inside the buildings. The militants walked into the midst of the carnage, firing off quick bursts into those al-Askarin fighters who were obviously wounded.

Now Kumandan Naguib and Mabood Gamassy joined the crowd to inspect the carnage. It quickly became obvious that all the inhabitants of the bucolic garrison were dead. Boudiaff and the two team leaders waited for their commander to join them.

Kumandan was pleased. "Excellent, Brother Boudiaff. All the infidels are now in hell feeling the first agonies of the eternal flames."

"I will not be so distrustful of our friend Jaafari in the future," Boudiaff remarked.

Kumandan looked at the team leaders. "Tell your men they performed excellently, then get them back on the trucks. We must return to Sharqmed as quickly as possible."

The entire group, laughing and congratulating one another on the great victory, headed down the hill back toward the road, where the trucks were parked around the lone olive tree.

ISRAEL
LATITUDE 31° NORTH, LONGITUDE 34° EAST
17 OCTOBER
1800 HOURS LOCAL
1600 HOURS ZULU

Major Arshad Zarimad and his six Bedouin trackers had begun what looked like an impossible task. Mossad agent David Mofaz had taken them to the western border area between the West Bank and Israel, making an educated guess as to where they should begin their search for the elusive party of five Americans and the Arab defector from Barq-min-Islam.

When Mofaz left them, the Bedouins looked out over the western horizon, trying to sense where the fugitives might have gone. Nothing sparked their basic instincts, and Zarimad got everybody into the stripped-down RBY Mk 1 infantry vehicle they used for their missions. All the weaponry had been removed from the conveyance, with only benches for seats, a radio transmitter-receiver, and a storage area in the interior. This was strictly for tracking purposes instead of combat, and was used mainly for the convenience of teams out seeking intruders and fugitives.

Zarimad, who did all the driving, began by dropping off two-man teams to see what they could discover. After a half hour, he went back to pick them up. For most of the morning they found absolutely zilch. But a little before noon, a strip of tread marks was discovered in a soft spot between two rocky spreads of terrain. The major got out his proprietary notebook of information that he had been using and organizing during his fifteen years of service. He had a special section on military tires, and he pulled it out to see if he could find a match to the marks on the ground in his private reference material. After jumping down from the RBY, he began thumbing through the pages. He perused a dozen examples, then smiled widely, announcing, "These are Michelin Run-Flat military models. Definitely not Israeli army."

Now began a slow process of making sweeping searches of the ground to find more tread marks in the sparse amount of soft terrain scattered among the large areas of firm, rocky ground. It was touch and go for a while, but by shooting back azimuths with his lensatic compass, Zarimad was able to determine the evaders' direction of travel fairly accurately.

Then, up ahead a hundred meters, his sergeant signaled excitedly. Zarimad sped up to the man. The sergeant pointed to a pile of brush in a deep gully. The major joined him and they went down to investigate. After removing a small portion of the camouflage, a deep, medium, and light brown pattern could be seen. When the vehicle was completely exposed, there stood a Portuguese UMM Alters command car for the entire world to see.

Now the other five trackers showed up, grinning widely at the find. One walked around, keeping a short distance between himself and the vehicle. Then he announced, "Major! There are more than six in the party we seek. There are seven!"

Zarimad went over to examine the footprints. "One is a very small person."

The sergeant examined the tracks. "Perhaps a woman." Then he laughed. "Of course it is! In the cinema Americans are very romantic fellows."

Zarimad went back to the RBY, where he had left his map case. He selected one of the area where they now stood. He spread it out and put himself in the evaders' heads. Where would they go? He sighted map symbols of a stream with vegetation around it that was located in the vicinity of a kibbutz.

"Did you find something, sir?" the sergeant asked.

"Indeed," Zarimad said. "I expect to catch up to them within twenty-four to forty-eight hours." He quickly worked out the correct azimuth to the site near the farm, and gave it to the sergeant. "Take the men along that track. I will follow at a distance in the vehicle. We do not want to alert our prey by the sound of the engine."

The trackers quickly formed up and moved out.

CHAPTER TWENTY-ONE

ISRAEL
DESERT BIVOUAC
18 OCTOBER
0545 HOURS LOCAL
0345 HOURS ZULU

It was light enough for a fire to be lit to brew the day's first cups of coffee. The fuel used was dead branches of scrub brush that gave off only an occasional wisp of smoke. Because of the need to conserve water, each evader was limited to half a canteen cup. This would be the only refreshment for the evaders until midafternoon, when Jonas Blane would allow the day's single meal of dehydrated rations.

Food wasn't the main problem at this particular location. In spite of the cutback on coffee drinking, water was eventually going to be critical unless they moved to a reliable source, such as a stream or oasis. The longer they stayed in the gully, the more acute would be the predicament. Attempts at finding water had come to naught, despite energetic digging into the wadi's soil. At one point Carlito had gone down almost four feet before Jonas ordered him to knock off the useless labor.

Now, with everyone's canteen cup half-filled with instant coffee, the seven people savored the hot brew's caffeine kick. Mack Gerhardt took a long, slow sip and exhaled. "We'd be real sorry dudes if it was summertime," he remarked. "There ain't any shade in this dry crick."

"If it was summer on this desert, we'd probably be dead by now," Joe Saada stated.

"I hate to think about it," Jonas remarked.

"How much water we got left, boss?" Bob Brown asked.

"Well, we started out with twenty-four canteens four days ago," Jonas said. "And we're down to twenty. That's a total of forty liters. So if I issue one liter per person a day, that's a total of seven liters daily. We can go between five and six days at that rate. So! I want everybody to turn in your canteens. You'll get a half cup at coffee call and half liter at the afternoon chow call. That builds in a bit of a pad we might need if things suddenly turn worse."

"Christ, boss!" Bob Brown exclaimed. "We got to find some water."

"More'n that," Carlito said. "We got to find good cover and concealment *and* water!"

"These short recons ain't getting us squat," Mack said.

"Yeah," Jonas agreed. "I've been thinking about that. How about a couple of volunteers for a RON?" Everybody but Shakeel Bashir raised his hand. Even Jaleela Qazi and Joe Saada were willing to go. "I appreciate the positive attitudes, and I'll give the honors to Mack and Carlito,"

Jonas said, choosing. "But don't prowl around out there for more than thirty-six hours."

"Roger, boss," Mack said. He nodded to Carlito. "Ready to go?"

"There's no time like the present," Carlito commented.

The others watched as the pair readied themselves to be gone for a day and a half.

The evaders had done the best they could to fortify the sparse bivouac area. Entrenching tools were used to hollow out two earthen bastions on each side of the wadi. The earth excavated from these digs was piled on each end of the bivouac area to provide flank protection. Jaleela Qazi, toughened up by her field training in al-Askarin, did her part and more in wielding the digging instruments. Additionally, a pair of shallow trenches were dug twenty meters out to each side that led to OPs, to increase security. Jaleela Qazi would continue her observation duties in one, while the others, with Bashir excluded, rotated duties in the other.

The whole thing was camouflaged with dry desert scrub brush wrested from the soil a good distance from the bivouac proper. If the covering were taken too close to the wadi, it would attract attention from aerial observation by the patches of bare ground. At least in the desert, unlike in jungle and temperate-zone forests, there was no problem with dying or dead plants showing up starkly in green areas. That would have meant almost daily rework, but the scrub life of Israel at that time of year looked pretty much the same dormant or alive. An unexpected blessing came from the lack of IDF choppers in the sky above the site. It was as if the Israelis had suddenly forgotten all about them. The situation was puzzling but welcome.

Now, doing their best to ignore the discomfort of short rations and little water, along with primitive living conditions, the seven evaders were in limbo; the success of their mission more doubtful than ever.

FORT GRIFFITH, MISSOURI
THE CAVE
19 OCTOBER
2245 HOURS LOCAL
18 OCTOBER
0445 HOURS ZULU

The three people in the communications room—Colonel Tom Ryan, Brigadier General Stan Beckons, and Sergeant Kayla Medwar—had put in a tedious evening. Their efforts throughout the long hours had been totally dedicated to trying to find out the status of Sergeant Major Jonas Blane and his team. Every known station, net, and/or frequency in the special operations commo system had been raised through microphones and keypads; and all inquiries about Jonas, et al, had resulted in negative responses.

Kayla made the final attempt, raising a SEAL detachment aboard a general-purpose assault ship in the Mediterranean, but once again the transmitted reply brought no information. The sergeant swung around slowly on her chair in front of the bank of communications apparatus, shaking her head. "It's like they walked off the face of the earth."

Ryan and Beckons sat next to her, and Ryan used his ballpoint pen to cross out the last on the list of frequencies the sergeant tried. He glanced at Beckons. "Well, sir, not even the Jordan Station had any news about 'em. That

leaves our old pals Delmar Munger and Norman DeWitt."
He looked at his watch. "It's after office hours. Those two
won't be available until the morning. We have no listing of
their home phones."

The general leaned forward. "I have another CIA contact. The guy isn't supposed to be called except in extreme
cases. And I'm not sure this is an acute enough situation to
warrant bothering him."

Ryan spoke with a hint of irritation in his voice. "As
their commanding officer, I consider this of the utmost importance. And I don't give a damn what he's doing right
now. I say that with all respect, sir."

"All right, Tom," Beckons replied. "I can't say that I
blame you." He sat for a moment more, then stood up and
walked across the room to the telephone, picking it up.
"I'm going to have to be patched into a secured ground
line." He punched in a series of a dozen numbers. After a
pause, his index finger once more danced across the instrument's buttons. Then he sat down. It took three minutes
before he spoke into the handset. "Ed, this is Stan Beckons. . . . Right . . . Sorry about the late hour. . . . Uh-huh, it
is important. . . . There's a team of the Unit that's gone
missing. . . . The mission to pick up the defector . . . Nothing, huh? . . . Okay. Thanks and out."

The general hung up. "As I'm sure you've surmised,
Jonas Blane and his guys have evidently done what Sergeant Medwar suggested, and walked off the face of the
earth."

"I should have said something at the initial briefing,"
Colonel Tom Ryan said. "DeWitt and Munger told us no
communications with the Cave. Only the Jordan Station.
And they don't have a clue any more than we do. This is
the last time anybody draws a curtain over any of my operatives."

"Don't beat yourself up," Beckons counseled. "When it comes to train wrecks, Israel and West Bank and the Gaza Strip are the surest places they'll happen."

TEL AVIV, ISRAEL
MOSSAD HEADQUARTERS
0730 HOURS LOCAL
0530 HOURS ZULU

Kalman Mandler, the director of special projects, gazed incredulously across his desk at the visitor. "Will you be kind enough to run that by me again, David?"

David Mofaz showed a slight smile. He wasn't a bit surprised by Mandler's hesitancy. "Certainly, Kalman. I want to coordinate with the IDF on allowing the Barq-min-Islam terrorist group to enter Israel and proceed to a specific location to launch an attack."

"Excuse me while I utter an obscenity in Yiddish," Mandler said. "*Drek!* I chose that language because the words sound exactly like what they mean."

"I am familiar with the term," Mofaz said. "I would like to explain further."

"Please do, by all means!"

"I have a target I want to hit in such a way that it will not appear that the attack was done by us Israelis. I want Barq-min-Islam to claim full responsibility for the operation."

"What target and why?" Mandler demanded to know.

"The American escapees," Mofaz said. "Even though they have been classified as renegades, it is still a diplomatic problem. Better if an Islamic terrorist group attacks them. I am convinced the evaders are heading west toward the Mediterranean Sea."

Mandler was not in a receptive mood regarding the request, no matter what the reason was. It was preposterous, and running it up through channels brought the possibility of not only a demotion for him, but an immediate dismissal from the service under dishonorable circumstances. He showed Mofaz a furious frown. "Would you be terribly inconvenienced if I had the temerity to inquire as to exactly where this target is?"

"I find that quite a reasonable question," Mofaz said. "But I do not know at the moment. However, I have a group of Desert Patrolmen tracking them across the desert."

"What group?" Mandler asked. "And who authorized this operation?"

"I have a detachment from the Bedouin Desert Patrol at this very moment busy finding out where the fugitives have holed up," Mofaz replied. "I did not request authorization to assign the patrol to the mission."

"Now, here's something out of the ordinary," Mandler said. He was used to taking shortcuts, so he wasn't quite as upset as he sounded. "Are the Bedouins the only Israeli outfit to be engaged in the operation?"

Mofaz shook his head. "I shall also need an armored rifle company to back up the Barq-min-Islam if they fail. I realize the defector might be killed in an all-out attack, but if this is not done, he will be taken to America. The idea is to betray Barq-min-Islam and take the defector away from them when they approach the West Bank border."

"But the Americans will be scurrying around the desert, will they not? They will certainly not be sitting still."

"I have had all IDF aerial patrols called off," Mofaz informed him. "The Americans will feel secure if they find any cover at all. By the way, I had no authorization to do that either."

Mandler shook his head. "Why am I not surprised?" He leaned back in his chair for a moment. "All right, David. I shall have an operations order drawn up."

Mofaz smiled and shoved a ten-page document across the desk. "I have already taken care of that."

Aaron Jabit, the owner of the fruit-and-vegetable sales company, stood at the window of his office gazing down at the parking lot. He hadn't uttered a word since Behraam Taimur, the commander in chief of Alifhedal's al-Askarin, had walked into the room. After a couple of minutes, Jabit turned and looked at the Lebanese who was standing on spread legs, his arms folded across his chest in a defiant manner. Jabit walked over to his desk and sat down. "You have made some grave errors, Behraam."

"The decisions I made out at the base camp had to be put into effect immediately," Taimur said angrily. "There was no time for consultation or long contemplation."

"The board of directors is infuriated," Jabit said. "You were instrumental in the complete destruction of al-Askarin."

"These were unfortunate incidents, to be sure," Taimur grudgingly admitted. "But I am sure that anyone in my situation would have done the same."

"A good number of our most dedicated fighters were wiped out," Jabit said emotionally. "No! Not *wiped out*— they were *massacred*! *Slaughtered!* When I think of the loss of valuable people like Peer Zeroual and poor little crippled Hanaa Maamon I could weep! And the disappearance of Jaleela Qazi, who had so much to offer, is in itself a tragedy of giant proportions for Alifhedal."

"I am convinced that Jaleela Qazi betrayed us!" Taimur

exclaimed. "If she had not given aid to the Americans, all this would have gone as planned, and we would have Shakeel Bashir in our grasp."

"I am not convinced of Jaleela's infidelity," Jabit snapped back. "And neither is Haleefa Nasser. He is of the opinion that she has been kidnapped and murdered."

"I am not going to argue the point."

"It is best that you do not," Jabit said. "When the Americans return to their country, their report on what happened out at the camp is going to cost us Washington's support and approval. The United States government was under the impression that Alifhedal did not have the goal of destroying Israel. You told the Americans that we are as dedicated to that as we are to wiping out the Islamic extremists, and there are witnesses who heard you say so. And that included Nasser. If those Americans who escaped are CIA, the revelation is going to cut off American funding and equipment for our struggle."

Taimur shrugged. "There are enough wealthy Arabs worldwide to make up the losses."

"But not the prestige of American support, you idiot!" Jabit bellowed. "Now get out of here! Go back to Lebanon!"

Taimur spun on his heel and left the office.

CHAPTER TWENTY-TWO

Mack Gerhardt and Carlito Grey's RON patrol had been an exhausting bust. For some thirty-four hours they had trodden across flat, rocky terrain surrounded by a shimmering horizon on all sides, discovering absolutely nothing except that the sameness of the desert seemed infinite. No streams or oases with sheltering trees and sweet, cool water were there to be discovered. Not even a single dry wadi that offered at least a semblance of cover and concealment could be located. The Israeli desert in their direction of travel had been nothing but a tabletop of rocky desolation.

Even though they were burning more calories and perspiring more heavily than the others back at the desert bivouac, they still had to stick to consuming the same amount of food and water. Only their superb physical conditioning gave them the ability to carry on as they now headed back toward the bivouac with combined feelings of acute disappointment and more than just a little hopelessness.

At one point, while sucking on a pebble to keep the saliva in his mouth flowing, Mack Gerhardt had growled, "Why in hell did the people of Israel leave bondage in Egypt to come to a godamn place like this?"

"They were following Moses," Carlito remarked.

"Well what damn fool wrote the OPORD for Moses, huh?" Mack demanded to know. "Didn't the dumb-ass ever hear of the word 'reconnaissance'?"

Carlito burst out laughing. "I wonder if he put in the parting of the Red Sea as a contingency."

Mack grinned back at him, seeing the humor through all the misery. "It was prob'ly in the transportation annex."

Now, continuing the return portion of the patrol, the duo kept a sharp eye out for anything untoward to appear, but the terrain was as bare as the sky, where not even a single recon aircraft made an appearance in the sun-bleached, cloudless expanse overhead.

The trudging came to a sudden stop when Mack dropped to the ground, and Carlito joined him in an instant. Mack pointed off at two o'clock. "There's some guys out there."

Carlito peered in the distance. "Yeah. Looks like maybe six of 'em. They don't seem to be coming this way."

"No," Mack agreed. "They ain't moving very fast. Let's crawl in that direction to see what they're up to."

"We got no pads," Carlito complained. "Our knees are gonna get sore."

"Not as sore as our asses after Jonas kicks 'em if them guys sneak up on the bivouac," Mack stated.

"Your point is well-taken," Carlito said. "Lead on, ol' buddy."

They crawled forward a little over a hundred meters before coming to a stop. Mack took another look from the closer range. "Man! Them guys must have all the time in the world."

Carlito also surveyed the six men. "Wait a minute! They're not hurrying because they're following a trail, godamn it!"

"You're right," Mack said. "And I'll bet a swallow of water they're searching for our little group. They got to find patches of soft dirt where we left sign among all that hard-packed terrain. C'mon! We got to make a circuit around 'em and get back to the bivouac."

The two Unit operators moved rearward far enough to be off the horizon, then began a roundabout trek toward the wadi, where the other evaders waited.

DESERT BIVOUAC
1900 HOURS LOCAL
1700 HOURS ZULU

Jonas Blane, with Bob Brown at his side, sat with his legs crossed as he leaned against the wadi's earthen wall. He had just heard a quick but thorough AAR on the patrol from Mack and Carlito. After mentally digesting the information, he asked, "You say there were six trackers?"

"Right, boss," Mack answered.

"How far away were they?" Bob asked.

"I'd say maybe ten kilometers," Mack said. "But they're moving slow as hell."

"Yeah," Jonas agreed. "It'll take 'em a lot of time to scour around out there to find soft terrain where we left spoor, then shoot back azimuths to figure out our actual direction of travel. It could take 'em as much as two more days to find us." He was thoughtful for a moment more, then asked, "What about vehicles?"

Carlito shook his head. "We didn't see any."

"That makes sense," Jonas commented. "Engine noises would give 'em away. Any transportation they have is following at a good distance." He sighed. "Well! Evidently some smart guy figured out we'd gone west toward the Mediterranean rather than east to Jordan."

"We're stuck here," Mack said. "There's no place to go. Me and Carlito didn't see nothing at all that offered any shelter or water, and I estimate we went fifty to sixty kilometers."

"Six guys aren't gonna attack right off the bat," Jonas said. "Once they locate this position, they'll have to send for reinforcements."

"Christ!" Bob exclaimed. "That could mean air strikes."

Joe Saada joined them after coming in from watch at the northern OP. "What's going on, guys?"

"Well, Joe," Mack said, "there ain't any good news to write home about. Sit down and we'll give you our tale of woe."

CIA CONTROL CENTER
SOMEWHERE IN VIRGINIA
1300 HOURS LOCAL
1800 HOURS ZULU

Norman DeWitt and Delmar Munger had ordered lunch sent in to the former's office from the Control Center's cafeteria. Both were in such uneasy frames of mind that even Munger picked at his food. He started to take a bite out of his BLT sandwich, then set it down. "Did Ed Pullini say anything definite?"

DeWitt shook his head. "He just mentioned that General Beckons had called him in the middle of the night and wanted a sitrep on the Unit. He didn't have any information for him, and said so. He wanted to know what we could tell him, and I said we had no idea what was going on."

"I kind of wish Pullini were clued in," Munger remarked.

"Are you nuts?"

"Hell, no," Munger snapped back. "If we knew the Unit's status we could take steps to alter the situation to our favor if we had to. Or if they're laid out dead and buried somewhere, we could take deep breaths and relax. I keep telling myself that no news is good news."

"And I keep telling *myself* that no news is the dreaded unknown," DeWitt said. "The only thing I want to hear is that four dead Unit operators have been discovered with their brains blown out. And that goes for Joe Saada too. Since he's also among the missing, you can bet your bottom dollar that he's sharing their same fate."

"What are we going to do if they suddenly make an appearance, all hale and hearty?"

"It'll be tough," DeWitt said. "But we'll stick to our guns and say that we instructed them to turn over the defector to the Mossad."

"They'll deny it," Munger said. "But it'll be our word against theirs, and that's got to count for something. Of course, Colonel Ryan will back them up."

"That won't help them out a bit because of their reputation. It'll just look like he's backing up his erring boys to cover his own ass."

"What about Joe Saada?" Munger asked.

"With a little luck, he won't want to get involved, so he'd say he also thought the defector belonged to the Israelis. Besides, we can always blame the communications section for sending erroneous instructions to the Jordan

Station. And, with them staring that in the face, maybe they'll back us up too. Anybody concerned with this mission is going to want to stay away from any controversy."

Munger turned his attention back to the BLT. "I sure as hell hope Blane and his guys get wasted."

SHARQMED, WEST BANK
CITY DUMP
21 OCTOBER
1015 HOURS LOCAL
0815 HOURS ZULU

Captain Khursheed Jaafari had just gotten into David Mofaz's Fiat and, after an exchange of greetings, the two said nothing as they stared through the windshield at the large heaps of trash to their front. Jaafari figured the Mossad agent had something very important to impart to him. And he was right; it was Mofaz who broke the silence. "I can give you the exact location of the defector Bashir and his escorts."

Jaafari's head snapped around, and he stared at the Mossad agent in startled surprise. He cleared his throat and asked, "Why are you willing to do this?"

"It would be to Israel's advantage if someone else attacked and wiped out the foreigners," Mofaz explained. "It is a political and diplomatic thing of great sensitivity."

"Mmm," Jaafari mused. Suspicion buzzed through his mind like hornets in a nest. There was no logical reason for Mofaz to make this revelation, and the fact that the Israelis did not wish to become involved made no sense to him, no matter what Mofaz said. He gave the matter some careful thought, then said, "Of course, you expect the Palestinian police to do the job, correct, David?"

Mofaz shook his head. "It would be impossible for them to perform the mission."

That also seemed odd to the captain. "Why not? We have tactical units that could easily mount a raid. And I can guarantee that there will be enough policemen to do the job quickly and completely. I do not understand the problem."

"The problem," Mofaz said, "is that the target is not in the West Bank or the Gaza Strip."

"Ah!" Jaafari said. "Now I see. They are in Jordan, are they not?"

"They are not," Mofaz said. "They are in Israel."

"Then whom do you wish for me to give the location to?" Jaafari inquired. "There is no one else I know about who has that capability, if not the IDF." He asked again, "Who?"

"Barq-min-Islam."

Now Jaafari was speechless, and he stared at his companion with wide eyes and an open mouth. He sputtered as he tried to speak, then finally asked, "How can such a thing be arranged?"

"That is not your problem," Mofaz said. "You are to go to Barq-min-Islam and say you've learned from a reliable source where Bashir has been taken. It is an isolated area in the desert that will allow Barq-min-Islam to get into Israel, do the job, then get back across the border as quickly as possible."

"Do you guarantee their safety?" Jaafari nervously asked. "If something happened to them, my life would not be worth the lowest piece of trash in this garbage heap."

"We will not interfere nor engage them in combat," Mofaz lied. "And they can keep Bashir."

"They will not believe it!" Jaafari exclaimed.

"Why not?" Mofaz asked angrily. "If we wanted to, we could move a parachute brigade against the evaders and the defector. Or a tank battalion. It is just that the situation has become very sensitive, and the government wants the foreigners to disappear for good. Bashir is not worth a diplomatic flap with the United States. But we do not want the American CIA to think they can act with impunity within our borders. That's it, plain and simple. Plus, there is that international-relationship thing I mentioned to you."

"Shall I tell them Israel will guarantee their safety when they return to the West Bank after the attack?"

"You may tell them that," Mofaz said, handing him an Israeli map with grid coordinates scrawled below the marginal information at the bottom of the page. "Does Barqmin-Islam have GPS capabilities?"

"Of course," Jaafari replied. "The Iranians send instructors to take care of such matters. And, of course, there are training camps in Pakistan."

"Then they will have all the intelligence and assurances they need."

Jaafari took a deep breath, then exhaled. "Whew! Very well, David. I shall see what I can do."

Israel
Desert bivouac
1030 hours local
0830 hours Zulu

Sergeant Major Jonas Blane was a man with a hell of a lot on his mind. The news of expert trackers following him and his charges across the desert had alerted him that something very special and very unpleasant was in store for the bivouac. No one had sighted the hunters from the OPs, but a couple of short recon patrols done by Bob Brown and Carlito Grey had discovered that the trackers had gotten close enough to have discovered the site, then just as quietly and mysteriously disappeared. That meant whoever they worked for would be showing up at any time. That was what worried him the most. Could it be Israelis, or perhaps an Islamic terrorist group with superb intelligence capabilities?

Jonas put the group on a 50 percent alert. Even Shakeel Bashir stood guard, and he pulled the duty with a great amount of fervor. The idea of his fellow Muslims catching up to him gave him a jolt of adrenaline that sparked every nerve in his body to the utmost in alertness. He not only pulled his shifts on watch, he stayed on duty well past the time he was relieved. Rather than have one person at each OP situated out from the wadi, Jonas decided that two would be better. With one on duty while the other rested, the posts could be manned the maximum amount of time.

And this was fine with Carlito Grey.

He and Jaleela Qazi were assigned to the northern position, even though Jonas knew some hanky-panky would probably be going on. But between some making out, their affection and attraction for each other would most certainly keep them almost as vigilant as Bashir, since they would want to protect each other.

With the precautions set up, there was one more thing for Jonas to take care of, and this could be the most difficult. The team leader had to weigh all the possibilities and contingencies and decide what reaction he would have for each. There were the alternatives he could choose of unlimited resistance, outright surrender, making a deal where the defector was concerned, or pulling off a night exfiltration out of the area in the hopes that somehow it could be pulled off.

And all this with a shortage of rations and water, while Blane had to face up to the fact that an armed showdown would drain the ammunition supply in a distressingly short period of time.

Carlito and Jaleela knelt side by side in the OP that was masked by an irregular mound of scrub camouflage around it. The couple had been able to carry on intimate conversations while maintaining complete surveillance of their area of responsibility out to their front and flanks. All of these tête-à-têtes had involved their future plans.

"We can get married in the post chapel at Fort Griffith," Carlito said, slipping his arm around her waist. "After that we can figure out our options."

"There are many uncertainties, Charles," Jaleela said. She had begun calling him by his given name rather than the nickname hung on him by his buddies in the Unit. "You mentioned the Federal Witness Protection Program, but will that work for us at Fort Griffith if Alifhedal really starts looking for me?"

"It will be best there, darling," Carlito said, kissing her cheek. "It's a secure area, and we can get a house near where Jonas, Mack, and Bob live. It's a neighborhood called Belleau Wood that's well guarded. There's real nice places available, and you'll like their wives. They're a cool bunch of gals, believe me. You'll fit in real good with Molly, Tiffy, and Kim."

"I think they must be very nice ladies, Charles."

"Yeah," Carlito said. "They sure are."

The couple dropped into silence, their eyes gazing out over the desert, both of them nervous and uncertain about the future they spoke about in such a carefree manner. Carlito's mind clouded over when he recalled Jonas asking him if he would shoot Jaleela if she were badly wounded and had to be abandoned. He consoled himself somewhat with the thought that it would probably be Israelis who attacked them. They, at least, were civilized enough to see that she was given proper medical care if left behind.

The fundamentalist Islamic mujahideen would not be so kind.

CHAPTER TWENTY-THREE

SHARQMED, WEST BANK
BARQ-MIN-ISLAM HEADQUARTERS
21 OCTOBER
1400 HOURS LOCAL
1200 HOURS ZULU

Kumandan Ishtiaq Naguib was huddled in his private office with Operations Officer Taqqee Boudiaff and Supply Officer Chiraagh Fahmy. Outside in the staff room Captain Khursheed Jaafari waited at the conference table for their answer to the proposal he had just brought with him.

Boudiaff was skeptical as usual, but a strong feeling of excitement buoyed up his attitude to one of near optimism. "This is too good to be true."

"I know!" Kumandan exclaimed. "So, could it be a trick?"

"There is always that possibility," Fahmy said. "But Jaafari has never steered us wrong in the past."

"That is true, but having the Israelis give us carte

blanche to cross their border is unheard-of," Kumandan said. "It has never happened before. However, I admit there are diplomatic considerations and political intrigue involved in all this. It is a complicated situation."

"Then perhaps similar arrangements have been made in the past with other Islamic groups, but was kept a secret," Fahmy suggested. "The Jews will certainly not discuss this openly if we accept their offer. After all, they will want the world to think that the Americans were killed by mujahideen without their aid. And it will enhance our reputation when we take responsibility for killing Americans *inside* Israel!"

"But what if the Jew infidels lie in wait for us at the border when we return from the mission?" Boudiaff asked. "They could then wipe us out and still have proof that the Americans were killed by our brotherhood."

"Use your heads," Kumandan said. "They want Bashir as much as they want the Americans killed by Arabs."

"If only we could take a hostage," Fahmy said.

"Wait a moment, brothers!" Boudiaff exclaimed. "We will have a hostage—if we will tell Jaafari to inform the Jews that if they attack us within twenty-four hours of the time we destroy the Americans, we will kill Bashir. Then they cannot get him as a prisoner to interrogate, and that is one-half of their goal."

"But what if he is accidentally killed in the fighting?" Fahmy asked.

"They will not know that," Boudiaff said. "We will dress one of our mujahideen to resemble him when we head back to the West Bank. The Jews will not dare attack us for fear of killing him. And we shall cross back over the border safely, having avenged ourselves on Bashir. That is what I want." He looked at Kumandan. "What do you think?"

"An excellent suggestion!" Kumandan said happily. "Follow me!"

The trio left the office and went into the meeting room. Jaafari looked up at them, noting the smiles on their faces. He grinned back. "Am I right to assume that you have accepted the terms offered by the Israelis?"

"You are correct," Kumandan said. "But you inform them that if they attempt any attacks on us within twenty-four hours of the conclusion of this mission we will kill Bashir. Having him in our custody is the motivation for agreeing to kill the Americans for them. Everybody benefits if no treachery occurs."

"I shall tell them," Jaafari said. Then he reached inside his jacket and pulled out the map Mofaz had given him. "Here is the exact location of the target. That includes the grid coordinates."

Kumandan nodded to Fahmy. "Fetch the GPS."

BEIRUT, LEBANON
1500 HOURS LOCAL
1300 HOURS ZULU

The ice-cream vendor slowly pushed his handcart along the street, seemingly unperturbed by the lack of clientele in the commercial neighborhood. He stopped once to tie a shoe, then a second time to pull a handkerchief from his cap and lazily wipe the sweatband inside, and once more to look into the cart and slowly count the contents in a leisurely impromptu inventory.

His attention suddenly turned to a door that opened in a small commercial building twenty-five meters down the street. It was a business electronics firm that had computer supplies, iPods, cell phones, and other items displayed in its front windows. The man exiting the firm was Behraam Taimur, the disgraced former commander in chief of the now-defunct al-Askarin of Alifhedal. He strode rapidly across the street to a small red Porsche parked next to the curb. He opened the door and climbed inside.

At that exact moment, the vendor reached into his cart and pulled out a small electronic device with a tiny antenna and a button on one side. He pressed the button, holding it down while pointing the aerial toward the Porsche.

The detonation of the bomb under the automobile went up through the floorboards, and was contained by the car's interior for just a millisecond, which was enough to allow it to double its explosive strength. The doors flew off, whirling through the air erratically due to the violent dynamics of the bending and twisting given them by the force of the blast. Everything still inside the car, including Behraam Taimur, was vaporized, except for his right hand, which spun upward over a hundred feet before arcing over and falling to the sidewalk to land in front of a startled and horrified middle-aged lady on her way to her apartment building two blocks away.

The vendor turned to leave the area, smiling to himself and softly calling out, "*Buza gelati*—ice cream for sale."

NEW YORK CITY
ANCS STUDIOS
1845 HOURS LOCAL
2345 HOURS ZULU

Maggie Donahue, the outspoken political columnist for the *Washington Beacon* newspaper, was in the green room prior to appearing once more with Hal Brassey on his *Hal Brassey Interviews* show. Maggie went to the refreshment counter at one side of the room and poured herself a cup of coffee. After picking up a doughnut, she went back to sit on the sofa.

Her scheduled appearance was a result of a quick meet-

ing with Senator Herbert Kinkaid's aide, John Fredericks.
But rather than get together at the Del Fontaine Restaurant,
they met in a small, dark bar in Elizabeth, Virginia, to make
sure they were not observed by anyone from the local political scene. Fredericks had another "leak" to pass on to the
lady journalist. This information had been concocted by the
senator based on his last conversation with Delmar Munger
and Norman DeWitt. The old politician was putting as
much distance between himself and the Unit as he possibly
could, and he knew of no better way than to use Maggie as
an instrument of deception and misinformation.

During the short session, Fredericks informed Maggie
that mysterious outside forces had blocked all access to
Colonel Tom Ryan and the Unit. Because of this clandestine pressure against him, Senator Kinkaid was forced to
bring his investigation to a halt. Although the senator's man
could not identify the unknown entity, he informed her that
the Unit team in Israel had committed a crime or crimes
against the local government and were now fugitives. This
passing of information had occurred the day before, and a
quick phone call to Hal Brassey had resulted in Maggie's
appearance on his show.

Now, sipping coffee and nibbling the doughnut, Maggie
waited to be called to the set.

1900 HOURS LOCAL
2400 HOURS ZULU

Hal Brassey faced Maggie across the table on his unadorned set as opening credits were run for the home audience. At a signal from the floor director, Brassey smiled at
his guest. "Welcome back to the show, Maggie." He turned
to the camera to address his unseen audience in their

homes. "Ladies and gentlemen, Maggie Donahue of the *Washington Beacon* needs no introduction. This is certainly not her first appearance on this show, and as usual, she has some rather striking information to pass on to us. I believe we could refer to it as breaking news." He poised a pencil over his customary clipboard and asked, "So what have you brought with you this evening, Maggie?"

"As you know, I've been following the story on those brigands known as the Unit, Hal. And a completely unexpected occurrence has suddenly exploded over the scene that puts this investigation at a disadvantage. Some phantom power, either military or possibly political, has thrown up a quasi-legal barrier to forestall the hearings that were being conducted by Senator Herbert Kinkaid and his Committee on Intelligence and Special Operations. All access to information or persons who could be helpful in this vital inquiry are no longer available."

"I see. Give us a brief summation of what you know about the Unit's present activities."

"We know they are operating between Jordan, Israel, the West Bank, and the Gaza Strip," Maggie replied. "However, what is masked in secrecy is the purpose of their presence in that area of the world. But you can be sure that whatever reason attracted them there bodes ill for other people."

"Do you consider your source or sources for this information reliable?"

"Of course!" Maggie exclaimed. "*Totally* reliable! I am in communication with top political and diplomatic echelons from which concerned individuals leak important items to me. This comes from contacts I have made over years of covering the Washington scene."

"Would these contacts include intelligence services?"

Maggie displayed an enigmatic smile. "I have no comment on that, Hal." Even though her only source of information was John Fredericks, it was to her advantage to give the impression that she had access to many sources of top-secret data from highly placed informants.

"Let's turn our attention to Colonel Thomas Ryan," Brassey said. "I read your article about the investigation regarding him being suddenly canceled. What is his status as of this date?"

"Ah, yes, Terrible Tommy Ryan," Maggie said with a disdainful laugh. "I don't know his present activities or location, since he was quickly and quietly released from federal custody. He simply dropped out of sight. I wouldn't be a bit surprised if he were over in the Middle East personally leading those bandits of his on that nefarious operation that is taking up all their time."

"Well, Maggie, it appears to me that as far as the Unit is concerned you are at an impasse."

"Not at all, Hal!" Maggie snapped at him. "I still have sources that will eventually provide me with the full information on Ryan and his gang. And when I have all the evidence and substantiation that I need, I will pounce on the Unit like a tigress attacking a band of jackals!"

"You be sure and come back when that happens, Maggie," Brassey said. He looked into the camera. "We'll be back after the break with our next guest, Dr. Watson Fremont, noted sports psychologist, who will give us his opinions on the use of steroids in today's sports scene."

When the cut to the commercial was made, Maggie stood up. "It was nice talking with you, Hal."

"You keep in touch, Maggie," Brassey said. "We've been getting a lot of mail about this situation regarding the Unit."

Maggie walked from the set feeling very satisfied and smug as thoughts of a Pulitzer prize in journalism loomed in her mind.

The camp was far enough out of the operational area that light discipline was no problem. Major Arshad Zarimad, commander of the Bedouin Desert Patrol outfit, sat around a small fire with Mossad agent David Mofaz. The stripped-down RBY Mk 1 infantry vehicle used by the Bedouins for special assignments out in the hinterlands was parked nearby, gassed up and ready to roll if and when needed. The only other individuals nearby were a half dozen of Mofaz's men in their sleeping bags, dozing warm and comfy in the cold night air.

The rest of the Bedouins were concealed out in the desert at special observation points, where they had moved just before midnight. Their assignment was to keep an eye on the target area where the Americans and the defector were located, and report any unusual activity.

Mofaz wore the usual set of Israeli army fatigues without insignia, but had a hooded field jacket on for extra comfort. Zarimad had on the traditional woven robe of sheep's wool worn by his people. He reached down to the coffeepot on the fire and poured himself another cup of the thick, black coffee preferred by the desert dwellers. He held it out to Mofaz, who presented his own cup for a refill.

The Israeli grinned. "You could strip paint off an army truck with this stuff."

"That is what makes it so good and stimulating, David," Zarimad said. "If you drink another cup, you will be removing that jacket from becoming too warm." He started to speak again but was interrupted by a voice coming over the small radio transmitter-receiver at his feet. He picked it up and spoke into it. After listening to a short message, he acknowledged the transmission, then set the radio down. "One of my men reports that Barq-min-Islam has passed his position, and are moving straight toward the target area. They should reach their assault position in another hour or so. They are in pickup trucks, and there appear to be a couple of dozen or perhaps thirty of the mujahideen."

"They will probably wrap this up pretty quickly," Mofaz commented. "Hit-and-run raids are a specialty of theirs. They will be facing only six men."

"Seven," Zarimad corrected. "I forgot to tell you that we discovered another person's footprints. Rather small, perhaps a boy or a woman."

"One more will make no difference," Mofaz said. "This is a big gamble. Our real purpose is to get the defector, but he may be killed in the initial battle or murdered by Barq-min-Islam when they encounter our troops just before they reach the West Bank."

Zarimad frowned in puzzlement. "There is much about this operation that I do not know."

"There is no sense in keeping secrets at this point," Mofaz said. "The Americans are renegades who must be killed or they may hand over the defector to the highest bidder. But the politicians and diplomats have stuck their noses into this mess. What we are doing gives us the best chance of getting the fellow for ourselves or having him killed outright to keep him from others."

"It is times like this that I am glad I was born a Bedouin," Zarimad remarked dryly.

0430 HOURS LOCAL
0230 HOURS ZULU

Kumandan Ishtiaq Naguib lay on the ground with Operations Officer Taqqee Boudiaff. Both had night-vision binoculars and studied the exact area where the grid coordinates indicated the Americans were situated.

"I see nothing!" Kumandan complained.

"They are out there," Boudiaff said. "The extent of the wadi can be seen both to the west and east. That is the only cover available for them. I have no doubt that they have put up extra scrub brush for camouflage."

"Ah, yes!" Kumandan said. "That is what we learned at the training camp in Pakistan."

Boudiaff took out his lensatic compass and shot an azimuth. Then he consulted his GPS and the map. The man was an expert in fieldcraft, having taught at the same training camp Kumandan had just mentioned. Boredom with training boys from the slums and the countryside to become mujahideen had driven him to join Barq-min-Islam to see some real action. He glanced over at the chief. "I have found the exact spot they are occupying, if the grid coordinates written on the map are accurate."

"Very well," Kumandan said. "I put you in command of the attack."

The two men got to their feet and went back to where the three Toyota pickups and Kumandan's automobile were parked. The thirty mujahideen riflemen, eager to begin the coming battle, stood around the vehicles and watched them approach in happy anticipation.

CHAPTER TWENTY-FOUR

The evaders under Jonas Blane's command were now beginning their fourth day on short rations. They had only enough eats and water for two or three more, and the sergeant major had sunk into a deeply contemplative mood about the situation. Even the weather was beginning to turn against them, with temperatures now hovering near freezing at night. In less than a week they would find the water in the canteens frozen in the morning. Without proper sleeping bags, the hours of darkness would be filled with wakefulness and misery.

It had become painfully apparent to him that there was no way in hell they were going to be able to reach the Mediterranean coast under the present circumstances. If they did manage to go across the desert undetected, by the time they arrived at the sea they would be near exhaustion. Plans to steal a boat for a blind run out across the water in the wild hope of finding a United States Navy vessel had deteriorated from a risky scheme into an impossible gamble.

The mission was compromised, plain and simple.

Jonas glanced at the others sitting close by in the wadi fixing their one cup of coffee for the day, and he now knew how Robert E. Lee must have felt in 1865 before surrendering to Ulysses S. Grant. The Confederate Army was beaten down, starving, short on ammo and shorter still on hope. Lee must have agonized for a night, as Jonas was doing, about wanting to save his troops further suffering and shedding any more blood unnecessarily. That had been in April 1865. And there had been another commander, Lieutenant General Jonathan Wainwright, who surrendered his famished, battered forces to the Japanese on the island of Corregidor in the Philippines in May of 1942. With no food, ammunition, or medical equipment, and mounting casualties, the general knew it was over. His troops were marched off to the hell of Japanese prison camps, where they would suffer unspeakable atrocities for more than three years at the hands of the cruelest and most savage troops of World War II.

At least if Jonas gave up to the IDF, there would be no mistreatment of his team. There could well be some uncomfortable interrogation and maybe a punch or two at the outset, but there would be no prolonged torture or starvation. The whole affair might even be kept under wraps as arrangements were made for their release through diplomatic channels. But Jonas, the Unit, and Colonel Tom Ryan would all know he had failed to accomplish an assigned mission. Of course, Shakeel Bashir and Jaleela Qazi could make deals with the Israelis as defectors and probably come out pretty well in the end.

Jonas was jerked from his unhappy reverie when Carlito called out, "Hey, boss. Your coffee is ready."

"Right," Jonas said. He walked over to the group and took the proffered cup. "Listen up. I have an announcement to make. There's nothing left for us to do but—"

He was interrupted by Mack Gerhardt suddenly crawling into the wadi from the south OP trench. "We got company coming, boss. And they're moving this way in skirmish formations. A couple of dozen or more."

"Okay," Jonas said. "It's time for a chat with the Israelis."

"These ain't Israelis," Mack said. "They're mujahideen."

Now yells of "*Allah akhbar*" could be heard in the near distance.

"Go to your fighting positions," Jonas ordered calmly. It appeared that this situation was going to be comparable to General Wainwright's. If the fight was lost, they would be at the mercy of murderous suicidal zealots.

Bashir's voice was close to a shriek when he begged, "Give it to me back my AK-forty-seven!"

"It's back at the command car where I threw it away," Jonas said. "You lie low, and if we have a casualty you can use his weapon. And you'd better fight. Those guys out there are after you more than us."

Bashir physically shuddered, then quickly found a place next to the wadi wall to cringe.

As far as ammunition, the Unit operators, along with Joe Saada and Jaleela, were in questionable shape for a sustained battle. There was a total of 5,400 rounds of 7.62-millimeter in 180 magazines. They would go into action with five bandoliers over their shoulders for the coming fight.

Joe, who had been at the north OP, was quickly called in, and when he joined the others he said there were perhaps ten to a dozen mujahideen on that side of the wadi.

Jonas understood what was going on. "The main attack will be coming from the south. Those on the north will cover that area in case we try a breakout in that direction."

Incoming rounds suddenly whipped the air above the wadi, zinging off into the desert. Jaleela was at the west end, where the dirt from the south trench of the OP had been piled as a barrier. Carlito was on the opposite side using the soil from the north as cover. Joe was in a bastion at the north side of the wadi to keep an eye on the smaller group of attackers, while Jonas, Bob Brown, and Mack manned the south side of the shallow field fortification in their own fighting positions. The heaviest of the attacks would be directed at them.

COMBAT

Kumandan Naguib and Taqqee Boudiaff were 150 meters back from the target area, using one of the Toyota pickups as cover. Both senior and junior rifle section leaders were in charge of the twenty attackers on the south side. Each commanded a squad of ten men. Over on the north, positioned for sniping and interception, a senior mujahideen supervised seven other fighters. All expected a swift victory that would result in a long, lingering death for Shakeel Bashir.

The main attack group had gone into prone positions as per instructions from Boudiaff, and was now low-crawling toward the objective. Through the use of fire-and-maneuver, they were able to keep up numerous fire bursts as they inched forward.

The defenders were unable to get good a sight on the enemy. The mujahideen were lower than the shrub as they approached on their bellies. Jonas, Mack, and Bob fired single shots into the general area of the enemy, hoping to score bullet strikes on at least a couple to make their comrades more hesitant.

THE BEDOUIN BIVOUAC

David Mofaz and his six men were ready to board the RBY Mk 1 infantry vehicle the moment word came in from the Bedouin scouts that the battle had climaxed. An Israeli armored infantry company with American M2 Bradley AFVs that had been redesigned to fit IDF needs was stationed a dozen kilometers to the east near the West Bank border. There were a total of sixteen of the vehicles carrying 112 riflemen ready to unass the M2s to take on the Barq-min-Islam when they made their break to reenter the West Bank after the battle.

Major Arshad Zarimad had called in three of his scouts, leaving a trio out as observers of the attack. The tribesmen had dug hasty spider holes in the desert floor a scant fifty meters from the wadi, employing ponchos and two-and-a-half-by-five-centimeter boards as bracing. Soil and brush had been piled on by their fellow tribesmen, who then withdrew to the bivouac. The infiltrators were so well hidden that when the mujahideen rolled into the area, the hiding places were not discovered. In fact, one of the concealed Bedouins was almost urinated on by a mujahideen answering nature's call. He had cringed at the splattering of urine on the cover of his position.

Zarimad walked up to join his Mossad friend at the vehicle. He had hooked his small transmitter-receiver on his web harness to be ready for any word sent in by his scouts out in the battle area. "How goes it, David?"

Mofaz glanced at the major. "It is that monotonous routine of having to wait that now occupies us."

"Noncombatants do not fully realize that much of war demands patience," Zarimad remarked. Suddenly his radio's dead-air hissing was broken by three short bursts of silence. He answered the covert summons, listened to the message, then signed off. He nodded to Mofaz. "The Palestinians have launched their attack on the Americans."

Now Mofaz gave his attention to his own communications gear he had put in the infantry vehicle. "I will alert the IDF armored infantry to be prepared for action within a short period of time."

"How long do you think it will take the terrorists to wipe out the defenders?" Zarimad asked.

"Not long, if the Americans are foolish enough to surrender to them," Mofaz said. "A little longer if they try to bargain a deal with the defector. And perhaps a half hour if they resist bitterly."

"They do not stand much of a chance, eh?"

"No, friend Arshad, they do not," Mofaz commented with a feeling of deep satisfaction.

COMBAT

Off to Mack's left, three mujahideen suddenly leaped up to their feet and made a wild charge at his position. He kicked off two fire bursts, killing the men on the flanks, while an intermediate pull on the trigger by Jonas kicked the middle man over. During this quick incident the entire attacking line of the terrorists leaped to their feet and made a quick ten-meter advance.

Carlito Grey out on the east flank was distracted by worry about Jaleela. Lately he had been fantasizing about how it was going to be when they got back to Fort Griffith. His passion for the woman blocked out any pessimistic truisms, and he concentrated on how great it would be to return from missions to be greeted by her at their home in the Belleau Wood housing complex.

Now, with shooting all around, Carlito kept glancing her way to make sure she was all right on the opposite end of the defensive position. The third time he took a look, he found himself gazing into Jonas's angry eyes. The sergeant major bellowed, "You keep your concentration on your field of fire, Sergeant Grey!"

"Yes, Sergeant Major," came a subdued reply.

A lone mujahideen on the north side of the battle took matters into his own hands, as undisciplined fighters who were more warriors than soldiers were wont to do. He crawled at an oblique angle toward the defenders in an effort to outflank them. His plan was to reach the wadi undetected, then make a quick charge toward the enemy, firing long bursts. He reasoned he would either be a hero if he shot most of them down, or go to paradise immediately for dying in combat against infidels.

Jaleela had yet to fire her weapon in the battle, but she was ready. The young woman had the selector on full-auto to use the skills she had developed during training at the al-Askarin base camp. Her unusually delicate touch enabled her to fire short three- or even two-round bursts that were deadly, yet saved ammo. Jaleela kept her eyes moving in left and right directions to be ready for any sudden appearance of a mujahideen attacker.

When the lone raider rolled off the desert floor into the wadi, it was so unexpected that Jaleela was startled into inaction. The man let out a wild, primitive yell and ran toward her, firing wildly. This was not like a silhouette target. Rounds splattered the dirt around her, and when Jaleela responded, she inadvertently kept her finger down on the trigger. The entire magazine of thirty rounds hit the mujahideen without a single miss. His upper torso separated from the bottom, and his head and body hit the ground as his legs ran on for three staggering strides before stumbling into the dirt.

Jaleela felt bile come up into her throat, but she managed to keep it down.

Not too far from her Joe Saada nervously covered his area of responsibility toward the north. He had not seen any discernible targets except for an instant when he fired at what he perceived as movement to his direct front. His selector was on semiauto, and he wasted only a single round that tore up the dirt about ten meters in front of his position. It was a personally embarrassing moment and he was glad no one else saw his panicky action. Shakeel Bashir was nearby, but he didn't see exactly what happened, since his eyes were closed shut in terror. However, the sound of the shot startled him and he squirmed backward farther down the wadi.

The pickup truck was a safe haven for Kumandan and Boudiaff. They could stand up and get a good view of their men's actions during the attack without fear of receiving fire from the defenders. Kumandan leaned toward his operations officer. "What is your assessment of the battle?"

"Our men are progressing slowly but steadily," Boudiaff replied. "I think it is almost time for an all-out rush from the south. I am certain it will force the enemy to pull back into our ambush group on the north."

"Will that finish them off?" Kumandan asked eagerly.

Boudiaff nodded. "It should do the job."

THE BEDOUIN BIVOUAC

Major Arshad Zarimad, sitting idly in the driver's seat of the infantry vehicle, received another notification on his radio of a transmission. He responded and listened to a quick report from one of his men in the three spider holes around the battle. When the scout signed off, Zarimad called Mofaz over to him. "A new report, David."

"Excellent," Mofaz said. "What is the situation?"

"My men advise us to proceed to the scene," Zarimad said. "It is almost over."

Mofaz hollered at his six agents, who were lounging on the ground. "Notify the armored infantry to prepare for the withdrawing Barq-min-Islam. The end approaches."

In less than ten minutes the seven Bedouins and seven Israelis were in the vehicle rolling across the rocky terrain toward the battle.

Combat

Operations Officer Taqqee Boudiaff hit the transmit button on the truck-mounted radio. "Attention, all section leaders. Launch final phase. Repeat, Launch final phase. That is all."

The surviving twenty-six mujahideen on both sides of the defensive site suddenly leaped to their feet and charged wildly toward the evaders' fighting position. As per Jonas's prior instructions, Jaleela joined Joe Saada, while Carlito Grey pooled his weapon with those of his three teammates.

The shrieking mujahideen from the south were formed into a single spaced-out skirmish line of seventeen men. Their weapons fired unaimed quick bursts to their direct front at Jonas, Mack, Bob, and Carlito. The Unit operators, with the advantage of the cover provided by the bastions dug into the sides of the wadi, calmly returned fire, sending six of the attackers tumbling to the desert dirt.

Carlito suddenly left the firing line and ran down the wadi to join Jaleela and Joe. Jonas cursed in rage at the sight, but had to continue to fire along with Mack and Bob. The attackers were insane with religious fervor now, and cared nothing about their safety as they ran toward their infidel enemy. Three more spun under the impact of the Unit team's volleys.

Carlito, Jaleela, and Joe had their hands full with the seven mujahideen from the north who had begun their attack only a scant twenty-five meters from the defensive position. This time Jaleela controlled herself and made steady trigger pulls, as if she were shooting on the al-Askarin base camp range. The young woman dumped two attackers in as many seconds.

Every round that Joe cut loose missed. The slugs buzzed off into the distance, but Carlito recognized that the crazed men rushing at them were running amok without control or discipline. He calmly brought three down while the last one took a head hit from Jaleela.

To the rear of the trio of defenders, the last eight of the attackers were swept by crisscross sweeping fire delivered coolly and efficiently by Jonas, Mack, and Bob.

Suddenly the entire area was wrapped in silence except for sobs of relief by Shakeel Bashir.

Back at the Barq-min-Islam vehicles, Kumandan and Boudiaff looked at each other in wide-eyed alarm. The whole final phase of the attack was over in less than three minutes. Boudiaff jumped into the pickup and started the engine. Kumandan had barely gotten in before his operations officer pressed down on the accelerator and the vehicle sped eastward toward the West Bank.

CHAPTER TWENTY-FIVE

ISRAEL
DESERT BIVOUAC
22 OCTOBER
0700 HOURS LOCAL
0500 HOURS ZULU

Sergeant Major Jonas Blane and a much chastised Staff Sergeant Charles "Carlito" Grey were on the other side of the wadi by themselves, some twenty meters from the rest of the group. Carlito stood at a strict position of parade rest, while Jonas was so close to him their noses were almost touching.

"I am considering pressing extremely serious charges against you, Sergeant!" Jonas hissed.

"Yes, Sergeant Major!"

"You left your assigned fighting position and went to Jaleela, leaving us one weapon short on the south side!"

"Yes, Sergeant Major!"

"I knew damn well when you fell for that girl that something wrong and crazy was gonna come of it, and I warned you about that, didn't I?"

"Yes, Sergeant Major!"

"You made one of the biggest mistakes a soldier in the United States Army can make, Sergeant!" Jonas continued. "You have personally, irrevocably, and inexcusably pissed off your sergeant major! And I want you to fully realize that from this moment on I am going to devote the rest of my army career to making you contrite, miserable, and a lost soul in the hell of military outcasts!"

"Yes, Sergeant Major!"

"Get out of my face!" Jonas snarled.

"Yes, Sergeant Major!"

Carlito wasted no time putting space between himself and Jonas, running so fast that the adrenaline pumping through his veins gave him the impetus to leap completely across the wadi to join the others. Jonas strode back furiously, jumping down into the depression and crossing it to climb out on the other side.

Mack Gerhardt looked at him. "We checked out the enemy, boss. Twenty-four dead and six wounded."

"How bad are the WIAs?"

"Two don't have long to go," Mack replied. "But three of 'em could survive with proper medical care."

Jonas snapped, "Well, we don't have the equipment to give them *proper medical care*, do we, Sergeant?"

"No, boss, er, Sergeant Major!" Mack replied, sensing Jonas's fury. "You want to end their suffering?"

"If you're talking about bullets in their heads, forget it," Jonas said. He took a deep, calming breath. "All right, let's just everybody cool it."

Out on the perimeter, Bob Brown called over, "A vehicle approaching. It's IDF!"

"Okay," Jonas said. "Everybody put your weapons

down in a pile and fall in. Fold your hands to your front to
show you are unarmed."

"What are we gonna do?" Mack asked.

"We are going to greet them in a friendly and peaceful
manner!" Jonas said. He gestured to Jaleela, Joe, and
Bashir. "You three get off to the side and do not—I say
again—*do not* make any hostile moves!"

Major Arshad Zarimad, with David Mofaz beside him,
drove into the area. The Bedouins and Mossad agents in the
back of the vehicle were on their feet, looking in awe at the
sprawled mujahideen spread around the area.

Major Zarimad brought the vehicle to a complete stop,
and, being the senior military officer present, he stepped
out. "Who is in command here?"

"I am," Jonas replied, though he purposely did not mention his rank or organization. "We have ceased all resistance. Our weapons are over there."

"I see," Zarimad said. "It would appear you are the vic-
tors in this battle."

Jonas remained silent, then saw David Mofaz walk up.
The sergeant major spoke in a flat, unemotional tone. "I
know you."

"And I know you," Mofaz said. "Our meeting was not a
particularly happy occasion, was it?"

"That wasn't our fault," Jonas said, pointing to Shakeel
Bashir. "There is the defector you are after. We will not
interfere with your taking him into custody, but I want you
to know I'm releasing him under protest."

Bashir happily walked forward with his hands high
above his head. Two of the Mossad men took him into a
rather gentle form of custody.

"You have much to answer for," Mofaz said in cold anger to Jonas. "Identify yourself."

"I will say nothing until I've conferred with a representative from the American embassy."

Mofaz grinned sardonically. "Do not show too much arrogance, American, or I will personally bring you down to a very respectful level."

"If you want to fall out on the green, just say so," Jonas said.

Further conversation between the two was interrupted by the distant sound of an approaching helicopter. In ten minutes a Westland Lynx chopper bearing the Star of David insignia on its fuselage appeared overhead, then went into a hover, blowing dust all over everyone before landing. The pilot politely cut the engine to end the irritation, which was an unusual courtesy for a helicopter driver to show anyone.

One man stepped to the ground from the aircraft and approached the gathering. This was Mofaz's boss, Kalman Mandler, the director of special projects. "David!"

Mofaz trotted over to him. "We have quite a shock here, Kalman. The Americans defeated the mujahideen."

"I am aware of that," Mandler said. "We received a report from the armored infantry commander saying that they had intercepted a Toyota pickup and captured two men in it. They were the leader and a senior staff officer of Barqmin-Islam. Mujahideen are good at attacking isolated kibbutzim and villages, but fade quickly when facing a determined and disciplined enemy."

"I had hoped that everything about this enigmatic situation would be cleared up today," Mofaz said.

Mandler smiled at him and shook his head. "I have a couple more surprises. A different contact has been assigned to us by the CIA. He informed us that these Americans are not renegades, as we were first told. They are members of the American army. They had been ordered to bring the defector back to the States, even though we had been advised of the opposite. The Israeli government has ordered their release and return to the States. And that includes anybody with them." He looked at the Americans. "Which is the leader?"

Mofaz pointed to Jonas.

Mandler walked over to Jonas and offered his hand. "My name is Mandler."

"Mine is Blane."

"Orders have been issued to return you to the American authorities," Mandler said. "And authorization has also been given for you to take the defector Shakeel Bashir with you. You have completed your mission, Mr. Blane."

Jonas smiled slightly. "Y'know, I always figured that one way or the other, I would do exactly that."

CHAPTER TWENTY-SIX

Jonas Blane, Mack Gerhardt, Bob Brown, and Carlito Grey sat in the isolation area, fortified by a cooler of beer they had brought with them from their team room. All were in civilian clothing that consisted mostly of athletic gear suitable for a fall day. Light jackets and sweatpants were the fashion choices of the Unit operators. The summons that brought them to that particular spot at that time was unexpected and caused more than a little uneasiness among them. Carlito was particularly nervous, because Jonas was still furious with him regarding his conduct at the show-down with Barq-min-Islam.

The door opened rather abruptly, and Colonel Tom Ryan entered the room, followed by Sergeant Kayla Medwar. The NCO carried a briefcase, and she laid the heavy article down on the table by the podium. With that done, the young woman walked over to a chair by the wall and sat down. She grinned over at the guys and gave them a wink. Ryan didn't seem so friendly.

"What the hell's going on, sir?" Jonas asked.

"Are we going out on another mission?" Carlito worriedly inquired. He had some plans in the offing concerning Jaleela.

"Relax," Ryan said. "You've been called into isolation for a special meeting regarding all the confusion about this latest operation. You'll be dismissed from duty when this session ends, and nobody—I say again—*nobody* outside of this room is to know about what we're gonna discuss." He opened the briefcase and pulled out a sizable stack of papers. He held up one document. "This is your after-action report involving the operation in the West Bank. Which, as you well know, inflated into a sojourn across Israel where you evidently wiped out a bothersome terrorist group as well as accomplished your assigned mission. All this was covered in eight pages."

"Thank you, sir," Mack said.

"That isn't a compliment, Sergeant," the colonel said. "It is a statement of fact."

Now the team knew what a bad mood Ryan was in. Next he pulled out a sizable bundle of papers six inches deep. "And these, my noble sergeants, are additional after-action reports regarding that same mission. One is from the Central Intelligence Agency's headquarters in Langley. The second is from the Central Intelligence Agency's Jordan Station. The third is from the Central Intelligence Agency's Control Center, and the last is from the Israeli government. I estimate all this comes to about fourteen hundred pages."

"Mmm," Jonas mused. "What we have here is an example of bureaucrats hard at work."

"What we have here, Sergeant Major, to quote the great statesman Winston Churchill," Ryan growled, "is a riddle wrapped in a mystery inside an enigma. Some incidents have occurred about which I have not been given any information."

Master Sergeant Mack Gerhardt shrugged. "That's not too surprising, sir. The mission started out smooth with no wrinkles; then the Israeli Mossad showed up demanding our defector. That's when all the troubles began."

Bob Brown nodded his agreement. "They started the shoot-out, sir. One of 'em went for his weapon and we responded."

"Yeah," Ryan said. "Even the Israelis admit that."

"Question, sir," Jonas said. "If the Israelis admit it was their fault one of their agents was killed, why did they come after us at the second safehouse? Especially with tanks."

"According to them, the American CIA informed their highest echelons in the Mossad that you guys were out of control," Ryan explained. "The CIA even strongly intimated that you were renegades acting on your own. Perhaps this was a subtle way for the Agency to take no responsibility for your actions; I do not know for sure."

"Who in the CIA did that?" Mack asked.

"That hasn't been determined," Ryan said. "It could be that the Israelis are lying to take some of the pressure off themselves. But that's another matter." Now the colonel picked up the CIA Control Center report. "In this paper, it is alleged that you were supposed to turn the defector over to the Mossad. This bit of startling news comes from our friends DeWitt and Munger."

"That raises some suspicion," Jonas said.

Then the colonel grabbed the CIA headquarters document. "The highest staff of the Agency insists they had no interest in the defector, and had no requirement that he be brought back to the States."

"Now, that information is completely new to me," Jonas insisted.

"But Jordan Station is telling us that they were supposed to help you pick up the defector and get him out of the West Bank," Ryan said. "They also emphatically state that nothing was told to them about the Mossad being involved."

Now Kayla Medwar, who had also perused the paperwork, interjected, "And they also state that an American helicopter with previous Israeli approval would fly in and pick up everybody for a flight out to the fleet."

"And this," Ryan said, waving another sheaf of papers, "is from the Israeli government, stating they had been notified about the defector and told they could pick him up from you guys at a safehouse in Musalmar. The CIA even gave them the address of the place."

"And that really pissed off Joe Saada," Carlito said. "That compromised the location."

Ryan shook his head. "I've never seen anything like this. I was here for the mission briefing by DeWitt and Munger. They most definitely said that you were to pick up the defector through Joe Saada's efforts, and that chopper would come in and take you out to an American warship."

"That should be enough to clear things up," Mack said. "We can back you up on that."

Ryan shook his head. "Don't forget I was hauled before Senator Kinkaid's committee and thrown in the slammer for not answering questions. And the leak to that reporter Maggie Donahue resulted in lots of negative publicity for the Unit. She hasn't given up yet either. She's threatening to do her own digging into our activities. If this came to a hearing that would be publicized, the public's trust in our veracity would be nil! Zero! Zilch!"

"To hell with the public," Mack said. "What about the government and military authorities who would judge us?"

"We have no friends," Ryan flatly stated. "The president of the United States says he knows nothing about us."

"Then where is this thing going?" Bob asked.

"Nobody knows at this point," Ryan said. "Do any of you remember anything—*anything*—that can pull undeniable evidence of the truth out of this morass?" He waited for a reply, but received none. "Think! If this thing starts building up steam, not only will the Unit be deactivated, but a few of us will be going to jail. The people who could clear us will turn on us to keep from compromising this vital program we belong to." Again he studied the team before him. When the silence continued, Ryan put the papers back in the briefcase. "We are caught between dirty tricks, dirty politics, and dirty journalism." With that final statement, he walked out the door. Kayla Medwar stood up and followed, pausing only long enough to give the team a smile of support.

If there was still any feeling of humorous optimism among the operators, it evaporated with those last words from their commanding officer.

ELIZABETH, VIRGINIA
POTOMAC VIEW SHOPPING CENTER
1400 HOURS LOCAL
1900 HOURS ZULU

The driver pulled off Lee Parkway into the shopping center parking lot, driving to an available handicap space. After he hooked the proper placard over the rearview mirror, he got out of the Honda Civic. His passenger, Jaleela Qazi, also left the vehicle and joined him to walk down the row of storefronts. She was a little confused about the placard, but figured it would divert any suspicion that the sedan in question belonged to a government intelligence agency.

After passing the Albertson's Supermarket, they went into a little place that was identified as the Rightway Employment Agency. A sign in the window gave notice that all their clients' hiring needs were filled until further notice.

The receptionist recognized the driver and they exchanged greetings. Jaleela was told to go to a door marked INTERVIEWS. She went to the entry, knocked, and was invited to enter. A heavyset man with an athletic appearance sat at a desk. He stood up, offering his hand. "Hello, Ms. Qazi, I am glad to finally meet you. Please sit down."

"Thank you," Jaleela said. She had already been briefed about the special interview that had been set up for her, but had no idea what it was all about.

"Would you care for coffee or a soft drink?" the man asked as she seated herself.

"I'm fine, thank you."

"My name is Ed Pullini, a deputy director of protocol for the Agency," the man explained. "That's a rather all-encompassing position that covers lots of details and areas. In this case, I'll get straight to the point and let you know we are interested in offering you employment in the CIA. I am talking about a career."

"Oh!" Jaleela exclaimed. "I am surprised."

"You shouldn't be," Pullini said. "You were very instrumental in the success of that mission in the West Bank. And I should add that this includes the Israeli desert episode as well. You risked your life to save some operators, and that's a very convincing way to demonstrate that you are on our side."

"I do have a special affection for the United States," Jaleela said. "But I am sure you know I am not a citizen. And I fear Alifhedal will wish to revenge themselves where I am concerned."

"That won't be a problem," Pullini said. "They have reorganized their leadership echelon and have reversed their attitude toward Israel. They do not consider you a traitor."

"I am relieved to hear that."

"And if you decide to become an American citizen, that can be arranged in an accelerated manner." He patted a dossier in front of him. "We have a lot of information on you, Ms. Qazi. You were a brilliant student at Columbia and received a bachelor's degree in journalism. May I ask why you didn't go on to obtain an advanced degree? You were certainly qualified, and you would have had no trouble getting your student visa extended."

"My dream was to become the first significant female Arab journalist in the Middle East," Jaleela explained. "My idol has always been Christiane Amanpour, and I wanted nothing more than to be her counterpart in the Arabic world. I was in a rush to find a position, and had no interest in spending any more time in classrooms than was necessary. So I took my degree and returned home to Jordan, where I found a place on a national television channel."

"I see," Pullini said. "I would imagine you ran into quite a few stumbling blocks in that environment."

"I am afraid so," Jaleela said. "In fact, the only assignments I received were inside the studio making weather reports and public-information announcements. I could not even read news stories over the air. And to make things worse, I was required to dress modestly with a head covering. I should have known that would happen, but my excitement of making a meaningful career for myself got in the way of facing up to reality."

"That must have been frustrating."

"It was," Jaleela said. "I reached a point where I decided to emigrate to the United States and pursue my professional interests here. But a young man at the station told me about Alifhedal."

Pullini nodded. "I am very familiar with that secular organization."

"Since their self-appointed mission was to rid the Middle East of Islamic republics and the tyranny of the mullahs, I joined them. That way not only would I be helping myself, but other Arab women for generations to come. I became a writer for their official newspaper, called *Hurriya Arabi*. That means *Arab Freedom*."

"Uh-huh. But you were in Alifhedal's combat wing when our operators came on the scene. How did that come about?"

"I decided to become a fighter after Benazir Bhutto was assassinated in Pakistan," Jaleela explained. "Her death so infuriated me that rather than fight with words, I was ready to take up arms against the oppressors of my ethnic sisters. If women like her were willing to risk their lives, then I could do no less."

"I can understand your motivation and enthusiasm," Pullini said.

"If I take a position with the CIA, what might I be doing?" Jaleela asked.

"You would begin in a location that must be undisclosed for the present," Pullini explained. "Your duties would consist of several things; but mainly monitoring the Middle Eastern media. That would include mostly newspapers and magazines, but also tapes of all news broadcasts, Web sites, messages on the Internet, and certain cinematic productions would also be included."

"That's quite an undertaking."

"You would have a staff of a dozen or so people who are also fluent in Arabic and English," Pullini informed her. "Some might have university degrees, but most will be ordinary men and women who share your views. At least half are native-born American citizens who have been motivated by horror stories from their parents and grandparents about life in the Middle East."

"Would I ever be able to actually go to Islamic countries as an agent?"

"Such assignments would come later," Pullini said. "And that would require special training. After spending some time in the monitoring job, you could be assigned operatives in that part of the world. You would stay here and supervise their activities at first, then go to an embassy to be closer to your teams. That would be the preliminary phase of your actually going on missions."

"I can see the logic in that."

"What about Charles Grey?"

Jaleela wasn't expecting that, and was slightly taken aback. "Charles?"

"Yes," Pullini said. "Are you two, shall we say, an item?"

Jaleela hesitated. "Well, we have a romantic attachment right now."

"Excuse my bluntness, Ms. Qazi, but I'm sure you understand I must inquire about this relationship."

"Of course."

"Is this a long-term affair?"

"I do not honestly know, but as of this moment I hope so."

"You said a 'romantic' attachment," Pullini said. "Would that also be sexual?"

At first Jaleela was offended, but she realized that if she accepted a position in the CIA, she would have to give up much information about herself. "No. I have not slept with Charles. I suppose it is a hang-up on my part because of the way I was raised."

"Actually it makes no difference," Pullini said. "The great majority of our employees have significant others or are married with families. But we closely scrutinize those relationships. Any breakups or divorces can affect certain types of individuals in negative ways."

"I truthfully cannot tell you where Charles and I are going, since our relationship is in a new environment."

"I appreciate your candor," Pullini said. He stood up and offered his hand. "We'll be in touch."

"Thank you," Jaleela said.

When she left the office, the driver stood up and opened the front door. They walked back down the row of stores in the shopping center to the car.

CHAPTER TWENTY-SEVEN

The room, normally used for conferences and meetings, had been rearranged for a hearing. The large table that usually dominated the center of the room had been moved to the end of the rectangular chamber to serve as a sort of judge's bench. A pair of chairs, two glasses, and a pitcher of water for a moderator and an observer were situated on the heavy piece of mahogany furniture, while a stenographer's station, complete with a stenotype, was off to one side. Additionally, more seating had been made available to the front of the bench with the positioning of a fixed row of folding chairs. A single chair was to the direct front of the table for witnesses.

A rather large, beefy man who appeared to be a sergeant

at arms, had his own accommodations by the door. He was already in position, sitting passively and waiting for the proceedings to begin.

Ed Pullini came in through a side door, followed by Harold Collier, the assistant White House chief of staff. A middle-aged lady entered a moment later, going straight to the stenotype. As soon as the stenographer was settled, she glanced at Pullini to let him know she was ready to begin her chore. At that point, Pullini nodded to the sergeant at arms.

The large man opened the door, standing back to allow four people to enter. The first were Colonel Tom Ryan and Joe Saada, with Delmar Munger and Norman DeWitt on their heels. As soon as they were seated, the sergeant at arms shut the door. He announced, "Mr. Fredericks and Mr. Dayan are presently outside waiting to be called."

"And the other person of interest?" Pullini asked.

"Down the hall in the last office."

"Thanks, Pete," Pullini said. He settled in his chair and gazed at the people to his front. "I know you were all caught unawares by the summons that brought you here, but it was necessary to serve the papers unexpectedly in order to inject some spontaneity into this hearing."

Norman DeWitt didn't like the sound of that. "Just what sort of hearing is this? There was no indication in the directive that these are legal proceedings."

"I wouldn't describe this event as legal proceedings, Norm," Pullini replied. "I believe *informal* legal proceedings' is a better elucidation."

"What is the subject of today's business?" Delmar Munger inquired.

"If you and your learned colleague will settle back and show a little patience, I'll get to the substance of this occasion," Pullini said. He cleared his throat and took a drink of water. "Everyone out there was actively involved in a recent mission to Israel to retrieve a defector from the Palestinian terror group called Barq-min-Islam. The man in question, whose name is Shakeel Bashir, was brought to the United States and is now being held while a final disposition for him is arranged. This situation is complicated by the fact that there is a great amount of confusion involving this case. Was the team of operators from the Unit supposed to pick him up from CIA operatives of the Jordan Station to bring him back to the United States, or was that same team supposed to have him turned over to them by the aforementioned office, then deliver him to Israel's Mossad? Frankly, the question seems ridiculous, since Jordan Station could easily have given him over without having the Unit even involved in the proceedings. If that is the case, it is most perplexing to try to figure out why this U.S. Army detachment was ever involved in the first place." He paused thoughtfully, then said, "Mr. Norman DeWitt, please come to the witness seat."

DeWitt did as he was told, protesting, "I have brought no documents or notes with me for reference."

"Please reply to the situation I just discussed by telling us which scenario involving the defector is the real one," Pullini ordered, ignoring the witness's protest.

"The defector was supposed to be picked up by the Unit team and turned over to the Mossad," DeWitt said. "Yusuf Saada of Jordan Station was to assist in the delivery by providing a safehouse."

"I see. But why did you not have Saada or some of his people simply turn the guy over to the Mossad by themselves?"

"It was thought that the Unit operators would come in handy in case the situation deteriorated," DeWitt said. "Once Bashir was in the custody of the Israelis, Saada could bring the operatives back to Jordan for return to the United States."

"And did the situation deteriorate?"

"Yes," DeWitt replied. "A firefight ensued inside the safehouse, and a Mossad agent was killed. This happened when the Unit team leader, Sergeant Major Jonas Blane, refused to comply with the request to give the Israelis the defector."

"And why would he do that?" Pullini said. "Since this isn't a regular trial you can speculate, guess, opine, or give any hearsay you desire."

"Well," DeWitt said hesitantly, "I'm sure he had an ulterior motive. Maybe he wanted to keep the guy and get a reward by returning him to the Islamic extremists."

"So you are telling me that Sergeant Major Blane disregarded a mission order?"

"Evidently."

"Thanks, Norm," Pullini said. "That's all for right now." He pointed to Colonel Tom Ryan. "You're next."

Ryan, who was sick and tired of such procedures after his experience in front of Senator Kinkaid's committee, walked to the chair and sat down. "How's it going, Ed?"

"Too much work," Pullini responded with a grin. "Now, what is your understanding of the mission orders?"

"My first team, under the direct command of Sergeant Major Jonas Blane, was to go to Jordon and meet Joe Saada of Jordan Station. Joe was to take them to a safehouse in the town of Musalmar in the West Bank, where this Bashir guy would be waiting. When the defector was in custody, a radio message was to be sent that would result in a U.S. Navy helicopter flying in and picking everybody up."

"Did the Israelis know about this operation?" Pullini inquired.

"We were told they had approved the flight through their airspace."

"Who told you that?"

"Norman DeWitt and Delmar Munger," Ryan replied with a slight sneer on his lips. "It was during a briefing they gave the Unit team at our home station of Fort Griffith, Missouri. That occurred on the seventeenth of September."

"And what happened in the OA after the Unit operators married up with Bashir?"

"When they got the defector, the Mossad suddenly showed up expecting him to be handed over to them. The sergeant major naturally refused, since his mission orders were to bring the guy back with him and his team. Things got testy, an Israeli agent went for his handgun, and an exchange of gunfire at short range occurred. The agent died, and the other Mossad people bugged out."

"That's all, Tom," Pullini said. As Ryan went back to his seat, the CIA deputy director of protocol glanced over at Harold Collier. "Anything to say, Harold?"

"It would appear we have two stories that contradict each other," Collier replied. "It could be that someone is lying, or perhaps there was a bureaucratic bungle in which conflicting orders were issued."

"Well, I guess we'd better check another source," Pullini said. "Joe Saada, come on down! And I hope you don't have a third version of this sad affair."

Saada, grinning, took the witness chair. "No, Ed, I'm on the side that says Bashir was supposed to be taken to the USA by the Unit's team."

"Okay, then. Tell us how you became involved in all this."

"We received word about the defector, and were told to arrange a place for him to be picked up in the West Bank," Saada began. "I used one of my operatives, who was a UN relief worker, to contact Bashir and take him to the safehouse in Musalmar. Later, my guy was taken prisoner by the Palestinian police, and his body was found in a trash dump. He had been tortured. I lay the blame for that tragedy, as well the safehouse being compromised, on certain people in the CIA. Namely, Norm DeWitt and Delmar Munger."

Munger jumped to his feet, but Pullini yelled, "Sit down and stay quiet, godamn it, Delmar!" He turned back to Joe. "Why do you feel they're responsible?"

"Because they are the ones who contacted Jordan Station with the instructions that the defector was to be flown out by the Unit team."

Pullini looked at DeWitt. "Is that the truth, Norm? Just keep your seat and answer the question."

"No!" DeWitt desperately exclaimed. "He's probably conspiring with Blane and those other cowboys to sell Bashir back to Barq-min-Islam!"

Harold Collier, making notes, shook his head. "This is getting more confusing by the minute."

"I have to agree," Pullini stated. He gestured to the sergeant at arms. "Have Mr. Fredericks come in."

John Fredericks had been kept outside because he did not have the proper clearance to hear all the testimony being given by people of the CIA and the Unit. He walked in almost cockily, going up to stand in front of Pullini and Collier. "I'm all set to be sworn in, gentlemen."

"This isn't that sort of procedure, Mr. Fredericks," Pullini informed him. "Have a seat."

Fredericks sat down, brushing imaginary lint off the sleeves of his suit jacket. Then he crossed his legs and grasped his knees, looking up into Pullini's face.

"You are an aide to Senator Herbert Kinkaid, are you not?"

"That I am," Fredericks replied. "He is the chairman of the Senate Committee on Intelligence and Special Operations."

"Exactly," Pullini said. "Now, a few weeks ago the senator had Colonel Tom Ryan appear before that same august committee to answer a few questions regarding his activities, as well as those of his command."

"Yes, sir."

"And the end result was that the colonel was hauled off and confined in the Federal Detention Center in Elizabeth, Virginia."

"Yes, sir."

"Now, those proceedings were highly classified, but news of the sessions ended up on the front page of the *Washington Beacon*."

"Yes, sir."

"As I recall they were written by the well-known journalist Maggie Donahue, and were quite inflammatory."

"I know," Fredericks said. "I read them."

"How do you figure Ms. Donahue got that information she wrote about?"

Fredericks shrugged. "I suppose there was a leak somewhere."

"Do you have any idea who might have given that information to the lady?"

Fredericks shook his head. "I'm at a complete loss. I wouldn't even hazard a guess, sir."

"Do you know Ms. Donahue?"

"I am acquainted with her," Fredericks said. "Of course, I have met many journalists in the course of my career. This would be mostly at news conferences and social occasions."

"Have you ever spoken at any length with her?"

"No, sir. I can't say that I have."

"I see," Pullini said, leaning forward toward the witness. "While you've been out there in the hallway, there has been a detailed discussion going on about a secret mission over in Israel. Some grave charges could be brought against some people that Ms. Donahue has skewered in her column. They would be at a serious disadvantage if they were indicted and the case went to trial, since they had been accused of outright murder in the press."

"I suppose so," Fredericks said calmly.

"Why did Senator Kinkaid suddenly cancel the hearings against Colonel Ryan and order his release from custody?" Pullini said, asking a question he already knew the answer to.

"I do not know."

"Did you tell Ms. Donahue what went on when Colonel Ryan appeared before that committee?"

Fredericks's face reddened; then he swallowed hard. "No, sir, I most assuredly did not."

"There is an excellent chance that the same question will be put to you at a trial while you are under oath," Pullini said.

"I stick to what I just said," Fredericks said defiantly.

Pullini said, "You're dismissed." Fredericks got to his feet and left the room with a lot less aplomb that he'd demonstrated when he first came in. Pullini nodded to the sergeant at arms. "Have Mr. Dayan come in."

The next man who entered was middle-aged but without any of the softness of that stage of life. He walked in a steady, almost military pace as he went up to the front of the room. When Pullini asked him to sit down, he settled easily into the chair, sitting with his back straight.

Pullini nodded to him. "You are Mr. Maxim Dayan, are you not?"

"I am."

"What is your profession, sir?"

"I am a representative of the Israeli Ministry of Culture stationed at the embassy in Washington."

All the CIA people grinned. Ninety-nine percent of people serving in cultural capacities in embassies were intelligence agents.

"I see," Pullini said. "Are you acquainted with the situation in which a member of Barq-min-Islam wished to defect from the West Bank?"

"Yes, I am."

"The American CIA contacted your country's Mossad organization about that situation, did it not?"

"I believe it did."

"Are you aware of the information sent to the Mossad?"

"Yes. Mossad agents were to go to a safehouse in the West Bank to have the defector handed over to them by the Americans. It was all arranged."

"Was there any information passed on regarding the safehouse?"

"We . . . er, that is, the Mossad was given the location," Dayan said.

"And when that meeting was made, the Americans refused to release the man into their custody," Pullini said. "An exchange of gunshots resulted in which one of the Israelis was killed. Correct?"

"That is true," Dayan said. "We know he was the one who instigated the violence. I believe my government has already issued regrets. Surreptitiously, of course."

"All right," Pullini said. "Now, besides the location of the safehouse, what other information did the American CIA pass on to the Mossad?"

"They told the Mossad that the Americans who refused to release the defector were out of control and not to be trusted. The CIA also passed on the location of the second safehouse, where the American agents had gone after the incident at the first."

"Do you know the name of the CIA man who did this?"

"Yes. His name is Norman DeWitt, and he identified himself as a senior controller at large," Dayan explained. "He also knew the correct communication challenges and passwords that were changed daily. For that reason he was trusted as far as the information given us. There was no doubt that DeWitt was in command of the mission, and he had a thorough knowledge of the American agents participating in the operation."

"Thank you very much, Mr. Dayan. We appreciate the Israeli Ministry of Culture allowing you to visit us with this interesting information."

Dayan stood up. "See you sometime, huh, Ed?"

"You bet, Maxim. Give my best to the rest of the guys."

After Maxim Dayan left the room, Pullini waved at the sergeant at arms. "Fetch the witness from down the hall, please." He stood up. "But first, let's take a ten-minute break."

Everyone, with the exception of Pullini and Collier, raised their eyes in surprise when the next witness entered the chamber. Pullini smiled at the young lady who carried a notebook. "Please give us your name and assignment in the CIA."

"My name is Dora Petchley, and I am the administrative specialist in the office of Norman DeWitt. I coordinate all paperwork involving the operations that go across his desk."

"Was that your only function in that capacity?"

"No," Dora replied. "I was placed there to gather intelligence on Mr. DeWitt and his subordinate, Mr. Munger."

"You were spying on them, were you?"

"Yes."

"Who assigned you to that mission, Ms. Petchley?"

"You did."

By now both DeWitt and Delmar were close to going into shock. Their skin was clammy, and beads of perspiration appeared on their pale faces. Munger instinctively reached up and loosened his tie.

"What methods did you use to obtain information on their verbal exchanges and activities?"

"Mr. DeWitt's office was bugged to the max," Dora said. "There was a recorder positioned on the floor above."

"I see that you have a notebook with you," Pullini said. "What is in it?"

"It is a summary of the transcripts of conversations between Mr. DeWitt and Mr. Munger regarding the activities of the defector and the Unit."

"Would you be so kind as to give us a brief rundown of what is noted there?"

"Yes, sir," Dora said. "Mr. DeWitt and Mr. Munger—whom I shall refer to from here on as the subjects—had been informed that a defector from the terrorist group Barqmin-Islam wished to defect to the United States. However, the subjects were fully aware that the CIA had no interest in the man. But instead of closing the file, the subjects decided to use it as an excuse to create a situation that would embarrass the Unit."

"Are you aware of their attitude toward the Unit?" Pullini asked.

"They hated it. They were always discussing ways of getting the Unit deactivated and its personnel humiliated and dismissed from the service. It was obvious they would use any means available, no matter the morality or legality of the methods. Thus the subjects formed a plan to send the Unit to the West Bank to get the defector, without informing the operators about the Mossad's part in the mission. The original idea was that the Unit operatives would turn the defector over to the Mossad and come back to their home station empty-handed, having failed the mission. It would bring down the Unit's reputation and prestige in the special operations and intelligence community. The subjects considered this a good start in their campaign."

"In other words, DeWitt and Munger set them up for failure," Pullini remarked. "But it seems things got out of hand when the firefight occurred in the safehouse. What happened then?"

"At that point the subjects decided it would be to their advantage if the Unit operators were killed," Dora continued. "They told the Mossad that the operators were out of control, with their own agenda, and should be eliminated. This was done through official communications to the Israelis."

"At that point the Unit personnel had been placed in mortal danger," Pullini noted. "Is all this evidenced in the recordings?"

"All that and much more," Dora said.

Pullini glared at DeWitt and Munger. "You will both leave this room immediately and turn yourselves over to the security people who are waiting for you outside." He waited as the two stunned men stood up hesitantly before walking unsteadily to the door. Pullini grinned. "I wish I had a gavel, but I don't, so my knuckles will have to do." He rapped on the tabletop. "This hearing is adjourned."

EPILOGUE

Norman DeWitt and Delmar Munger disappeared from view. DeWitt's wife and children, stunned by this unexpected situation, were forced to endure the humiliation of having agents swarm all over their house during an intensive shakedown in which the agents ripped things apart in their eager search for anything incriminating. The very emotional protests and complaints voiced by Mrs. DeWitt got her nothing but curt orders to keep her mouth shut. After five hours the CIA men and one woman left with certain items in boxes. No explanation had been given the family, and the wife was unable to find out where her husband was or what he had done to bring this down on his home.

Munger, as a bachelor, was unaware of what went on in his condo, but would have been dismayed when his carefully nurtured and stored collection of pornography ended up in a CIA storage unit "somewhere in Virginia," with other personal and valued items that he had accumulated over the years.

Because of the sensitivity of the situation, both men were now confined in the Federal Detention Facility in Elizabeth, Virginia, as special prisoners kept away from prying eyes and ears. They were lodged in the same block, but occupied separate cells at opposite ends. The new prisoners were kept locked down twenty-three hours a day, allowed out for one hour in a caged exercise area. Since the pair of conspirators were on opposite sides of the facility, they were unable to see or speak with each other. However, the guards Mickey Dempsey and Terry Nolan had access to both, and made the inmates' collective lives miserable. This was done in hopes that Colonel Tom Ryan would hear of the harassment and forgive the pair for the way he had been treated during his confinement.

Meanwhile, arrangements were being made to charge DeWitt and Munger with embezzlement of government funds in order to keep the real truth of their crimes from the public. The CIA was very sensitive about being embarrassed, and thus allowed the two miscreants to plead guilty to the contrived charges and receive sentences of three to five years in a federal prison. Failure to cooperate would have resulted in accusations of their real felonies of treason, attempted murder, and abuse of authority. In that case, life imprisonment without the possibility of parole was the alternative.

Because of the massive exposure of his activities in Jordan Station, Joe Saada was totally compromised. He was transferred back to the United States and given an assignment as a CIA attaché to the Homeland Security Commission. His consolation for losing a position he had systematically and painstakingly built up over several years was that the new posting was a promotion with a good raise in pay. This meant he still had a bright future in the Agency. However, the Israeli government also issued an order to no longer allow the Nijmi Engineering Limited to do business in Israel, the West Bank, or the Gaza Strip. No explanation was offered to the puzzled Saada family, who were already perplexed about Joe's return to America.

Senator Herbert Kinkaid suffered a heart attack and resigned his Senate seat, as advised by his personal physician. His toady, John Fredericks, joined a lobbyist's firm, representing tobacco corporations; various land development companies; petroleum interests; and a mortgage investment consortium. Olivia Brandon, the sexy receptionist, got her own cable television news show as an anchor. The thing she liked best about the new job was that she could wear the same style of clothing that she had in the senator's outer office.

Palestinian police captain Khursheed Jaafari's initial fears about revenge from Barq-min-Islam dissipated because of the complete destruction of the organization. Kumandan Ishtiaq Naguib and Taqqee Boudiaff rolled over, betraying Chiraagh Fahmy, the driver Sura Jettou, and the bodyguard Mabood Gamassy, among others. All were put away for life terms in the Israeli penal system. Jaafari went back to his larcenous ways, still saving his money for the investments he hoped to make when Palestine won its sovereignty. Visions of skateboard parks and fast-food franchises danced through the cop's head each night before he drifted off to sleep.

Shakeel Bashir was taken back to Israel by the Mossad for a rather intensive debriefing. After being wrung dry, the defector was allowed to leave the Middle East and seek asylum in Sweden.

Maggie Donahue's efforts to find the real reason behind the dropping of the investigation against the Unit came to naught. In fact, she ended up close to becoming a laughing-stock during appearances on several talk shows in which she tried to keep the case alive in spite of flagging public interest. Maggie was obsessed with Colonel Tom Ryan and the Unit to the point that she was beginning to appear a little on the crazy side. The publishers of the *Washington Beacon* eventually warned her that if she persisted in those activities, she would be fired. Ms. Donahue, finally noting her slipping popularity, went back to being simply a news writer.

FORT GRIFFITH, MISSOURI
13 NOVEMBER
0130 HOURS LOCAL
0730 HOURS ZULU

It had been a short date, ending before midnight. The evening had started out awkwardly for both Carlito and Jaleela in spite of their putting on happy faces. Each had already realized that their relationship had gone over a hump and was now slipping down into meaningless oblivion, with no hope of revival for the romance that had begun in desperate circumstances. The problem was that the couple did not know they both felt the same about the situation. They truly liked each other, and neither wanted to cause the other any emotional pain.

The truth came out during the drinking of the after-dinner dessert wine. Their eyes locked, and they gazed at each other for long moments. Then Carlito set his glass down, speaking in a low voice. "It's over, isn't it?"

At first Jaleela didn't understand what he meant, but then she nodded slowly. "Yes, Charles. It is over."

He showed a slight smile. "Well, you're going to start your junior-officer training with the Agency in a couple of weeks, and only God knows where I might be heading." He paused. "It's not enough to build a marriage on, is it?"

"No, it is not," Jaleela agreed. "I feel sad, Charles."

"Me too."

"Maybe you should take me back to my hotel."

After he paid the bill, they left the restaurant and drove to the downtown area. He found a parking place near the entrance, and escorted her into the lobby. There was no reason to say anything else or waste time. The couple embraced, kissed, and parted.

It was that simple and plaintive.

Twenty minutes later, as he turned off the highway into Fort Griffith's main gate, Carlito didn't want to go to the barracks. There would be somebody up or maybe a pool game going on in the dayroom. He just wanted to be alone. The best place would be the team room, since Jonas Blane, Mack Gerhardt, and Bob Brown would be at their homes in the Belleau Wood Housing Development. Now the only good thing in Carlito's life was that Jonas had finally lightened up on him about the incident at the firefight.

Carlito made a quick turn and headed for the Cave. When his headlights hit the sign proclaiming, THE 303RD LOGISTICAL STUDY UNIT, he pulled into the parking lot. After switching off the ignition, he sat gazing through the windshield at the empty building. One long sigh later, he left the car to stroll up to the front door. After flashing his ID at the guard on duty, he headed for the stairs that led down toward his destination.

Carlito was surprised to observe a light under the door of the team room. He stepped inside, then stopped short at seeing Jonas, Mack, and Bob sitting at the table drinking beer.

Jonas smiled. "We've been waiting for you, buddy."

"What's going on?" Carlito asked.

Mack slid a can of beer over to him. "We reckoned that you and Jaleela was gonna break up tonight."

Carlito grinned slightly. "Why? Is it written on the wall around here someplace?"

Bob shook his head. "We sensed it over at Jonas's party a couple of nights ago. Our wives had figured it out too."

"We thought you might like some company," Jonas said.

Carlito didn't acknowledge the remark. He just treated himself to a swallow of beer, suddenly liking those sons of bitches a whole lot.

Outside the Cave, Fort Griffith was locked into its usual quiet nighttime routine, with the streets deserted. Over in the infantry area a disgruntled CQ had come out on the steps of the barracks with a stepladder to replace a burned-out firelight. Better to do it then, before the officer of the day or sergeant of the guard spotted it and wrote him up.

Back in the team room in the Cave, the four Special Forces men sat drinking beer and murmuring softly in conversation. The spirit of soldierly camaraderie lay over them like the comfort of a poncho liner on a cold night in the field.

De oppresso liber!

GLOSSARY

AAR: After-Action Report.

ASAP: As Soon As Possible.

ASL: Above Sea Level.

Assault position: Last site of cover and concealment before reaching the objective.

Asset: A person who, for various reasons, has important intelligence to provide operators and/or teams about to be deployed into operational areas.

Bastion: Part of a fortification or fortified position that juts outwardly.

Battle rattle: Combat gear carried on the body by troops.

BDU: Battle Dress Uniform.

BOHICA: Bend over; here it comes again.

BOQ: Bachelor Officers' Quarters.

Boots-on-the-ground: This refers to being at a specific location, ready to get down to the business at hand.

Briefback: A briefing given to staff by a team regarding their assigned mission. This must be approved before it is implemented.

CAR-15: Compact model of the M-16 rifle.

CAS: Close Air Support.

CG: Commanding General.

CO: Commanding Officer.

CP: Command Post.

CQ: Charge of Quarters.

The Dozens: A word game of insults, generally about girl-friends and family.

E&E: Escape and Evasion.

GPS: Global Positioning System.

Hors de combat: French for "out of the battle."

IDF: Israeli Defense Force.

Kaffiyeh: Arab headdress (what Yassir Arafat wore).

LZ: Landing Zone.

Mossad: Israeli Intelligence Agency (*ha-Mossad le-Modiin ule-Tafkidim Meyuhadim*—Institute for Intelligence and Special Tasks).

OA: Operational Area.

OP: Observation Post.

OPLAN: Operations Plan.

OPORD: Operations Order. This is what an OPLAN morphs into.

POV: Privately Owned Vehicle.

PX: Post Exchange, a military store with good prices for ser-vicepeople.

RON: Remain Over Night. Generally refers to patrols.

Run-Flat tires: Solid-rubber inserts that allow the vehicle to run even when the tires have been punctured.

SERE: Survival, Escape, Resistance, and Evasion.

Sitrep: Situation Report.

SOP: Standard Operating Procedures.

WIA: Wounded in Action.

Zulu: The time at 0 degrees longitude, i.e., Greenwich mean time.

ABOUT THE AUTHOR

Patrick Andrews is an ex-paratrooper who served in the 82nd Airborne Division and the 12th Special Forces Group of the U.S. Army. As an "army brat" during his boyhood, he attended schools in Oklahoma, Arizona, Alabama, and North Carolina. Later the family moved to Wichita, Kansas, where he completed his education, then enlisted in the service. After release from active duty, Mr. Andrews became a professional writer, living in California and Florida. He now resides in Colorado on the front range of the Rocky Mountains with his wife, Julie, and two indolent cats.

THE UNIT

**SEASONS 1-3
NOW AVAILABLE**
SEASON 4 COMING SOON

 © 2009 Twentieth Century Fox Home Entertainment LLC. All Rights Reserved. TWENTIETH CENTURY FOX, FOX and associated logos are trademarks of Twentieth Century Fox Film Corporation and its related entities.

Also Available

THE UNIT: SEEK AND DESTROY

by

PATRICK ANDREWS

First in the brand-new series based on the CBS television series conceived by Pulitzer Prize winner David Mamet

A European syndicate has launched a well-financed revolution to take over the Democratic Republic of the Congo. Their strike force: professional, high-caliber European mercenaries and disaffected soldiers of the Congolese National Army. Their plan: to neutralize the Republic's armed forces and become the new rulers. Their opposition: the Unit, which must wrestle control from the insurgents in a jungle hell. There's only one option: to follow the order of intervention to the extreme—and make it out alive.

Available wherever books are sold or at penguin.com

The *New York Times* bestseller and
gripping personal story behind
Black Hawk Down.

IN THE COMPANY
OF HEROES

by
Michael J. Durant
with Steven Hartov

Piloting a U.S. Army Special Operations Blackhawk
over Somalia, Michael Durant was shot down with a
rocket-propelled grenade on October 3, 1993. With
devastating injuries, he was taken prisoner by a
Somali warlord. With revealing insight and emotion,
he tells the story of what he saw, how he survived,
and the courage and heroism that only soldiers under
fire could ever know.

**Available wherever books are sold or at
penguin.com**

Penguin Group (USA) Online

What will you be reading tomorrow?

Tom Clancy, Patricia Cornwell, W.E.B. Griffin,
Nora Roberts, William Gibson, Robin Cook,
Brian Jacques, Catherine Coulter, Stephen King,
Dean Koontz, Ken Follett, Clive Cussler,
Eric Jerome Dickey, John Sandford,
Terry McMillan, Sue Monk Kidd, Amy Tan,
John Berendt…

You'll find them all at
penguin.com

*Read excerpts and newsletters,
find tour schedules and reading group guides,
and enter contests.*

Subscribe to Penguin Group (USA) newsletters
and get an exclusive inside look
at exciting new titles and the authors you love
long before everyone else does.

PENGUIN GROUP (USA)
us.penguingroup.com